THE VARIOUS LIVES OF MARCUS IGOE

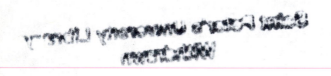

THE VARIOUS LIVES OF MARCUS IGOE

BRINSLEY MacNAMARA
Afterword by Michael McDonnell

Dufour Editions

Published in the United States of America 1996
by Dufour Editions Inc.,
Chester Springs, Pennsylvania 19425-0007

Library of Congress Cataloging-in-Publication Data:
MacNamara, Brinsley, 1890-1963
   The Various Lives of Marcus Igoe / by Brinsley MacNamara.
      p.   cm.
   ISBN 0-8023-1304-3
   1. Men—Ireland—Psychology—Fiction. 2. Villages—Ireland
—Fiction. I. Title.
PR6025.A3134V37 -1996
823'.912—dc20
                                                          96-772
                                                          CIP

                  paperback ISBN 0 8023 1304 3

          Printed and bound in the United States of America

CHAPTER I

A MAN! But, upon examination, perhaps only the semblance of a man, with little, if any, suggestion of immortal quality in his lineaments or gesture. He did not suddenly strike the onlooker as a man who had ever done anything in the past, or as one who might ever rise to action in the future. He was as one fixed immutably in the uneventful present, in his way, a perfect specimen of that type, for had he not lived for what were already a great many years behind a little squinting window in the very middle of Garradrimna?

His was, perhaps, the ugliest of all the squinting windows in the village, yet he himself, Marcus Igoe, was by no means the ugliest man in the whole place. Sometimes, and particularly at certain angles and in certain lights, the curious optical quality of the window seemed to endow him with a visual squint which was in itself disquieting, an indication to many of a mental state that could, quite easily, be interpreted as a denial of the meagre wisdom that might be in him. For, after what could be made to appear as a great expanse of the most intensely concentrated observation of the little, continuous pageant of the street, it could not be said with truth that Marcus Igoe, although he had never made any use of his experience, had not learned a few things about life.

His way of going on being sufficient only to bring him a bare subsistence, his mind had no opportunity of ever becoming rose-hued or filled with false valuations, and so he was enabled to see life fair and square, that is, stripped barely of its mantle of illusion at every turn, with his laugh, when he did take a laugh at it, not a little sardonic.

In addition to his rather dismal general circumstances he had a wife, Mary Margaret or "Margo," as she was called, who had a tongue, they said, like the lash of a whip, and it seemed a pity, if he had ever had any hopes of becoming a philosopher, that his wife's most marked quality had so often the effect of causing him to withdraw his eyes and his mind from contemplation of the show which passed on the street outside to concentration of his every faculty upon the main purpose of his life, upon himself and upon the causes which had made him what he was.

Thus ensued a kind of clash whose reverberations, going with clattering echo down into his very soul, made a mood in which he seemed to be permanently fixed. This was his mood of combat with the life around him. But there was another condition flowing over this, which, in a sense, otherwise determined him. For, often, the actual performance beyond the little squinting window would grow dim, and people whom he knew only too well in flesh and blood would become as the silent figures of a fantasy... and then, also, would be forced upon his consciousness that he himself, Marcus Igoe, the shoemaker, if you liked to be euphemistic and wished to use that term, an entity, an inhabitant, a citizen, was nothing more than the outlandish ghostly chimera of a crystal-gazer's dream. For it had been borne in upon him, after long pondering, that, when a passing neighbour looked in at him askance, he was nothing more than a hint, a mere suggestion, a shadowy symbol of the catastrophe that might evolve, through the manipulations of Fate, in any life that ever was.

He was, in a sense, through realisation of his remoteness from place, and power and influence and importance, a warning of the thing that might happen to any man—if he did not mind himself. If only looks of envy or amazement fell in upon him from the street outside he would know then that he had achieved a desirable destiny, a fulfilment, a condition that men might dwell upon with something of hope and desire stirring them at the end of any gaze... For the look out of any pair of eyes, is, maybe, more than half in dream. With much else, after long pondering, he had learned that, but he had made no reality out of the dream of his life. He had achieved nothing and he was nothing. There were moments when he could remember only that he had done one thing—he had married Margo...

But then his sense of combat, however sadly diminished, would struggle back into him, and he would be driven to remember that, in his queer way, he had had a past, a quaint and quiet little past perhaps, but he had done things then. And it was the thought that people passing by the window must have remembrance of him as he was in those days that always stirred him back into life again. They knew... but look at all he knew about them! All the same, he had made a holy show of himself that time...

CHAPTER II

IT seemed that, at the beginning of it, no man had ever been better fitted for the curious kind of career he had begun to embrace. He remembered well the proud title, in the slang of the time, which had distinguished him enviously in the 'seventies of the previous century — "Marcus Igoe, the lady killer." His mother had always insisted upon the full and correct use of his Christian name, and, because it was somewhat unusual in these parts, it helped still further to mark him. They said that his mother had spoiled him, but no matter about it now, for maybe only for his father he could never have come to be the way he was at present.

His father, Denis Igoe, had once owned the thriving boot shop and drapery in Garradrimna, as well as a fine house and farm at Harbourstown. His father, wise man that he had been in ways, had put him early to the "trade," while his mother had fought for his establishment as a little gentleman in their "country place," as she called it, at Harbourstown. In a sort of way he had learned the trade and the business by the time his father had died and his mother could have her way. She left the "business" to the care of a couple of assistants, and went with her lovely son to live at Harbourstown, but not before she attempted to give him, even at a late stage, (although he had been through the Diocesan Seminary), a final coat of mental and social varnish at an expensive college for young gentlemen.

When he came out into the world, with as much as they could manage of the stamp of "trade" rubbed off him, he entered into the exclusive society of the strong farmers, and was most popular with their sons and daughters. From the very beginning he began to gain a reputation as a ladies' man. When he was about twenty-five his mother died, but she did not leave him a desolate orphan. He could afford to pay men to look after the farm, as well as the shop, while he went gaily about the country in quest of joy. His physique inclined him to effeminacy, and he always said that he adored the company of the fair sex. He was little and mean-looking, but this did not prevent him from being acceptable to the ladies, and they thought him very good sport.

He was a bit of a character, and he adorned himself most tastefully after the fashion of his kind in those days. In the late 'seventies he was a fashionable figure, and, about the year 1880, he would appear to have attained to the height of his reputation. In the more strenuous excitements of the earth he was not a conspicuous figure. But the ball-room was his place of power. All over the countryside he was in demand for dancing. No list of invitations was ever considered complete without the name of Marcus Igoe appearing therein. A dance devoid of his presence would be quite impossible. And he was always organising dances.

It may be somewhat difficult for anyone to realise him as he appeared in those days, for the long perspective of the years produces a misty and somewhat unbelievable figure, but if one thinks of him mainly as a dandy, a "masher," to use an alternative description then prevalent, some kind of definite impression will prevail. If one could think, too, that there existed always just a little touch of satirical appreciation of himself by himself one may be further helped towards at least a glimpse. A dandy he most certainly was. He was moustached and side-whiskered after the fashion of the period, and his manners were faultless by comparison with nearly everything around him.

His thin hair was always Macassared to resplendence; he wore several inches of a high collar as straight and stiff as the armour of a knight of old, and with it a puce tie with spots of delicate tint; a "swallow-tailed" coat, which looked perilously like a morning coat although it suited him; trousers of wide pattern conveniently fashioned to hide the slight bend in his left leg; and shoes which were notable examples of the cobbler's art. The few enemies he had could say nothing worse of him than that of course he made his own shoes. The most delicate silk gloves completed his conquering attire, and when he opened his mouth to say: "Could I have the—the *esteemed* pleasure, Miss—?" or "Would you be so *very* kind as to give me the next dance, Miss—?" he always spoke in the authentic tones of gallantry. Although the broad, heavy accent of County Meath still stuck to him, his words always fell musically upon the ears of listening ladies, and there were very few who could resist the gentle lure of him. He was a good dancer, but it was not merely as a "Terpsichorean," as the *Meath Reporter* once described him, that he was captivating. He was most concerned to see that all were in perfect enjoyment of the occasion, and perfectly at ease, tea for the ladies... drinks for the men... every sort of entertainment and satisfaction. Indeed, to see him amid the flock of ladies at a tea-table was to realise at once what a gallant he could be, almost a hero of romance, a veritable cavalier.

"The floor is just in *neece* order, Miss Merlehan," he would say. (He always pronounced "nice," a favourite word of his, in this way.)

"Lovely, Mr. Igoe."

"Thanks to you, Mr. Igoe," Miss Marcella Plunkett chimed in now.

"Merci, Mademoiselle!"

This with a bow. (He spoke French to the extent of about ten words, and it was considered very genteel amongst the strong farmers' daughters.)

Miss Marcella Plunkett was one of his greatest admirers, and moreover many said that it might easily result in a match between them.

"This is a better dance than the one at Clunnen. Happily, fewer sets of quadrilles... getting dreadfully common now... schottisches yes... and the waltz... Ah, the waltz, divine. Thanks to your exquisite musical taste, Mr. Igoe."

"Merci, Mademoiselle."

When all his responsibilities as organiser were discharged, he would be the outstanding figure upon the floor. And, as he entered into the mood of the night, his words to any girl with whom he might happen to be dancing became charged with an effulgence of sentimentality. It would often appear to those who witnessed that he was about to fall under the influence of sudden impulses. Strangers at the dance would think that the great surrender was upon him, but those who knew him better simply smiled. To them he was merely retaining his title of "Marcus Igoe, the lady killer."

And yet there were times when he deceived even these, and they thought that at long last he was seriously fond of some girl he had just met. (This had happened already in the case of Miss Marcella Plunkett.) It became a matter of prevalent gossip that he was sending her frequent and bulky letters through the post, as well as numerous presents of plums and pears from the gardens of the Hon. Reginald Moore. (Chocolate, that more convenient mode of affectionate giving, had not yet come into vogue.) But at the very next dance their illusions would be dispelled, for there they would see him behaving as usual, but with a different girl.

Those who, rightly or wrongly, were supposed to have the knack of seeing into the future imagined for him, out of their gift of divination, a curiously undistinguished and unromantic end.

"He'll be going on like this until no young girl will look at him any more, and he'll finish up, mebbe, by marrying some ould-fashioned lassie that'll mebbe be remembering it all against him... heart-scalding him about it for the remainder of his days."

In Garradrimna a man of sense and understanding like Bartle Boyhan would say, to clinch the matter and dispel any possible suggestion of marriage: "Is it Marcus married indeed? Why, there isn't an ounce of married man's flesh on his bones!"

And thus did he dally with serious things until he had slipped into his thirty-fifth year.

CHAPTER III

IF he ever looked at himself now, it was only, as it were, the very beginning of himself that he saw. He had no great concern for the future, for he had no reason to dread. But there were those to whom he was an anxiety, especially matchmaking mothers with lovely daughters who had not a penny. Yet, for all the wiles of these creatures, he refused to be captured. He made love to all of them; he was constantly very deeply "in love" with one or other of them, but he never once thought of marrying any of them. His esteemed worth as an organiser of dances and other forms of genteel amusement had merely increased with the years. He kept pace with the fashions, and always arrayed himself, as he thought, tastefully in the prevailing vanities, and he did not seriously observe the silver that was just beginning to creep into his hair.

When he was nearing forty, an extraordinary thing happened to him. For the first time in his life he fell intensely and genuinely in love. This time it was with Olive Fetherstonhaugh, the daughter of an impecunious sporting gentleman of the neighbourhood. He had become acquainted with her at the dance of a charity bazaar where she was helping with some of the local gentry and their ladies. It was the most splendid moment of his whole career when he was permitted to lead her to supper speaking his best French the while. She did not mind in the least; one must put up with a good deal in the interests of charity. He was such a funny little man, she thought.

15

Later she danced with him quite remarkably often, and he spoke to her in gorgeously-coloured language while she permitted him to attend on her. He was hopelessly in love. He thought of her with such a desperate tenderness of intention as he had never before experienced. A wiser man would have realised the somewhat startling immensity of the social gulf which divided them, and felt, however sadly, that his was as impossible as the desire of the moth for the star. But he was blind, blind as a bat going wildly through the dusk.

The circumstances of his passion most seriously affected the whole grand manner of his life. Hitherto, he had been content with the social aspirations of the strong farmer or shopkeeper, and was satisfied to dwell somewhere near the apex of middle-class existence. But now, his consuming infatuation lifted him far beyond. It is strange and fearfully disturbing when a man finds the desire of his heart when in the neighbourhood of his fortieth year. Yet so it was with Marcus Igoe.

He began to rush himself into all kinds of expense to help his dream of Olive Fetherstonhaugh. He began to use his substance, the means that his wise dead father had left him, in a vain attempt to become a real gentleman. He was accepted as a member of the Hunt Club, and proceeded to keep horses that were immensely costly. Of course, Olive Fetherstonhaugh always smiled graciously in his direction at Hunt meets, and this divine condescension seemed to repay him sufficiently for the money he was spending. It may have been that he still amused her, for he was a comical figure on horseback, with his great silk hat and insignificant person. He was sent invitations to the County Balls, and this was an honour which had never before been conferred upon him, for all his wide fame as a lover of, what the *Meath Reporter* termed, "the light fantastic."

Once or twice the lady of his dreams went so far as to give him a dance at these exclusive assemblies, and he had passed with her in a maze of exaltation through the excited onlookers. He never realised why there should be such an amused expression upon every face, nor why she, beyond any of them, had been so merry. After one such transportation, he rushed over to London and bought her a pearl necklace of high price, which she was very pleased to accept. He invited her father and her father's friends to shoot over his land and specially employed a man, indeed a full-blown gamekeeper, to develop its sporting possibilities. He gave dinner parties, which were really drinking parties, to these gentlemen, and to all of which the Hon. Reginald Moore was pleased to accept his invitation and behave as a notable and brilliant guest.

All this time his bank balance had been diminishing rapidly, but he took no serious notice of it until Olive Fetherstonhaugh suddenly married a Captain who had distinguished himself in the Zulu War. So that had been her fancy all the time, a tall Guardsman, like in a novel, and he could realise it now, even if he had not been able to realise it then, that he was no figure of Romance. He could look at himself now just a little differently. But, even so, he had just been on the verge of declaring his grand passion to the adored one, the loveliest little girl in all Ireland! Indeed, he had already given the contract for the rebuilding of his house in Harbourstown upon a grandiose plan to an expensive Dublin firm in the distant and pathetic hope that she might be enticed... Oh, he was modest in his hope and only said to himself that she might...

It was a hard blow, the whole thing, and helped him, swiftly enough, to experience an accountable desire to descend from the grand life of a country gentleman. He sold his hunters in a somewhat belated attempt to recover his losses, but he had been well fleeced. His old means of enjoyment and distraction had deserted him too—the times he had had at the strong farmers' dances—these had fallen beneath him the while he had been aspiring, and this, too, was a bitter realisation.

For what must have appeared long years to him, but which were in reality only a couple of seasons, he effected, not without a hard struggle, retirement from the life around him. But at length—well, he could not stand it any longer. He returned, at first somewhat meekly and apologetically, to those well-nigh forgotten places in which he had once been such a successful figure. He was again attracted to the simple and substantial amusements which he had disdained the while he was following the shadow that was Olive Fetherstonhaugh. He was gladly welcomed, for he had been missed. The anxious mothers again permitted him to enter their thoughts, although they knew that he was not now the great match he had been. He was again, to his shame almost be it said, Marcus Igoe, "the lady killer," falling in love and forgetting just as of yore.

CHAPTER IV

HE looked older, almost, than his years, that is to say, he suggested almost at a glance, the sere and yellow period, people might easily say, for he was in the vicinity of his forty-fifth year, when he was struck by the notion of attending what turned out to be a particularly memorable dance. It had never suggested itself to him for a moment that the occasion might come to be momentous, but it did.

There was a certain lady in attendance who had come from far places in America, and it was she, beyond all the others, who, upon this occasion, caught his amorous fancy, and became the object of his most pressing attentions for the remainder of the night. She disclosed herself, of a sudden, as the most clever and charming of all the girls he had ever met anywhere. Her quickness of perception appeared to him as most desperately surprising. As she spoke to him in her smart, slangy American way she appeared absolutely delightful. Her name was Dorothy Hanratty... Oh, such a night!

In the days that followed the dance, there ensued the usual series of communications between them. This time—he knew it even as he wrote—he was more tender, more explosive, more deep, more everything, in his professions of undying affection. It may have been that the heavy sense of his disappointment had not yet been fully lifted from his mind, and that some of the very things he had once desired greatly to write to Olive

Fetherstonhaugh he now wrote to Dorothy Hanratty. He referred more than once to the happiness of "something, some day."

Miss Hanratty was delighted... Imagine, on the very first night she had "tried out"! She was immediately looking forward to a speedy termination of the "Romance" into which she had just strayed. She had no desire to return to America, but on the contrary was real glad of this opportunity to remain so suitably in Ireland. He was pretty crabbed, to be sure, but he had a nice place, with every opportunity of comfort, and these were exactly what she wanted. She was very pleased that he had so soon begun to mention "something, some day." As for him, he merely thought of her as he had thought of countless others—with, of course, one grand exception—not at all seriously, for he was still the great philanderer, but just as a passing fancy.

After a month or so, his letters began to dwindle, but not so her thought of him. Her face just looked only a little harder by way of regard, and every thought and every scheme concerning him came a little more firmly to the forefront of her mind. Although he did not know it, she had gone, in his absence, to have a look at his place, and had come away decidedly pleased... Yes, by Jiminy!...

He met her again, at another dance, towards the end of the year. He said he was very glad to see her, but this was not strictly true. Nor did it perceptibly increase in truth when she began to be "true to him" for the remainder of the night. He, the gallant, the inconstant lover of the countryside, who had never identified himself twice in succession with the same girl, save in the spacious and never-to-be-forgotten days of Olive Fetherstonhaugh, felt that this was not quite as it should be. It was a distinct encroachment upon what appeared now his real self. He felt that the night was the most wholly miserable he had ever spent.

He resolved to refrain from writing to her again. That was the way to settle it! That was the way he had always settled it! He consoled himself after this fashion, as he foolishly imagined that the regrettable affair had reached its conclusion. But he was thunder-struck, one morning, to receive notice that an action for breach of promise of marriage had been filed against him by Miss Dorothy Hanratty! It was, indeed, as a thunderbolt to the whole countryside. Even people, who, having observed how she had attached herself to him, and said that how she would be just the one to hammer some sense into him, although he had almost slipped past the days of such a possibility, now said that they were sorry for him, the poor little fellow, who had been such good fun in his way.

Oh, it was terrible, and, as the day of the trial drew ever nearer, he was continually attacked by thoughts of dreadful possibilities and apprehensions which scared him. His letters—of course she had kept every one of them—about forty. A grand show they would make of him when they were read in Court! She was claiming a thousand pounds damages! It meant that he might have to sell his farm in Harbourstown. His lovely farm! Of course, they would give it to her! They always did in such cases. He might yet have to go back and take up the business in Garradrimna that his mother had taught him to hate. Imagine, business in Garradrimna, with a name like his behind him, as well as the name that was going to be before him now!

He looked like a dead man as he took the train to Dublin, and never rightly knew how he managed to stumble down to the Four Courts. He was a crushed and timid and altogether pathetic figure as he made his appearance. With a chill feeling of horror he saw a reporter making a sketch of him. That was how he was going to appear before the whole country, a bad character, a villainous and abandoned scoundrel like in an English Sunday newspaper. He knew in his heart, too, that the others, so busy also with their note-books, had already begun to describe Miss Dorothy Hanratty as "a young lady of prepossessing personality."

It would all be in the papers next day. No defence could save him. There was never any such thing in a breach of promise case. She had on her side eminent Counsel with a reputation for ferocious eloquence. His letters were read for the benefit of the grinning crowd, all butchered there before his eyes to make a legal holiday. His poor little innocent letters that had never meant anything! Even his title of "the lady killer" which he had worn, not without a little pride, and to which he had come, in the course of years, to have an attachment, was dragged down before them as food for laughter.

"And this, gentlemen of the jury, is 'the lady killer,' " said eminent Counsel, without the faintest trace of delicacy, without consideration, indicating him with a coarse gesture: "This effete Don Juan, this remnant of humanity, who has danced his life away. Surely the punishment of the verdict we claim is certainly a slight one against a man who has so spent his life!"

The torture of it all at last came to an end. She had got her thousand pounds. He could have settled it out of court if Charles Delamere, his solicitor in Castleconnor, had not rushed him into fighting it. These cursed lawyers anyway!

As he passed up through the streets to his hotel on the North side he could hear the newsboys shouting: "Result of 'The Lady Killer' Case." As he listened to the awful sound, he thought sadly of the peaceful place far away in Meath, of Harbourstown, near the green banks of the Boyne, and then of Garradrimna. Imagine, they would be reading about him, a few evening papers there to-night, and handed eagerly from hand to hand. They would be crowding the steps of Andy Megann's newspaper shop to-morrow for the more extended accounts in the daily papers. He would be the day's great joke all over the country; everywhere they would be talking about it. It was a queer pity of him...

He had experienced the second great disaster of his life, and once more he felt a consuming desire to retire from the life around him. As soon as the talk died down, or as soon as he had a notion that it was dying town, there came for the first time in his life little moments of bitterness, little moments when he felt what he described as the worm turning in him, when he felt that, eventually, he might become a different man. He thought of them in Garradrimna as gloating over him and grinning. If ever he had to return to Garradrimna, he might find himself looking at them through eyes that might be very like their eyes, through glasses never rose-hued, through squinting windows...

CHAPTER V

YET so great is the power given a man to rehabilitate himself that, even now, the mind of Marcus Igoe did not become wholly submerged. It was true that he had to mortgage his farm in Harbourstown to the last penny, but he still had the shop in Garradrimna, and so he struggled to keep up his place and position. He could feel that he was coming to have the sympathy of his neighbours—if that counted for anything, but, no doubt at all, he was merely the ruin of the man he had been. He felt that he was allowing his appearance, such as it was, to fall into decay, and he resumed the wearing of clothes that he had cast from him on the early "nineties", yet there was a laugh in him still, some turn of the thing that was nearly his lost self. For the sake of old times, he was invited to all the dances about, and he appeared there in the swallow-tailed coat and high collar and the other apparel of his prime. But he was half a stranger in such places— now that he had been through what he had been through. Old, ceaseless, relentless, Father Time, too, had been working wonders around him. ... He felt himself moving, for the most, among sons and daughters of friends of his youth, and former "adored ones." It had come to pass that these were the *beaux* and *belles* of the moment.

Sometimes the young girls hauled him out upon the floor for a dance, playfully, and yet with tender respect for his different age, almost as they might behave towards their fathers. It hurt him. He could see now that he was not looked upon as he had been of old, but rather as a sort of elderly patron of the dances, and he was, by reason of this realisation, helped into a queer conspiracy with himself, that is, not his real self, but the self he had some notions, if not actual dreads, of becoming. But, quite unescapably, a conspiracy had sprung up between his mind and himself regarding the young girls. He was at times almost afraid of himself because of his remarkable intention.

At last, at one such dance he was having with Phœbe Hope, who was the charming daughter of the Miss Marcella Plunkett of his hey-day, he plucked up all that was left of his once indomitable courage, and those who beheld, with kindly sympathy, his faded figure wading through the waltz, saw that, most unaccountably, some noble resolve had taken possession of him. As he swung past them and they heard him make use of some of the old fine phrases of his tradition—the French and all, they saw in him again the figure of "the lady killer" newly arisen to surer glory. The thing that they had always been half afraid might happen had happened at last, and people were glad, a good many of them, for the sense of happy illusion it might bring to his mind. His end might easily be like the beginning of his life after all—supremely happy and care-free.

But this was not exactly what was happening to him, although it had been his grand intention. His thoughts of return to conquest had been pulled down to make way for a noble idea, and it made a thronging and brilliant movement into his mind, as his body moved rhythmically round the room.

He realised now that it was not possible for him to return to a period of second gallantry, even as a man returns to second childishness. But a little of earth's happiness still warmed his heart, and he began rapidly to develop his idea. Here was the fair daughter of a fine woman he had "loved," and he felt that he could love her now in turn, maybe for her mother's sake, and maybe because he was really and truly in love with her. It was a most courageous notion, particularly at the present time, when he was not without convictions of the inevitable sadness of human destiny.

He quickly considered that Phœbe Hope was at the very age when the female mind is, for the first time, just susceptible to the whisperings of Romance, and he continued to stay by her side when the waltz was concluded, talking to her in the light, pretty way that had been his grandest accomplishment. He spoke to her most eloquently of life and love, he who had placed a good deal of his life behind him, and love beyond him. She was pleased to listen. Then he went on to speak, in the natural course, of marriage, and, in what must have appeared as a fine, sudden frenzy, asked her to marry him… She seemed to think at first that he was only joking, and laughed pleasantly as if to maintain his amusement… But when she heard him refer sentimentally to the almost ruin of his life, and of how there was still time to turn over a new leaf and make her happy, the anger of all her girlhood flashed into her eyes and she withered him with passionate exclamations.

"Oh, I declare to goodness, the idea! Well I should just think not!… The idea of you having the cheek to think of wanting to marry me!"

With surprised and angry laughs to hide her real confusion, she hurried away from him, and he was left there alone by the wall while another dance had begun to move round and round… Yes, the young girls were finished with him, and he had never realised till now that this dreadful thing was sure to have happened some day… He heard a smart shop-boy from Dublin, ask someone who was the ridiculous old josser in the swallow-tailed coat—the faithful garment that had seen his rise and fall, and this, the crowning offence of his demolition…

He slipped away very quietly, and went away by himself through the youth of the morning. There was all around and about him a chromatic and orchestral brilliance, a brightness that was beyond any brightness he had ever known. He could almost feel himself swaying unsteadily, as one drunk with morning glory. But that was only what the birds might think where they were drunk with song and sunlight amid the green trees. For he swayed unsteadily simply because even the light heart seemed to have gone out of him and he was absolutely of no weight or importance in the world any more.

CHAPTER VI

WHEN he reached the house, he looked long into the glass. Yes, certainly, the things that had just been said of him were most amazingly true. His ancient morning coat that he had always fondly imagined to be part of a dress suit, was seedy and disreputable, and he was little and ugly and old and getting to be as grey as a badger.

He stood there beholding himself until he heard Farrel McGuinness, the post-man's, knock at the door. He went down and was handed an ugly-looking letter which he opened with fear clutching the little place where his heart had been... It was an official notice apprising him of the fact that the mortgagees were about to sell his farm.

The dismal reality of this ending was as a crushing blow after the Romance of all his drifting years. It was a mean consummation, such as might happen to a man who had done no gallant things at all. And an ancient, outworn figure of Romance would cut but a poor figure set here among the agricultural realities of County Meath. There was some queer little touch about him, but now, of a sudden, was it a big thing, an enormous malaccomplishment appearing to be the reef upon which the adventure of his whole life had been wrecked. His farm gone and nothing left now but the neglected shop! It had been doing so badly for the past few years, too, his old-fashioned assistants, John and Jane, running it, with John coming out to Harbourstown about twice a year to go into a whole lot of account books, just when he might be on the point of going somewhere for the day or the night. Now it was to be the shop again with John and Jane and the account books and Garradrimna. Above all, Garradrimna that he did not quite understand ... that he did not like in his heart of hearts. There would come a time he knew full well when he must hear them whispering around him.

"The ould fool, the poor ould fool, wasn't it a grand way, begad, that he went and lifted himself out of his farm?"

In such moments, would it be hard or would it be easy to maintain his once famous gesture, or to think with splendid pensiveness of his lost loves?

CHAPTER VII

TO come back to Garradrimna with nearly his whole life behind him, and to begin again. How could it be done? How could he face them? But he had to do it. He, who had so successfully removed himself from its codes, would have to learn all its ways just as if he had never lived in it, nor near it. The faded John, the faded Jane, what did they know? Beyond, the two sides of the Main Street of Garradrimna and all the squinting windows, men talking of him, women gossiping.

He began to think of his father. His father had intended him for Garradrimna. His father, a man of Garradrimna, without any of his mother's notions, who had thought of him hopefully. Even as a baby he had spoken of his son as "a great gosoon," meaning thereby a promising boy.

"Isn't he a fine gosoon, ma'am?" This to a customer.

"Oh! sure he's a grand gosoon!"

His poor father's vanity had been flattered by the very sound of the word, and it must have remained as a note of music in his mind long after Marcus had spoiled it by a loud screech.

And it was of these things he would be thinking as he stood by the counter now, trying to reconstruct himself. If only he had not gone to Harbourstown... Oh, if only he had not... with the remembrance of it always falling heavily down upon his mind now... Although he did not know what they were saying of him, he knew that they were talking, and he was adopting extraordinary means to protect himself, disguising himself ... growing a beard, standing still for long intervals as if nothing had happened to him. If only it had been his father who had had his way with him and not his mother, there might have remained the early promise of the "gosoon" ... But now only the beard, bringing gradually, however, the fantastic realisation that nothing had really happened to him at all.

His shyness in the presence of his father, as he grew up, was something which suggested the man he might become, before he had done anything in the world or before the world had done anything to him. He was possessed of a terrible shyness, too, in the presence of girls and women... But a promising gosoon, they all said, with the father's ways. The father's acquisitive ways, they meant, his business sense, his natural acumen, his deep perception of Garradrimna... It could be seen very soon that the false prophets of Garradrimna had been given the lie, and their sayings made to become as dust and ashes in their mouths, for everyone knew already that there was no chance that Marcus Igoe would begin to lavish his father's share, as soon as it came into his hands, although many had said wishfully, hopefully, while he was still a child, that this might come to pass. But they endeavoured to maintain their gift of prophecy and to excuse the unaccountability of this case by saying that it always takes a fond mother and not a fond father really to spoil a son... Mebbe... Aye, mebbe it does and then mebbe it doesn't...

Amid the conducive surroundings of his father's dominating personality the "gosoon" sprang towards manhood responsibilities with surprising rapidity. But, at the age of twenty, he was still "the gosoon", and, as if to express the extreme guilelessness of the age at which he was compelled to remain by his fond father's regard, he retained, as habits now, all the callow virtues of the gosoon stage. He neither smoked nor drank, shaved nor looked at a girl. There were occasional wild moments when he felt an almost overmastering desire to express the manhood which, nevertheless, he believed to be in him, but these notions were silenced, even, as they jumped into life, by realisation that he was Marcus Igoe, Denis Igoe's only son, and that his father was one of the great merchants of Garradrimna. His intimate relation to his father's renowned prosperity ought to be sufficient demonstration of his manhood without his finding it absolutely necessary to do any wild things. But it would not be a very "wild" thing, for instance, if he began to use a razor. His adolescent beard made his face look curiously ragged and "gommish," as he beheld himself in the glass...

He spoke of the matter to his mother, since it had begun to trouble him somewhat seriously. She looked at him quizzically... an offended fondness filling all her eyes... and she made him early ashamed of himself in a reply which seemed designed to pluck up the two flowering plants of his longing.

"To go shave, is it? Musha, Marcus, I'm surprised at you. Sure that'd be nearly all as one as thinking of looking at girls and you only a gosoon still."

He did not return to this importunity again, and by the time he had reached his twenty-fifth year, his full brown beard was an accomplished fact. His fond mother was just as proud of this beard as he himself had come to be, for it stood, in a way, for double obedience, the second aspect of which was by far the more gratifying to her mind, for although his eye held the sparkle of youth, it had not yet fallen in rapture, so far as she knew, upon any girl, although old gossips coming into the shop were never tired of dragging the matter around by saying:

"Musha, you're not looking well at all, ma'am, and isn't it near time that himself and yourself were thinking of letting Marcus bring in a woman to give you a hand?"

Her reply was, invariably, the same:

"A woman, is it? A wife you mean? For pity's sake, and him only a gosoon!" Sometimes they would take little smiles to themselves, when they thought of the beard which removed him outwardly from the gosoon state, as if with one swift stroke of a pencil by a master artist... But, as he pushed on to the age of thirty, it was his beard, extraordinary and expansive, and descending easily below the second button of the waistcoat, which still held him in a kind of satirical relation to the gosoon stage. Whenever his father said to a customer in the shop: "Oh, the gosoon will get that for you," or his mother would say: "Oh, the gosoon will see that you get exactly what you want, ma'am," his failing parents' implicit belief in their son's essential surviving relation to his young years would effectively prevent a strong, sarcastic smile from curling many a lip at sight of the great beard which now almost swept the counter.

"But sure he's mebbe really only a gosoon after all," one would say to another, with a puzzled shake of the head... "Sure when that's the way they see him, mebbe he is."

CHAPTER VIII

WHEN Marcus was turned thirty his mother died and, towards the end of the same year, his father, leaving his only son all his possessions in the world. And once more the false prophets, the Old Moores of Garradrimna, were baulked in their sense of divination. For it would seem, indeed, that, although his present perfect state of independence afforded him every opportunity for the spirit of youthful wildness, which the much concerned fondness of his mother had so successfully quelled, he remained unshaven, undelighted by either cigarettes or wine, and quite unenamoured of any lovely lady. His life, it would seem, was finally shaped and fixed. Besides, too, after a very short time, he did a significant thing— an action which, in its affirmations, almost prevented further surmise about him, so wise was it, so solid in the viewpoint that it expressed.

He saw the gradual decline of the bootmaking business in the disappearance of the gentry who had patronised him, in the dwindling custom even of the people who still stuck to the old ways in spite of the great influx of cheap boots from Northampton to the other cheap-jacks of the place. Henceforth, bootmaking in Garradrimna might easily become a declining business… A man must think of a way of going on that would never know this kind of setback… and there was one such business. In his observation, the advances of civilization had never seriously affected the sale

34

of drink. In good or evil fortune, too, it was the thing that men always supported, always would support in Garradrimna.

There could be no doubt about him now, anyway, for was he not announced as the purchaser of the extensive premises of Jimmy Merriman, who had just recently retired, they said, because he had too much money and did not believe in selling drink any more. Thereafter, Marcus Igoe was a fully made man, and well in line with John Higgins, who owned the biggest and most varied establishment in the village. It seemed that nothing further he might do mattered in the least. Still, you never could tell. It was most irritating to see a man so wise after all. There grew up a certain heretical feeling with regard to him promising certain excitement to Garradrimna, where little things had always been the really significant things. This matter of his beard, for instance, was still a constant source of anxious consideration, not to say hope, to many a one.

"Mebbe," some said, "he'll be ever and always striving to let on he's a gosoon by wearing the yoke that his mother would never let him cut off, for fear he mightn't look like a gosoon, by reason of him using the razor. And when a man pretends, when he has to let on he's something he isn't, he always finishes by getting to be something else."

"D'ye know now?" others would say, "there must be some method, after all, in the madness of his appearance, for, to begin with, d'ye see, it is a great saving of time for any man to grow a beard. He has that advantage out of it anyway."

This last not infrequent observation held a good deal of wisdom, for, in a place where time was not considered of very large account, Marcus Igoe was a visible proof of the value of time. He never wasted a day, or any part of a day; he never took a holiday nor ever attended any of the crude entertainments which helped, spasmodically, to brighten the life of the village.

"Fools, all of them, and fools and their money are soon parted!" He used to say this of those who made their poor attempts to be gay, for he was now a man of immense wisdom in little things, little observances, little tricks, little ways, little sayings.

His daily life was a complete and perfectly ordered sequence of habits. He rose punctually at seven to the exertions of the day and, a few minutes later, walked down the street to the shop which, before the purchase of it by himself, had been the property of Jimmy Merriman. He would stroke his fine beard in delight as he went, and it would often appear to some particular oracle of Garradrimna, Dickeen Crosbie, for instance, that the whole power of Marcus Igoe lay in his beard, and, further, that it was essentially related to whatever calamities with which the years might eventually afflict his head. For example, one morning, in a moment of real vision, Dickeen said:

"D'ye know what I'm going to tell you now, if he shaved it off, I'm of opinion that he'd lose his strength like Samson and wouldn't be worth a damn for anything any more. But when the grey begins to come into it, mebbe it's what he'll get afraid of the holy show he'll be and then... and then you could never know what he'd do."

"Mebbe," replied Bartle Boyhan, the boon companion of Dickeen, as both waited at Kafe's corner for the establishment at the north end of the Main Street to be opened, so that they might at least begin to quench the great thirst that was upon them.

"Mebbe, I say, only mebbe."

CHAPTER IX

AS one result of his perfectly ordered life, the premises which he had purchased were opened and their machinery in motion by the time that Marcus Igoe came down the street from the shop that his father had left him, and above which he still slept. Morning after morning, it would seem endlessly and forever, he would say the same words to the assistants, Ethel and Henry, who had been left behind him by Jimmy Merriman—

"Lovely morning, Ethel!"

"Lovely morning, Henry!"

Then, passing swiftly through the shop, and entering the nook of a room between the shop and the kitchen, he would sit down to what always had a suggestion to him of the little, irritating delay of his breakfast.

"Now, Kathleen Mavourneen!" he would call, and Kathleen, the servant girl, would appear bearing on the same old tray exactly the same kind of breakfast, week in, week out. He would spend the very same amount of time in consumption of it each morning, giving out the very same kind of dry old chat to Henry Abbott, his assistant, if he happened to be with him at table.

Occasionally, the accustomed routine would be broken, ever so slightly and not altogether irrelevantly to the intrinsic personality of Marcus Igoe. His devoted assistant would say, "Mind, sir, your beard!" as, in an unguarded moment, or in a moment when his mind was completely occupied by thoughts of

37

business, an inartistic dribble of tea, or it might be a stain of egg, would appear distressfully upon the rich and comely beard of the gosoon. Then, what was the wise man's only known turn of vanity would manifest itself... He would rise in some confusion and wipe his beard dry and clean with his handkerchief before the advertisement for Jameson's Whisky which served also as an overmantel...

Now and then, in such a moment, he would seriously examine his beard, as if for the traces of the silver which must soon be falling, Henry Abbott watching shrewdly the while with the corner of his eye. No, no, thank God! It was still the same. The years had not yet begun to run races past him.

By this time he had come to be regarded as "a shocking wise man entirely." And, certainly, the strongly imperturbable look in his eye fully consolidated the very convincing sweep of his beard. Even if, eventually and inevitably, it came to be grey, he must then look exactly like a wise man from the East, or a prophet out of the Bible. Yet, in spite of much convincing evidence of this possibility, the few remaining wise ones, the long established oracles of Garradrimna, said, out of their vast store of knowledge of such cases as his, that they had known of some of the wisest middle-aged men who had completely lost their heads over girls and the like, and done "quare" things.

There was no limit to the disturbing influence of women, as they well knew, most of them being women themselves. But it might still take a considerable amount of this kind of disturbance to move the mind of Marcus Igoe, for a petrified crust of commonsense was already over all his ways. But hope eternal sprang to the breast of Dickeen Crosbie, for instance, and, in contemplation of the wise man, he found it a great comfort to say the like of this to himself:

"It does be a kind of funny to think that it's often the very things that are after making a man smart and successful, succeed, after a while, in making an end of him as well. It's his habits, as it were, reinforced by his beard, that are after making Marcus Igoe, and mebbe now it might turn out to be his beard and his beautiful correct and business-like ways in combination that'll have something to do with making an end of him."

But Marcus Igoe went his way, as if not a word was ever being said about him. He was, surely, in his own person, a shining example of the futility of envy. Whatever anyone might say, it was his habits and nothing else which had succeeded in making success the foremost of his habits. Never, so far, for a moment, had he gone trespassing, as it were, beyond the mearing fence of his own rigid personality, never, even as he began to advance in years, was he heard to laugh out heartily like a man because of any remarkable comicality that he might suddenly have detected in the scheme of things. He was completely blind to the wilful and disconcerting twists of life, for it must be said, albeit with regret, that he had no sense of humour, having given himself no leisure in which to develop one.

And thus did the years pass on, yet not at all monotonously for him, but punctually and upon a definite plan that pleased him until a goodly quality of silver had crept into his hair... But now that this, the snow, had at last fallen, it did not greatly disturb him. He accepted the ravages of time, for his very nature compelled him to admire the habitual and correct way in which old Father Time held occupation of his appointed place, even as he himself occupied his place in the life of Garradrimna.

CHAPTER X

HE was just within four months of his fiftieth year when a most unaccountable disturbance began to make entrance into the life of Marcus Igoe, and, even as it had been hopefully prophesied, it was one of his habits that had much to do with its beginning, his admirable punctuality that had developed a certain movement of mind which caught him in its net now, and he so wise and all...

A new book-keeper had come to John Higgins's, the "Enormous Emporium" that was situated midway between the shop that had descended from his father and the new and different kind of shop that Marcus Igoe had bought. Now here was a thing, an aspiring circumstance of life in Garradrimna, which caused him to sneer almost unkindly, although he was not an unkind man— the very idea of anyone employing a book-keeper specially in Garradrimna, instead of letting the assistants enter transactions in the books anyway as they occurred! Besides, he was his own book-keeper, for he considered, and perhaps not unwisely either, that it also was one of the little ways by which a man might reasonably hope to attain to opulence in Garradrimna.

"Book-keepers, the Lord save us, sure them'd go near robbing a man with their salaries and mistakes."

Yet for all the strength of his firm conviction he had nothing very severe to say, personally, of this new book-keeper of Higgins's, Nancy Looram. He soon found that she was nearly always standing at the door doing nothing only looking out as he went by of a morning upon his blithe passage between his two shops. The girl had already fallen into acquaintance with him quite naturally for he was one of the institutions of the place, like the shop behind her or the forge or the pump or the young men's hall. From the very first he had nothing but the very nicest things to say (to himself) about her. He, the appraiser and idolater of habits, was glad to see that she was fondly devoted to at least one habit, that of standing at the door every morning doing nothing only looking out at him going by... It was grand to see her in particular, one of the earliest signs of life about the place...

People of Garradrimna still twisting and turning lazily in their beds could hear his voice raised in salutation of her, and ringing pleasantly into the tall green woods which stretched far away in soft and billowy delight beyond Clunnen Castle... At first it had been merely: "Good morning, Miss Looram!" and that was all. But, gradually, some unaccountable hesitancy had slipped into his stride, and now he often stopped to have a word with her... He sometimes laughed, too, and those who heard said it was a pleasant laugh, now that he had found it after all the years...

Frequently, he was seen to dally longer than was good for the precision of his habits. He often worried for the peace and careful conduct of his future life after such aberrant moments, and he firmly resolved to be more careful next morning... But in the morning the bulwarks of his determination would be shattered hopelessly if Miss Looram happened to be standing at the door of Higgins's, and she always was... gazing out over the tall green woods in the most delightful way ... until he appeared.

If it were possible that he could simply regard her as Higgins's book-keeper, he would have said that Higgins was giving her a lady's life, which might result in his finally disappearing from the scene as a business rival in Garradrimna... But being whom she was, he said nothing at all...

Unpunctuality, permitted to enter his life thus casually, affected him at every turn. His faithful servants in the shop that had descended to him and where he lived, John and Jane, and his housekeeper, Mary Margaret Caherlane, observed the extraordinary change with startled eyes. They had half longed for it hitherto... yet they were strangely sorry now that it had come... They felt that they were losing something that had been like an old friend. And it might easily be the prelude to drink, now that he had a public-house of his own.

A thorough and complete disintegration began to extend hurriedly through the whole of Marcus Igoe. He began to display a gayer trip in his stride, in an attempt, possibly, to catch up with the youth that he had permitted to slip past him while he had been cultivating his habits towards such extreme precision. He fell to wearing his well-preserved Sunday clothes upon week-days, and, in a remarkable fit of vanity, got a new suit made expensively in Dublin, which, he felt, must be an example to Tommy Price, the tailor of Garradrimna, for the remainder of his days.

This strange proceeding was followed immediately by another performance even more decidedly peculiar. He turned attention to the thinning thatch upon his head and spent upwards of a pound upon several bottles of a famous hair-restorer, in a strenuous attempt to recall it to luxuriance. He was not suddenly successful to any conspicuous degree, and, his desire to appear young in the eyes of Miss Looram being so great, he was prompted most unhappily, to the thought that the energy required for the maintenance of his beard was having an impoverishing effect upon the other part of his covering. One could not have it both ways... In these moments he would have visions wide and complete as those of men who had adventured or travelled far.

The things he had not done with his youth were the things he might do now, daring, astounding, even devilish things... But there were little moments of doubt. Could a man reasonably or decently do all these things in a beard? He often wondered, thinking so, but the great men of the past had been bearded, the prophets and the poets and many warriors. It was only a fashion, the fashion of a more niggardly time. Shaving was something that had been foisted on the world! But girls were always in the fashion and of the fashion. They must like it. Could he do it, could he say to her the words he wanted so greatly to say while wearing that beard? Often, as he spoke to her, he caught her eyes upon it, whether in admiration or in envy or in disgust he never could tell. She was always looking at it, anyway, the lovely little thing!

So, one fateful morning, driven to it by her eyes, he shaved off his fine, full beard.

It was only his customary whistle that Miss Looram recognised a little later as he came down the street. She smiled, with a kind of stifled graciousness, in his direction, for she was in reality driven to great straits to hide her amusement. She suddenly realised that this morning she could readily speak to Marcus Igoe of all the light things of the world—local jokes and commercial travellers' stories, at which she could laugh immoderately and at the same time make an attempt to disguise the subject of her amusement. He thought that he had never before seen her so perfectly charming... Ah! ha! It must be the removal of his beard. How well he had guessed what would please her most? Sure it had been a show anyway... He would "axe" her any morning now... But he would give her a little time to get used to his new appearance.

His assistants in the public-house scarcely knew him when he appeared before them, but they hid their laughter as best they could... Besides there was something that almost frightened them about his amazing metamorphosis... for he was really like one who had returned from a distant country or from the grave... He gave one a sense of some other life, a dream life, or a real life through which he had passed and with which he was quite finished. For a moment everything that was in his presence or around him seemed to fade... into a present unreality. The assistants were grievously perturbed, and looked, as it were, for help to the little accustomed cluster of morning customers... hopefully, for Garradrimna to re-assert itself again through comic means... If his customers recognised him, if they rose superior to the disturbing thoughts he brought into one's mind...

But they had recognised him ... some of them, Bartle Boyhan, for instance, and Dickeen Crosbie, two men who had the comic vein so deep in them that they could not be deceived by anything... Already they were congratulating him on the improvement in his appearance... He laughed thankfully, and said that he felt lighter anyway—without the beard... and wondered why he had not got rid of it long ago.

As soon as he went into the little nook of a room between the shop and the kitchen, Bartle said, with mock concern, as he gave a wide wink:

"Imagine, the ingratitude of that, and it nearly after making him, the same beard!"

CHAPTER XI

A FEW mornings later it was given to Bartle Boyhan to speak the bitterest word that had ever sounded in the ear of Marcus Igoe.

The men of the unquenchable thirsts and the satirical minds were already standing by the counter when Marcus came in from his morning passage down the street... There was an unsatisfied, unfilled look in the eyes of the man of two shops and many affairs, which the satirical leer of Bartle immediately caught.

"Good-morning, sir," he said, putting down his pint... after having waited and being hopefully disappointed by Marcus's failure to say:

"Lovely morning, Ethel!"

"Beautiful morning, Henry!"

There was certainly something wrong with the wise man... He mustn't, for how could he have seen Nancy Looram at the door of Higgins's?

There was no sign of the accustomed movement to the little nook of a room between the shop and the kitchen, no sound of the stereotyped command which was the way he ordered his breakfast: "Now, Kathleen Mavourneen!"

The wise man was, on the contrary, speaking strangely to the two of them. He was excited, different, even more different than was suggested by his absent beard. The very fact that he had not seen Nancy Looram this morning was the cause of his manner. But they knew it too. They knew it so well that they could not go on listening to him for long. They looked at one another in commiseration, as it were, of the imbecile behaviour of the great man and spoke, Bartle first:

"By the look of you, sir, I'd nearly say for certain that you hadn't heard the news yet. And, at the same time, I'd go so far as to say that what's after happening in Garradrimna, secretly, at six o'clock this morning in the bright sunshine and the birds singing beautifully, is preying, as it were, disastrously, upon your poor mind and you don't even know it...

"Tee Hee!" spluttered Dickeen, in spite of himself... "And I may as well tell you straight that I don't blame the little girl at all for what she's after doing on you in the heel of the hunt, because I know, I say I know, that she was dying fond of you all the while you bore that late glorious growth so proudly on your bosom... Musha, sure you were just like the grand little gosoon of your mother's affection. She felt, she must have felt, as it were, that that luxuriant performance, for all your reputed wisdom and the strong evidence of it that you have gathered round you, hid the face of a gosoon and the heart of a little child.

"But, as soon as you revealed yourself, as it were, in that unhappy moment when you attacked yourself with the razor, she could not bear to think that, after all her fondness, you were only a middling, dilapidated ould man, with a retreating chin and an ould grey mallet on you, and it bleaching bald with the dint of the years, so you see she married John Higgins at six o'clock this morning, and him with only a scrubby little bit of a whisker itself, but, maybe, in the course of time, it will grow into a beard of sufficiently respectable dimensions to be a memento for ever and always of the love of her heart that she lost in you, for that's the plain truth and nothing else; she was in love with your beard, and it broke the poor girl's heart nearly, and drove her to rashness and, eventually, to loveless marriage when you went and demolished it."

Bartle, in moments of magnification, claimed descent from the satirical bards, and this was out of his "songs," but its "singing" upon the ears of Marcus Igoe... Oh God! ... It was devilish... He found himself performing weak gestures that were almost the indication of pleas for mercy, for example, stroking the air in the place where his beard should have been. In any other calamity, it might have been as a staff to lean on, but it was not there now...

He could nearly cry... so, hurriedly, desperately, in case any calamity of that kind should betray the full and final wounding of his heart, he hurried from the shop and into the room where he had taken his breakfast through all the contented years before he had parted with his gorgeous beard in the hope of winning a woman's love, not knowing that, maybe truly, as Bartle said, what she had liked in him was what he thought she had not liked...

Even the command, "Now, Kathleen Mavourneen!" would not yet come from him, would not rise above the smother of his feelings... But, of course, he had not the faintest thought of the breakfast now... yet, for all that, he was intensely conscious... He could hear from the shop the jubilant noise of Dickeen and Bartle. These sounds were fully representative of the feeling towards him that had just been created by the marriage of Nancy Looram and John Higgins. Garradrimna, in spite of all his habitual wisdom, was going to have its sport at his expense after all.

As a melancholy solace, there, with his head upon the table, he had remembrance of the ancient words: "If I be shaven, then my strength will go from me, and I shall become weak and be like any other man." That was the little saying he would be remembering now... remembering. It was the truest expression that had ever come from the strongest man who had ever lived. He had learned it early in life, only to forget it, so desolately and with such loss now… for he now saw clearly what had happened. John Higgins, his big rival for the trade of the sixth or seventh public-house (there were seven but really room in the place for only six) had seen that his whole strength had lain in his beard.

Oh, he was relentless and remorseless, that Higgins. "To attack Marcus Igoe in his strength," he must have said, "and maybe finish him too," and he had had good help from that two-faced little girl, but two nice faces! They must have conspired, John Higgins and Nancy Looram, to finish him. How well they had not married until just after he had cut his beard? They had arranged it nicely. But, after all, had she said anything about his beard, had she requested him to do away with it? No, she hadn't, but she had hypnotised him into doing it, and that was worse. She had made him feel like doing grand things for her and that was what he had done … at the instigation of Higgins! Did ever anyone know anything like it? A show! That was what he was going to be, an absolute, holy show…

It seemed to him, all that day, that there was an unwonted stillness upon Garradrimna, as if, in a sense, some sad thing had happened. And there were moments when the silence was punctuated by another and very different form of sound, the sound of suppressed laughter, at the forge, at the dress-maker's, in every one of the other six public-houses.

Even upon the street there were little spurts of laughter that carried far, disturbing the listener, disturbing even the most anxious and concerned listener, Marcus Igoe himself, where he sat still in the room where he had so often taken his habitual breakfast, rising every few minutes to look at himself in either the whisky mirror or the port mirror, long and sadly… This was surely someone else, some dim and defeated man who had lived in another time… maybe powerful once, but now merely a figure of unreality and dream, who might never hope to hold again the influence over Garradrimna that he had once held. Was he there at all, or where was he, or what had he done with his life, or had he ever been?

It was again for him the mood entirely of dream ... Himself in other days, in other circumstances, with things he had done now undone, and a great sense of happiness splashing and gurgling through his mind, as of a mountain stream splashing in the sunlight over little stones... glinting in delight... If Mary Margaret Caherlane had only gone away to America that time she had threatened, when, as a mere boy, he had made love to her, and if he had remained lucky and becoming successful according to all the codes of Garradrimna... had yet remained himself, for all that, still, young and hopeful with the dream of a reality filling all his mind. Aye, that was the thing—the dream of a reality.

He could feel himself moving into thought of himself as the possessor of the one window in all Garradrimna which did not seem to squint. No gaze of malignant scrutiny ever fell from it in any attempt to still further warp the course of life in this small place, where even the most insignificant events seemed to pass in affright beneath that oblique, inquisitive stare... The squintless window was that of Marcus Igoe, who had the name on him of being a hard man. It might be that it was because of his hardness he lived so much to himself, as they said, and so had little leisure, when you thought of how hard he worked, to cultivate a vast interest in all the small affairs of Garradrimna.

But, although they respected all the money he had made, they loudly deplored the fact that he did not possess a squinting window even as each of themselves. Their windows were their very lives, for through them each looked into the windows of the souls of the others, often to the extent of shattering an enemy through the very vehemence of that long, stony stare... It was not a little queer that Marcus Igoe, alone of all the householders in Garradrimna, never attempted to exercise this sinister power over others towards their destruction, yet, although this would seem to suggest a certain softness, a certain amount of desire not to be the cause of hurt to any other, they called him a hard-hearted man.

"The Lord save us, but isn't Marcus Igoe the hard man?" they would say, with a curious, incessant emphasis, as if to insist upon the softness, by comparison, of themselves.

Never an eye would appear in any window of his little house all through the day, for he had always some money-making plan to occupy him through working hours, instead of gazing out with a wide look of wonder upon every passer-by, and, because he had not married, he had gathered no kindred eyes about him to take the place of his in any window... There was some kind of inter-dependence, surely, between the fact that he had not married, and the fact that he had no squinting window. But, strangely, it was not until all the windows were closed and all the blinds pulled down upon all the windows of Garradrimna that the absence of a woman in his life smote him with a full sense of his loss...

Then it would seem as if all the destructive power of the windows was turned upon him as he sat in his cold, dark house alone. On wet, cheerless nights it was his peculiar and sad fancy to sit by the fireless grate thinking, thinking. It was very queer indeed, that, although he had means in plenty, he had not attempted to surround himself with all the protective comforts which a man likes to place between himself and the grave. But the windows of Garradrimna had successfully prevented his contriving a window which might stand, somehow, as a protection from some of the more destructive forces of life. His hardness bespoke wisdom, but it was a sterile wisdom that had not made the world any easier for him.

"Isn't it a very foolish thing for Marcus Igoe to be so wise a man?" was a thing they would often say in Garradrimna.

In all his quiet moments by the fireless grate, his very heart would feel as if stared at by the windows of his own soul. It would seem to be shrivelling up within him. He had done a poor, mean thing with his life, and the thought of it continually burned into his mind as his punishment. He had not taken unto himself a wife, and why, in the name of God, had he not done that?

There was a day when he had been younger and even then he had had a house of his own and a promising share of the world. The little broken memories of that day would cause even his cowardice to stir reproachfully in his breast... But the windows were his excuse for himself always, the little, squinting windows of Garradrimna which he could think of only as having abridged his destiny. Even if he had attempted to maintain it, the offensive stare of his one little window would have been no match for all the rest of them, so powerfully arranged in combination... Beneath that awful, discouraging, defeating leer, how could he have sallied forth on any morning to the sacred ceremony of marriage, how could he have returned on any evening with his bride?

And there had been one girl, *his* girl in the days gone by, Mary Margaret Caherlane, the tidy little maid in his father's house. How bold he had been that time, how exciting it had been, that secret love affair? He could remember still, with a return of rare gladness always, the evenings he had gone walking with her in the silent woods beyond Garradrimna and how they had returned, arm in arm, towards the village, a brave and lovely intention warming his heart... until they were near the village... when the precaution would fall that their courtship must still remain a secret...

51

What would his father say, or his mother, or the whole of them in Garradrimna? How, one lovely night, they had gone almost together and sat near one another at Buzzanno's Circus. It was in some such a moment that Mary Margaret Caherlane had spoken of going to America... going away from him... and she had promised him her photograph, a tiny one on tin... and that, maybe, when she came back he would be his own master and master of Garradrimna too...

Ah, yes, his cowardice had conquered him, and that was why the windows always seemed to spoil his satisfaction with any triumph over Garradrimna he might have made — because they had defeated his dream, and very well did he realise it, now, in a powerful crush of feeling that was akin to remorse, but was not altogether despair.

He always seemed to think of her as having gone to America... that she had given him the little photograph and was far away from him in a foreign land, where she had found a man, maybe, who was not afraid... They did not seem to be afraid of anything in America!... She must have a big family by now... and she seemed to have come back, often and often, to Garradrimna with some of her lovely children... stopping to speak to him as he stood in his own doorway on summer evenings, and they had lingered there talking, until the fragrant dark had gathered in around them, about the beauty of the twilight time in Ireland... And he had listened almost dumbly to her splendid talk as she went on past him in the conversation, and gazed upon her grandeur, the hard look which his name had induced upon his countenance softened, somehow, as he heard her always ending on the wish that she could live in Ireland always...

But it seemed to be only her photograph that he had on cold, empty nights in Garradrimna, and was it any reason then that he had grown more and more to be a hard-hearted man? It was enough surely to excuse the fact that he had almost sold his very soul for money, and the reason, truly, why he had begun to buy up the whole of Garradrimna. They said it was the height of foolishness for a hard man to be doing the like of this with his money — just to be buying houses to leave them empty and let them slip into ruins.

He was destroying Garradrimna. Already he had purchased seven small houses in Nugent Street, and it seemed likely that he would buy the whole of it and Main Street as well, if he could scrape together sufficient money before he died. They laughed in enjoyment to think that his madness might waste every single penny of his hard-earned money before he had managed completely to purchase the squint of Garradrimna. But loud though they might whisper, bitter though they might sneer, it was not given them to see an explanation of the hard-hearted man.

It was his abiding conviction that it was the squinting windows that had brought him loneliness and loss, so it did not seem queer at all, at least not to himself, that he should be devoting his money and his life to purchasing the malignant stare of Garradrimna. But no one had ever heard him whispering in the evenings over her image in his mind: "And I'd marry her, ready so I would, if the man died on her over there, and she came back to Ireland — even if she had fourteen or fifteen childer itself. And something tells me that she might come back, even that way, some day, and mebbe, if I can manage it, there would be no squinting windows in Garradrimna but my own by the time she'd come."

CHAPTER XII

YET, in spite of all dreaming, all attempts however plausible, to fix himself and look at himself in other schemes of life he had only done one thing, he had "met" Margo... who had been Mary Margaret Caherlane and who had never gone away only remaining to become the plump and somewhat strong-tempered woman he had married after he had lost everything in real life. The adventures of his "lives" had brought him only to this. He was not even a shoemaker to the full extent of the "trade" he had learned... only a sort of a shoemaker, a cobbler, the small part of the precaution of his dead father, that he had retained, as it were, just barely to save himself.... There was no doubt about it; one way or another, Garradrimna had made bits of him. No matter what he might have done, it would, most likely, have made bits of him.

He knew all its rutted ways down which he had descended from every dream, but he had a notion that, at last, he had some claims to wisdom, that he had, somehow, grasped the meaning of things. His was, in a way, a philosophic occupation, the cobbling of the shoes of Garradrimna and half the parish. If it took more than he was capable of to look into the minds of a great many of them, could he not look at their boots and tell you something about them that way? There was a good deal of a man after all in his boots. He had come to learn the shape of men's minds, as it were, from their boots, and the things they were capable of doing.

He could examine a pair of boots as a phrenologist might examine a cranium, going over them with great care, and, by virtue of a subtle faculty which seemed to have developed in his fingers, tell you many a thing, and then there were the shoes of the ladies. He still used the "trade" terms to include the shoes of women and of "ladies" that is to say real ladies, for there were a few of the kind still in the locality — gentry and even farmers' daughters of good breeding and accomplishment. The shoes of maidens just beginning to court passed through his hands. And above all, but upon a much higher shelf of his speculation, there were the shoes of little children...

Often he would throw two or three pairs of shoes together and dwell upon them in calm speculation. They might be enemies or they might even be lovers, or else young people who had yet to face the world, which, in a sense, he had never entered, and yet he could almost tell you exactly from pondering their shoes, the kind of things that might ensue, the kind of gay or sad things that might happen to them and they going through their lives... Often, sitting there alone in the midst of crowds of shoes, a whole world of struggling, warring, loving, laughing, crying humans would be about him.

He could almost feel himself become of significance and account in the world as he gazed upon them... a gigantic power behind the scenes, knowing all about them, doing with them, manipulating them absolutely as he liked — only he wasn't let. And it seemed such a pity—when a man like him was compelled to renounce a speculative form of life in which he might have won to much excellence, for an actual one which precluded the possibility of any brilliant success. Speculation, wide and free, upon the feet of men was one thing, but the actual repairs of their shoes was quite another.

His mind might have brought him anywhere only that the wife made him earn his living. He could have come at length to know everything about life — if he had been let alone, yet it seemed scarcely possible now that any circumstance that might arise in the life of a poor cobbler of bad boots would call for any great exercise of wisdom, any nice occasion when the lifting of a finger, one way or another, at the bidding of the mind might be momentous, but even in the midst of the ferocious torture of work, it was Marcus Igoe's remaining means of solace to have hopes. Something might happen yet… It would be most gorgeous, for instance, if…! But his thinking, his half dreaming, which might so easily subside into his desired condition of pure contemplation was never allowed to proceed very far…

There would be a youngster standing by his side with the remains, as it were, of a pair of boots in his hand and there would be his wife, Margo, beside him giving out her command:

"Let you have the young lad's boots finished this evening, you idle, good-for-nothing old man! Musha, sure it's me heart broke you have!"

Or it might be a messenger from Rodolphus Keeling, the rich man, wanting an eyelet put into a hole in his left legging, or a thong tied to his riding whip (for he sometimes cobbled harness as well). Margo would always stand right over him while he would be doing a thing of this kind for Mr. Keeling, although he quite failed to see where he gained anything by letting everything wait upon a thank-ye job belonging to the likes of Rodolphus Keeling. But of course it was part of the unfortunate foolishness of Margo to fancy that a rubbing of shoulders with the "quality" secured even thus at obvious loss, contributed to her own worth in the eyes of the neighbours. The quality indeed!

Ah, ha, he knew the quality… since his dream of Olive Fetherstonhaugh. General Jim, The Hon. Reginald Moore, The

56

Hon. Benjamin Rand and that crowd! But maybe there might come a day even still when *her* lovely hunting boots would be sent to him for some slight repairs... and then he would remain for hours and hours with one little boot upon either knee talking to them with coloured talk, petting them until they would make movements like dancing steps...

Even after some such gayer moment of his labour, he would still be contemplating, still bothering his head seriously in attempting to puzzle out the nature of wisdom. But, what was it anyway, when all was said and done? From the most persistent observation of his neighbours it seemed to be a matter of money, pure and simple, like everything else in the world.

And so he knew moments almost of final despair, simply because, seeing that he could never hope to have any money, he could never hope to have any wisdom. Therefore, it was likely that, domineered over to his destruction by his wife, he would go down to history as the most undistinguished citizen that Garradrimna had yet produced...

There were times when he thought of this with a villainous and painful insistence, which became duly reflected in the quality of his work. And it must be said at once that, at no time at all, did he make a bad attempt to reproduce his state of mind... Ah, where the devil was the use in a fellow being alive at all if he did not leave some kind of a mark upon the world? (With this, a terrific clout to the sole of any boot at all upon which he might happen to be working!) A man doing his damndest with the boots of the whole countryside when he knew well, at the same time, that it was too late in life, he having put too much apast him, to think of making a reputation as a cobbler. (Now, with this, a fierce blow to a rivet that had gone sideways!)

So far as he was concerned, what did they think they were at, boots and people and all? (With this, savage hammering!) He could tell them, then, that his repairs to that particular boot would not be an advantage to any man's frame of mind! Mebbe, if he was spared, he would yet succeed in leaving a mark upon Garradrimna and the whole countryside! (There, it was finished now, and, after a fierce final skelp, he flung the boot from him!)

By degrees, he found himself making an extraordinary and quite unenviable reputation. For many a man who had become crooked with corns, twisted and physically squinted in the eyes of his neighbours, laid it all at the door of Marcus Igoe.

"As sure as you're there I'll go this way to my grave on the head of him, the savage and revengeful scoundrel! I'll never recover from the crooked feet he's after giving me, and, furthermore, it's mebbe what I'll be handing down the pair of feet you see on me to my children's children!"

In the more deeply burning moments of the vindictive way into which his mind had turned, Marcus Igoe had wild visions — visions of a great procession of cripples, each one most suitably bent in artistic agreement with the power of the squinting windows to produce a like condition in the mind. It would be an achievement certainly, but the more his thoughts became occupied with it, the more did it appear as a desired result that was destined finally to elude him. Each fresh production of a cripple was such a blow to his reputation as a cobbler, even as his reputation stood, that it meant the removal, by people taking the necessary precaution, of many possible cripples beyond the reach of his revengeful hands. It would appear then that if he could not withstay the purpose of his bitterness, his customers must all be gone from him very soon.

But, somehow, the failure of his life, the sad collapse of all his little attempts to be remarkable, had determined this subsequent quality of his life, and he felt that it was likely to remain always at the same level in spite of any attempt at amelioration.

If only he had been fair to Margo… from the beginning, instead of thinking of someone else, and then, on the head of that, subsiding, as he could think of it in no way other than that he had subsided, and surrendered in his business duel with John Higgins, becoming, God forgive him, even as Bartle Boyhan and Dickeen Crosbie, only without their accomplishment of saving wit… letting everything go until Margo had to marry him to save him…

He seemed to have had money once upon a time, but it was so long since, and he had not minded it. With money and some sense he could have beaten Garradrimna. Margo had the sense, and, he supposed, that was why she was always trying so hard now to make him earn. But the incurable twist in him still persisted. The endeavour to which she was forcing him towards the lifting up of his life again was producing an effect which doubly marked the declining quality of his declining years… If he had money itself… Ah, if only he had… But would he, in that event, be able to do anything with the self of him that had never seemed to become a reality?

CHAPTER XIII

WHEN he was just turned sixty-one a remarkable event happened in the life of Marcus Igoe. Indeed it might be said with truth that it was the only remarkable event that had ever happened to him … only it was outside him. He had had nothing at all to do with bringing it to pass. He was left a legacy by his aged uncle Paul, who had just died in New Orleans. He seemed to be working as usual on the morning that the news came to him, carried quite grandiosely indeed by Charles Delamere, the solicitor belonging to Castleconnor. His beautiful blue car, with the silver figure poised for flight upon the bonnet, glided softly to the door and Mr. Delamere prepared elaborately to descend.

A certain exaltation sprang into the mind of Marcus upon beholding this unaccustomed spectacle come to his own door. It coincided with a swift return of his thoughts to memories of Charles Delamere with him in the Four Courts in Dublin in the breach of promise action brought by Miss Dorothy Hanratty. As a sort of prelude to the satisfaction he might soon be having, he muttered to himself quite joyously: "He rushed me into torture that time, but I think I have him now…" Even a thing, so calculated to startle him, as the visit of a solicitor in state, he could not realise outside his scheme of revenge.

Could it be that, at last, he was going to have satisfaction for the annoyance and disgrace and loss he had gone through that time of the "case" by producing a monumental pair of corn-producing boots for the man who had been his own solicitor? It might seem a queer way of getting the better of his former legal adviser at this late stage... but he was confused by thinking that what business other than boots could possibly have brought Mr. Charles Delamere to his door? He was almost into the shop now. There must surely be left upon him, by way of marking his own peculiar, although belated, means of getting the better of all the circumstances that had afflicted his life, a mark that might never be effaced. It was the only chance he had ever had of marking his regard of the Law. Ah, ha, he knew the Law!

As it appeared to bear so directly upon the main purpose of his life, Marcus began to feel curiously sorry, as soon as disclosure of the purpose of the visit made it plain that the opportunity of producing a pair of boots of almost unbearable torturing power would not be afforded. His immediate disappointment was so great that it took him quite a while to realise at all the drift of what Mr. Delamere had begun to say... His uncle Paul dead in New Orleans... a wealthy bachelor with a great way of going on... minded himself... a shrewd man who had made discreet investments... his nephew Marcus Igoe of Garradrimna... Meath County, Ireland... sole legatee... a very considerable fortune... wished him joy...

Margo, eager in the foreground, displayed such an intensity of feeling as seemed fully to make up for her spouse's deplorable absence of emotion... This was where she was going to come in after all she had suffered... She had never held a very high opinion of her husband's grasp of things, but, in this moment, whatever lingering hope he might have retained of again connecting himself with reality faded from her mind... When great good fortune had come running towards him at the very last he was unable to meet it like a man and bid it welcome...

Ten thousand pounds! Why, it ought to be enough to drive any man near mad, let alone a cobbler that was going to hell! Why didn't he fling the hammer right through the little window and hit whoever might be passing by and the last after it to hit him again? Why didn't he do something... anything...? But there, not a word out of him! No expression of amazement or gratitude at all, only a queer, dreepy smile upon his face, and he giving light taps of the hammer upon the sole that he happened to be working on when Mr. Delamere came into the shop... She felt ashamed, so she did, of being the owner of such a man, especially in the presence of the solicitor...

By nature and by calling, suave and subtle, Mr. Delamere had always succeeded in demonstrating, by a remarkable display of coolness, a fine loftiness of character upon an occasion of this kind, but in the presence of such extraordinary behaviour on the part of Marcus Igoe, his customary self-possession was forced, as it were, out of balance... and he was compelled to betray a certain excitement, which, he thought, reflected somewhat upon his dignity in a very important moment. As a result he felt himself stuttering, not at all impressively, in giving preliminary instructions about the fortune... They might possibly require something to be going on with. He had great pleasure, he said, in advancing, out of his own pocket, whatever amount they desired... On second thoughts he said that perhaps a hundred pounds would be very acceptable for the present.

It was not, in the face of her man's queer behaviour, until this foretaste of the fortune was safely in the hands of Margo that her disturbing suspicion of the dream-like nature of the event finally disappeared from her mind. But Marcus grew more quiet in himself... until a smile that held a suspicion of derision, which might, and again might not, be the correct way to greet a harbinger of good tidings and great joy, began slowly to light up his face...

The harbinger himself felt, as he made his exit, that there can be uncomfortable moments, even in the life of one whose presence stands, upon rare occasions, for good fortune.

While Margo, wildly exultant, and certainly, at the present moment, the happiest woman in Garradrimna, counted the notes over and over, Marcus had a glimmering of appreciation and promise of what the legacy meant in a feeling of triumph, not in the fact that his wife had notes to the extent of a hundred pounds in her hand, but in the fact that he himself had just behaved more splendidly than Charles Delamere, the solicitor... Only Margo was saying things to him about that...

But he was silent, smiling the while... Indeed, he was so unusually silent beneath the castigation that Margo felt a scruple in the thought that the whole thing had turned the poor fellow's head, and that it was pure mad he was entirely with concealed delight... Thinking, for instance, of the things he was going to do with the ten thousand pounds... Ah, ha, but she would have something to say to that now! She had gone through enough watching him... waiting for him.

Mebbe, God only knew, mebbe, he was at the present moment thinking of some of his lost love affairs... Miss Plunkett, for instance, or Miss Plunkett's daughter, Phœbe Hope. That was all she ever wanted to remember to realise to the fullest the class of a man that Marcus Igoe was. Imagine, the mother first... and then, after properly making a show of himself twice, the daughter... Ah, ha, that upstart bit of a lassie was going to have plenty to torment her now... Think of her married to Rodolphus Keeling...! But where would Mr. and Mrs. Keeling be beside themselves now?... Yet how would Marcus himself be influenced by the money? What kind of pranks would he try to play? Not, of course, that she was going to let him!

But she would behave like a wife to him anyway, even from the very start. So she hurried out to John Higgins's and bought him a nice treat for himself of a dozen of stout... He could be taking them, she thought, nicely and quietly, while she went off to display her womanhood to advantage by purchasing some "style" (not that she was going to get much of the right thing in Garradrimna) preparatory to setting out to get more in Castleconnor. This, in itself, would be a way of killing two birds with the one stone, for it would be the means immediately of publishing their good fortune abroad, and it might be as well to make a beginning at once...

Thereafter, through the day, Marcus sat just inside his own window, while, hurried here gradually by Margo's essay in publicity abroad, were assembling all the children and ragamuffins of Garradrimna, gathered on the street outside to observe the first few moments of the brilliant spectacle of Marcus Igoe taking his ease... Even those who were too young to have known the background of him or to appreciate its richness, were amused...

He seemed to be holding converse with himself as, bottle by bottle, the first efforts of his attempt to recapture himself grew in splendour, until, at last, the crowd having been augmented by such notables as Bartle Boyhan and Dickeen Crosbie, a loud cheer rang all down through Garradrimna... The exultant sound might be taken as signifying that the new Marcus Igoe had arrived... and there was a great anxiety upon everyone to forget, even with a laugh at each putting away, some aspect or another of his earlier "lives."

But Marcus himself was not forgetting. He was remembering, or trying to remember, not exactly to remember, but to vision, to see as something that might have happened, something that Margo, for instance, might "kill him" for if she knew... But if he had married Miss Looram that time... or earlier in life — at the proper season, he wondered, would the decline which might have overtaken him, even if he had won her, be much the same as the condition he had experienced at her loss when he had let everything go to the bad? At length, he drew into clear contemplation of the life he had missed...

It was another rival that he had to contend with, for his capture of Nancy Looram had depressed and destroyed John Higgins... But still it was the same duel, and Garradrimna the same place. Out of the seven public-houses two only to the forefront, and upon his not the hurry of business but an immense disquieting stillness.

This was a remarkable feature of Garradrimna that, although there was a fairly good business to be done with the pretty considerable population in the fields behind the village, the carters and van-men and cattle-men going this way every day, as well as the droves of sportsmen passing through to the frequent races in Mullahowen and the numerous coursing matches at Brannaganstown, and although Garradrimna had notions of, one day, becoming a most important place, some curious twist in the economy of the place, or in the nature of the people, expressly laid it down that all the business was to be done by one house—at a time.

Presently it was the house of Ursula Wyse that was doing all the business, while Marcus Igoe was "nearly out on the door." They held that Mrs. Wyse was a wise woman, meaning no feeble joke either. For she was no joke at all as a business woman. The way, for instance, that she kept up the appearance of her place, getting expert, "classy" painters out from Mullahowen to give it every possible touch of importance and appeal. How neat and inviting the name "Ursula Wyse" looked in new gilt letters above the door... while the outside of Marcus Igoe's was so dilapidated, they said, that you would nearly want to get up on a step-ladder with specs on you to read his name above the door... it was that withered away!

As if in gradual anticipation of the general opinion that very goon he would be "out on the door" Marcus spent most of his mornings leaning against the jamb of it, in his shirt sleeves, looking out at the signs of Mrs. Wyse's gathering custom for the day... A useless little lump of a man, as his wife thought of him, smoking a short clay pipe and never doing a hand's turn before God or man. After a little while he would revolve himself around and say... "I'm bet!" repeating it as he went back into the empty shop. "Bet, broke and bewildered!"

Many a morning, as he stood thus, calmly filling himself with his accustomed gloom, he would be accosted by Dickeen Crosbie and Bartle Boyhan. Although customers also of Mrs. Wyse's, they stuck to Marcus Igoe's... through some feeling of old allegiance and because there was another reason. As a result of their chat, he would always feel obliged, in the way of friendliness, to bring them in for a treat.

Once inside, their chat was found to develop so heartily that either Dickeen or Bartle would be emboldened to return the compliment — on credit.

"Sure my name is good," he would say. And, this treat supplied, either Dickeen or Bartle would have the courage to ask for another — on the same terms.

"Put them down in the book too. Our two names'll look very suitable, now, and very nice alongside one another in the one book and we such chums!"

These two friends of Marcus were a morning torment to Mrs. Nancy Igoe... The patent foolishness of that Marcus, and they only codding him up to his two eyes! Nor did they find much favour either with the children of Marcus, Gertrude Igoe and

Norman Igoe, now grown up and both nearly marriageable but denied everything by their father's foolishness and uselessness. Their mother had been responsible for their distinctive christening, hoping thus to qualify them fully for the grandeur she had fondly fancied nothing in the world could prevent them having — only for Marcus.

There was little wonder that he sought release from his worries in the conversation of his two particular friends. And he had one desperate hope... If a place like Garradrimna had notions of lifting up its name, was there any reason why a man like him should not have notions of lifting up his name too?

CHAPTER XIV

... SURE our name is good...

... It's all in a name...

Marcus had begun to notice that expressions of the nature of these jumped, with great frequency, in and out of all the conversations he would be having with his friends. Even his wife looked up at him from the debris of account-books she was examining one morning and said, her eyes filling with tears that scalded him:

"Musha, Marcus, sometimes I can't help thinking of the lovely lessons I used to learn at the boarding-school for young ladies where I prepared myself for this class of a life, God help us. There was one by Shakespeare: 'A rose by any other name,' it went on, and oh, it was lovely, Marcus, lovely. Just think of that now: 'A rose by any other name.'"

He made a hurried escape from the onrushing flood of her tears... but he could not escape from this matter of the name, which was urging itself upon his consciousness at every turn. A fellow should have a bit of pride in his name! It was all a man had when he had nothing else, and maybe there was as much magic in the name of Marcus Igoe (if people were only made to see it) as in the name of Ursula Wyse... But he was anonymous, as it were, like a fellow who would be ashamed to put his name at the bottom of a letter to the papers. No wonder the missus was always crying... and the childer going pure mad with him.

He put on his coat now, and, as he went out the door, looked up at the name. It was the final touch to his making up of his mind... that glance. He hurried down to the workshop of Gilbert Gallagher, and found that ancient man deep in converse with his coadjutor, as they called him, Bill the Savage. One could not call it exactly "converse," for not an audible word was passing between them, yet there was a great flow of mood between them all the same. Here were the artists of Garradrimna, the men not altogether of its little ways who lived more or less in their own world.

Around Gilbert were many examples of the work out of which he made his living, carts, creels, wheelbarrows, box barrows, shop-keepers' shutters and window-sashes. But he did not stop at carpentry. Running all around the shop were shelves, holding pots of paint, but which the conventions of the place limited mostly to yellow ochre and Prussian blue...

Neither of the two men made the slightest breach in the silence as he waited... They seemed to be pondering themselves. Gilbert Gallagher, who did all the "tasty" jobs about Garradrimna, and Bill the Savage, who could do anything with his hands, they said, only he never did it. Bill's clothes were always at the uttermost stage of dilapidation, the soles of his boots held on by bits of twine, the coat collar turned up to his neck, and caught tightly by a safety-pin to hide the absence of a shirt. He was one who had reduced life to its barest, and yet they called him a savage, not a saint for doing so. But Gilbert Gallagher, the disappointed artist who had allowed Garradrimna, more or less, to conquer him in the work it demanded him to do, had sympathy with the other, this sad man with the craft in his fingers and the vision of the artist in his mind. On nights when he was too much afraid of the wind in the woods to go home to his hut outside the village, Gilbert let Bill the Savage sleep amongst the shavings of the workshop. He shared his meals with him... He felt that, somehow, Bill might yet do the thing in Garradrimna that he himself had not done, and, although he had to put up with much, he never failed to see in Bill his own blood warm when he felt it cold, and, always, one nearer and dearer than any child of his body could have been.

Here was a bit of Garradrimna that was almost beyond anyone. One might always be more or less sure of what one might think of or say about any of the best of it. But in the face of that cold silence, that remoteness... it left one not knowing what to say...

Marcus began to comment upon examples of Gilbert's painting that were lying around — new and re-habilitated sign-boards. Gilbert looked at him out over his glasses. The lips of Bill the Savage seemed to split a little into a cold, cutting smile. At length he came to the point.

"I'd like to have one of them done for myself, or the yoke I have over the door done up somehow."

"Well, and am I going to be ped?" said Gilbert suspiciously. "You know you haven't much of a name in Garradrimna by this, Marcus, no, not, much."

"Yes, you'll be ped!" said Marcus, almost shouting it, as if to induce belief. "Even if I have to sell out the shop, lock, stock and barrel, to pay for my own name to go above my own door."

"Ah, now I'm listening to you, Marcus, but remember this, that the devil an up it'll go until I am, and, if I'm not, then back with me to this place again and every inhabitant of your native village brightening the window with the handkerchief to have a good look at your newly-painted name and it returning sadly on my aged shoulder."

"Oh that'll be all right," said Marcus, with all the conviction of tone he could well summon in the emergency. But he got out of the shop with as much speed as the occasion permitted... They were strange devils them two, and one could never know what they might concoct between them, even without saying a word. He felt annoyed by the whole thing, and wondered was it wise to have set about rehabilitating himself at all... He spent a most sleepless night, with Nancy at him, too, about the cost that would have to be undertaken now to prevent Gilbert Gallagher making a show of them as he had declared.

He was, therefore, in a mood to enter for hope of comfort into conversation with the cronies next morning, when they bore down on him from Kafe's corner almost as soon as he had made his matutinal appearance at the door.

"We're after being down with Gilbert Gallagher," said Dickeen, "and Bill the Savage was there too."

"Is that so?" said Marcus nervously, his tongue beginning to go dry in his mouth.

"And we were both more than glad to see that, at long last, you're after taking our advice about the value of a name... It was near time... Gilbert is after executing the most wonderful name-board to yourself with the letters all curled like and the whole of it decorated with the quarest curie-caries... Bill the Savage was poring over it when we came in, and I wouldn't put it apast that unchristian devil if he had something to do with it too... And I suppose it's going to cost you a big penny, Marcus? And it'll be done shortly."

"And it's finished that soon?" He was already at his wit's end about the money.

Dickeen and Bartle replied simultaneously. "But wait a minute... what d'ye think but, after all his most beautiful work, in an endeavour to suit your taste properly, wasn't your grand front name spelt wrong."

A light of relief sprang into the eyes of Marcus. He saw a way out of the difficulty.

"Bedambut, I have him, now, I have him! When he arrives now with the yoke and his threat to make a show of me 'tis I'll frighten the devil out of him with a counter threat of an action for defamation for spelling my name wrong on me, so I will."

Both Dickeen and Bartle were forced to exhibit painful grimaces at this exhibition of sheer wrong-headedness on the part of Marcus.

"Listen!"

"Arrah, listen, will you to what we have to say? Marquis... M-A-R-Q-U-I-S was the way he had it spelt instead of Marcus. And there now, d'ye see, by a most wonderful stroke of magic, is the solution of all your difficulties!"

"Is it to have the scuts of Garradrimna calling me 'The Marquis Igoe' for a nickname all the dear days of my life?"

"Well, even so. 'Igoe, the Marquis' would sound better than 'Igoe, the bankrupt,' and the nickname coming on you now might save you from the actual description that'll surely be yours if you don't look sharp."

"Save me... I wonder can anything save me... I suppose I'll have to treat yous anyway..."

They moved, all three, into the little parlour at the back of the bar. Dickeen and Bartle immediately eager to bubble over with hopeful words. Marcus was silent and gloomy until Dickeen said:

"But he's not going to charge you anything for painting it at all..."

"What, you don't tell me? Is that so?"

"The devil damn the penny... He says now that that's the only condition under which he'll let it go up! There seems to be some big idea in this, as if Gilbert and the Savage had achieved between them without ever speaking a word, a sort of gorgeous inspiration like, a work of art. 'That's not a signboard at all,' says he, 'that's my soul,' and Bill grinned in agreement."

Now if anything like a miracle could have been effected to change the mood of Marcus at the moment it was this news. It blew his worry of the moment, the payment of Gilbert, from his mind. And so relieved and hopeful of himself did he appear of a sudden that the rest was easy enough for Bartle and Dickeen. With soft words they concocted a rose-hued picture all full of "The Marquis." They were bright with conviction. Yet, they did not quite succeed in chasing every turn of doubting from his mind.

"Ah, I dunno the devil. It'd be a shocking big venture," he said, as soon as the first flush of his enthusiasm had fled.

Said Dickeen:

"And is it possible that you're going to turn your back on your luck and you nearly out on the door?"

Said Bartle:

"Are you going to put yourself in the way of never doing another day's good? But mebbe... I say mebbe, you have a taste for settling down in the workhouse... and now look it, Marcus! I'll put it straight to you. You're aware, I suppose, that people'll believe nearly anything if only you put it before them in print.

"But a fellow has to live up to a name, even when he gets it that way. He has to have a bit of go anunder him, a bit of swank... And look at my best suit of clothes, for instance, look at the trousers!"

He made several gestures of exhibition.

"Of course, as you have truly remarked, Marcus, there's a lot in this idea of clothes but sure there's many a tailor in the city of Dublin would let you have all the clothes you want for nothing or for, should I say, the privilege of being allowed to show off a big gilt framed yoke in his window, saying how he was 'Tailor, by Special Appointment to his Highness or his Grace or whatever you might be — The Marquis of Clunnen...'"

"There's not many Marquises shopkeepers and general merchants, I suppose?..." This in a shifty, nervous, half-hopeful, half-despondent way.

"All the better then; you'll be something new, and novelty sways the world. A Marquis turned publican! Sure there's many a Marquis would turn worse, if only he could see the future before him that's before you now!"

"They'll go wild altogether in America and print headings a yard long over the news. Ten to one if you don't see an American millionaire or millionairess coming skeddadling over striving for to pick up the son or the daughter from you."

This last speech was almost a stroke of genius on the part of Dickeen. It fell intuitively upon one of the strongest inclinations of Marcus, his real desire to do well by his son and daughter — if only something would give him the chance of doing it. Now he was spurred to decision. Seeing that he absolutely must do something, it was just as well to do this, that they were asking him, for all the difference it made... He took the small, black clay pipe of depression from his mouth, and smashed it to smithereens as he struck the table a powerful blow of his fist.

"Boys, howsomever it's going to turn out, yous have me convinced at long last. It's a great idea! It's an absolutely huge idea!"

Bartle was equal, superlatively, to the moment.

"Look at that now, the most wonderful fortune that was in your name all along and you never to have seen it, until Gilbert Gallagher made the curious blunder. Why, sure a Marquis is between an Earl and a Duke."

Nancy hurried in.

"Begad, this is funny, Gilbert Gallagher and Bill the Savage is after leaving a new name-board outside the door without being ped or a ha'porth. It's spelled ridiculous and painted like the printing on a circus van. What does this mean now? Why didn't you tell me, Marcus?"

She really thought, did she, that it was the old Marcus she was speaking to. Well, then he'd let her see.

"Ahem… I suppose now, Nancy, you'd never credit me with e'er a drop of blue blood in my veins at all? What?"

"Well, indeed?"

"No, of course not. Well I may tell you this, that I'm just after discovering for the purpose of business, commerce and enterprise that I'm a… a sort of a Marquis."

"A what?"

"A Marquis, no less… Marquis Igoe. The Marquis of Garradrimna… if you'll take my word for it."

"Well, there now, imagine that! And I'm the Marchioness, we'll suppose, doing a big book business in the drinking line, and nothing in the till, and I not to get a new dress this three years."

"Oh, but we're going to change all that… Mebbe it's what you'd see yourself sitting beside me yet, and I driving around inside my coach and four and I in robes and uniform, and a shiny knee-breeches and a sash and a sword, and the people of Garradrimna bowing and scraping saluting to me, the very same as you'd see the King, for instance, on the cinematograph. I'm going to set up the name-board exactly as it's spelled and printed and… and…"

"… And you have only to exhibit a thing sufficiently long in print, ma'am, for people to believe it even though it may be the damndest lie in Christendom," said Dickeen coming to his assistance.

It was probably the unaccustomed air of decision about Marcus, rather than the extravagant notion of the moment that convinced Nancy... but certainly she appeared impressed. Marcus was keen to notice this, and said:

"Well, what d'ye think of that now, Nancy?"

"Well, begad, I thought I'd never be inclined to remember Shakespeare again and I looking at you. But I can't help thinking of that passage: 'A rose by any other name.'... And I won't have to be crying my eyes out nearly when I remember it now..."

The miracle was wrought. His wife, the very last one you would imagine, had already begun to accept him as "The Marquis."

"I wouldn't doubt you, Nancy," he said... "Get us three pints now, and put them down in the book to 'The Marquis.' Sure I'd never have met you at all only for this book-keeping anyway..."

CHAPTER XV

THE setting up of the name fell as a rather poor joke upon Clunnen, but when the laughter, which held as well a tinge of a jeer, appeared, at length, to die down, Dickeen and Bartle began to enforce themselves as publicity agents on behalf of Marcus.

"D'ye know where we're after being?" they would say running into one house after another, "well, we're just after being up at the Marquis's."

"What Marquis?"

"What Marquis?" either Bartle or Dickeen would repeat without the least flicker of a smile. "Surely you're not that ignorant... The Marquis of Garradrimna, who else?"

"The Marquis" or "The Marquis of Garradrimna," were words scarcely ever out of their mouths. They fully believed in the virtue of hammering a thing in well... But it was hard work in the case of an individual who did not give much assistance and who was beginning to be known locally as "Murksheen Igoe."

At last, one fine Sunday, their efforts in publicity began to show signs of having effect. People from Castleconnor and Mullaghowen, who were out for the day, and who had heard the extraordinary story of "The Marquis," were eager to see the name above the door... They stopped their bicycles or their cars or their motor-cars outside, and, looking up, saw that the amazing cheek of the man was a fact. They would have to see "The Marquis" for themselves. But, just yet a little while, "The Marquis" was not to be seen. He had employed Bartle and Dickeen as doormen, first of all as a recompense for their having made him a Marquis, and, in the second place, because they were most reliable men who could be depended on to say, without turning a hair:

"Oh, the Marquis is not quite himself to-day, he's slightly indisposed. But if you were to come next Sunday... or, some other Sunday..."

Curiosity thus created brought an ever-increasing crowd in long cars and motor-cars and char-a-bancs, and the broad grin of a full-blooded disbelief in the whole thing was soon turned in the face of Garradrimna. It had become impressed through the spectacle of this acceptance of The Marquis on the part of strangers, grand smart people from Castleconnor and Mullaghowen... and, for all its reluctance in the beginning, it began to follow the crowd.

Marcus, for all his earlier foolishness, was not without a good deal of adaptability, when face to face with an opportunity. So, the very first money he made out of the Marquisate he began to use towards its further development. He had the shop brightly painted and renovated, both inside and outside by expert, classy painters from Mullaghowen. He hesitated in his deflection from Gilbert Gallagher when it came to the signboard and it received a further embellishment from Gilbert or Bill the Savage.

They pondered long over it this time and when Marcus began to be anxious about its absence from over the door for even a day or two, he visited the workshop, only to be received stonily. "Ye could put your hand out and touch it absolutely," he said, a little later, in an attempt to re-create a sense of the atmosphere through which he had passed, "and I was in holy peril of my life, the way the Savage looked at me and then at the signboard, nearly the same as if he was going to chaw the two of us, myself and my name into little bits. Howsomever, I got the right side of Gilbert...

explaining the way I did, that his name was going to go down to history for all he was after doing for us."

"That seemed to anger the Savage something frightful, and the cowld sweat nearly began to come dreeping out through me... until I saw that Gilbert Gallagher was conquered by my words, and he said he'd do his best to have it for me to-morrow... Even if he had anything to do with it the first time, which I don't believe, there was no doubt at all that, be the look of him, he had nothing to do with it the second time. It was all the Savage's work. D'ye know that fellow is a devil, even if he is a genius itself, and he'll do harm to someone in Garradrimna some time."

It did not seem to matter now who might try to improve upon the idea of the Marquis, it was the courageous inception of the thing that mattered. It was an idea that would go on. And often, when Marcus saw the deplorable figure of Bill the Savage go shuffling down the street, the wind blowing through his rags, the lean hand fumbling at the safety-pin which caught the coat collar about his throat, the loose soles of his shoes slapping against the wet side-walk, he would have compassion and invite him in for a pint. But no word would come from him even then, no look in his eyes, but that of one seeing beyond the world. "God, it was queer, the poor devil," Marcus would think to himself, just before he proceeded to forget and go on with his business.

He turned his attention with great deliberation to development of the name of the Marquis. He had magnificently printed handbills done for general distribution, and large three-colour posters, prominently featuring his name, executed for exhibition in particular places. He had it printed even on a recently ordered supply of tea-bags THE MARQUIS OF GARRADRIMNA. These words stared you heavily in the eye no matter which way you turned.

And behind or, more truly, in front of all this show was "The Marquis" himself, well dressed, important, silent, inaccessible, and ably assisted by his business advisers, Dickeen and Bartle. The hidden population of Garradrimna, the carters, the van-men, the cattle-men, the tramps and the droves of sportsmen passing to the frequent races in Mullaghowen and the coursing matches at Brannaganstown were now his to a man. Everyone said that the house of Ursula Wyse was gone to the dogs anyway... no one going into it... no class...

Marcus went on building up the illusion of respectability... He dressed better and behaved more splendidly from day to day... and... fully convinced, many a one would say:

"Sure I suppose now, he's one of the most respectable men in Europe, and it's nearly a pity to see him only a Marquis."

Marcus felt himself in accord with the world and gay, gay beyond the expectation of his brightest dream, but his wife, "the Marchioness," was not so happy for she knew her man better than anyone. One morning she approached Marcus with a statement of her new trouble.

"I thought, as sure as anything, that, when we'd begin to do well, my worries would be over. But now the shop is always so full of customers that Norman and Gertrude are not able to attend them all."

"Let them wait...! It's what they should be glad of the privilege of being allowed to wait in The Marquis of Garradrimna's. Ha, cocking them up attending to them indeed!"

"But sure that's what Norman and Gertrude are beginning to think, too. People coming into the shop are beginning to give out cuts and hints. If they're not smart enough to understand the deep-down side of advertising, they're gabby enough to talk about what they can see."

No, it wasn't good enough, Marcus decided immediately. It was, in fact, an awful mistake. So now a bar-man and a shop-boy were employed while Norman and Gertrude, in complete fulfilment of their aristocratic names, were seen going off to play tennis with the *élite* of Castleconnor and Mullaghowen... It was another move for Marcus in the right direction. People seeing them go about idle and magnificent, would say:

"'There's the Marquis of Garradrimna's son!' or 'There's the Marquis's daughter.' Such style! The father must be doing immense. But sure he has a splendid shop and a great name. I must surely go over there to-morrow for a supply of things."

CHAPTER XVI

In reality, however, matters were not so bright. One could almost think of Norman and Gertrude as having superseded Dickeen and Bartle as advertising agents for the business. But in proportion to their value, they were disproportionately expensive. There was no standing Norman until he got a car; with Gertrude it was continuous spending of money upon new frocks.

"Lord, it's shocking expensive, this being a swell," Mrs. Igoe would say about a hundred and forty times a day.

And even though they had cost him a bit in the beginning, Marcus was not blind to the big mistake he had really made in substituting Norman and Gertrude for Dickeen and Bartle and the hand-bills and the three-colour posters, not to think of the still potent influence of the name-board by Gilbert Gallagher. They were now living beyond their means, and this was just as bad as when they had been doing nothing in the shop only "pulling the devil by the tail." They had the name still, of course, but a situation had been created in which the name could only be retained by extraordinary expenditure in the direction of advertising, which must increase rather than decrease if they were to stand at all. And yet, the business, such as it was, could not bear this. It had reached almost the full limit of expansion... yet if Gertrude put on a less expensive dress than her last, it would be noticed. If Norman showed the least trace of retrenchment in his lavish behaviour it would be noticed And, from such points, the decline of "the Marquisate" would begin. But even the faintest suspicion of decline would be sufficient to ruin them, so tremulously did they exist upon the verge of unreality.

There was a little hopeful turn in the situation which caught the consideration of Marcus… Mrs. Wyse, a fine woman still, only she had such a lot of young daughters, seemed to have some sort of a wild eye upon young Norman… She even got Dickeen Crosbie to hint the possibility of something to Marcus… Then there was Martin Ivory, who lived at Harbourstown, a good solid sensible man of fifty-five or so — with plenty of money they said… Gertrude! He had even gone so far, or at least so Bartle Boyhan said, to mention the matter to Bartle, so that he might mention it to Marcus. If only one or other of these excellent arrangements could be managed while there was yet time… But what could a man do seeing that the minds of his children were set upon some gorgeous "Lord" or "Lady" out of Castleconnor or Mullaghowen, and not upon good common-sense natives. And it would be madness for the moment to forbid them the foolishness of their ways.

"Uneasy lies the head that wears a crown," he would say to himself over and over again.

But as luck would have it, one day a happy accident came to divert the mind of Marcus from his worries.

On that morning a number of "American journalists" swooped down upon him in search of "copy."… It went forth immediately that they wanted to "syndicate" him all over the earth… Any little doubts concerning the "Marquisate" that might have begun to creep in were quickly dispelled. Wasn't he a great man entirely to have about the place?

After the departure of the "American journalists," who were really a few smart "go-boys" from Castleconnor brought over by Dickeen and Bartle to ease the situation, Marcus spent a few days anxiously closeted with his advisers. They had somehow felt it as a strain upon their reputations that the hidden genius of Bill the Savage had evolved a plan which had brought Marcus Igoe to his present condition. Could they not go a little further, they who had the brains, too, if they wore them on their sleeves itself... But they had thought it out and were come now to Marcus with whole-hearted assistance at a crucial moment in his career.

The result of deep and anxious consultations was that Marcus emerged a grievously changed man... He nearly frightened the life out of his wife Nancy on the morning that it happened by showing a complete inability to recognise her; he passed Norman and Gertrude as if they had become complete strangers... He began to ramble in his talk, using queer, high-flown words, like what one would meet in novels dealing with mediæval chivalry. "Beshrew me!" and " methinks" and "varlet" were amongst the expressions that came from his tongue. He talked of the shop as "my castle," and spoke of buying "a brand-new suit of armour and a sword." "To slay mine enemies!" he replied to a question of Nancy's as to "what on earth he wanted with a sword now, and it such a dangerous-looking yoke?"

Then what had happened fully dawned upon the wife of Marcus. *He really thought that he now actually was what he had been only letting on to be.* The strain of acting the part had "affected" him. This was terrible, and she with so many anxious thoughts of settling the children advantageously before the "smash" came. But this was worse than any "smash."... If the rumour of insanity in the family got abroad...! She was distracted.

They had a terrible job, the whole of them, in hiding him from the public for fear of the consequences. For the moment, the situation appeared to be a little too much for even Bartle and

Dickeen. Nancy, too, would say a thing to them as unhelpful as this:

"As sure as day it was all them lads from America. Peculiar and all as Marcus was, he looked sane enough until he heard of his name being broadcasted like that. This Marquising is after being the greatest curse from start to finish. But if we give it up now, we're ruined entirely. But where is it going to finish?"

CHAPTER XVII

To the apparent relief, however, of his "advisers" the madness of Marcus now took a promising turn. He spoke of a "banquet" to Bartle and Dickeen, calling them at the top of his voice in the shop before everyone, "Sir Bartle" and "Sir Dickeen," and asking them to bring their friends, while, immediately, they knew the friends they would bring… It was a plan that fully appealed to Mrs. Igoe.

"To get the two nice little childer settled is mebbe all that this cursed Marquising was ever meant for… And if I do get them settled now, mad or not mad, I'll make Marcus give up the whole thing. For it's surely a shocking strain on the nerves for anyone to be striving to make themselves out something that they're not. And sure, if himself was only to retire with his great name still strong on him it might be something to live on for the remainder of our days."

"Begad, you're a great woman entirely!" said Dickeen with enthusiasm. "If another woman got to be a Marchioness all of a sudden she would have gone madder than himself, and then where would the both of you be landed by this?"

On the day preceding the evening of the "banquet" "the Marquis" was very bad. His conduct in and around the shop had the effect of finally demolishing any lingering hopes which Norman and Gertrude might have had of his recovery, with its consequent survival of their aristocratic state. They were only too anxious to save themselves… only they were in dread that their father might do something to still further spoil their prospects at the "banquet." So when Bartle's and Dickeen's "aristocratic friends" arrived, as the sole other guests, they found no difficulty at all in getting on to the very best advantage with the objects of their hopes...

Indeed, everything was almost completely arranged before the "banquet" began, although there was really no "banquet" in it at all, but, instead, an ordinary sensible affair of settling two matches "at one slap" in accordance with all the best practices of the countryside... It was a great moment for the long-harassed wife of the Marquis, and Dickeen and Bartle discreetly withdrew, so that she might have full enjoyment of it.

They moved into the little parlour at the back of the bar, where they had had so much planning, as it appeared now, for no other purpose than to bring about the present situation.

They were confronted by "the Marquis" himself, a bottle of champagne in his hand, and a broad smile over all his countenance.

"Well, boys?" he said.

"Musha," said Dickeen, "will you tell us if it's yourself that's in it at all, or only the shadow of a lunatic?"

"Oh, I'm here all right, the whole of me, brains and bones, why?"

"The Lord save us," said Bartle, "we thought you were mad out and out, you acted the part that damn well."

"Hold your glasses, boys. This stuff wasn't a bad help, but it's the last bottle I'll take, for it's the last bottle that's in it... Well, boys, it was a great idea right enough, one of the best yous ever thought of, to let on I was mad entirely to get Norman and Gertrude to stop their gorgeous gallop through the country and settle down to my advantage."

"To go all out with the Marquis business was simply our advice to you and you follied it well. Damn it, sure you nearly deceived ourselves, as well as the Missus... But you never saw anything like the way them all rushed it... the two matches is fixed up perfect."

"That's very satisfactory, and so far so good," said Marcus, taking a long shrewd look at both, "but what would yous advise me to do now, boys, for now comes the crux of all my Marquising?"

They pondered the problem in silence for a few moments. At length it was Bartle who spoke:

"Now, if you were to retire, simply sell out the place to a big business magnate in Castleconnor or Mullaghowen... there would be a lot of them only too glad to have a lep at the chance of it now, and it having such a trade."

"No use, Bartle. I as 'the Marquis' am the whole thing. The whole contraption would fall asunder in a week without my name behind it, and then my name, my great and far-reaching name, d'ye see, would go down worse than ever with this downfall, and my new son-in-law and my new daughter-in-law mightn't like it at all."

"Therefore," said Dickeen, "if you were to retire in the full blaze of the Marquisate, it would be a most powerful thing for all concerned. People would have a kind of respect for you then as long as you'd be alive. And, anyhow, don't you want to give your son a chance of distinguishing himself in business now as the husband of Mrs. Wyse. Look at all the daughters of hers he has to get off his hands!"

"Good health, boys, my couple of wise men from the East, my cabinet ministers, my privy councillors, and is it possible that yous don't see the solution that's all grandly fixed up and ready, just made for me like a new suit of clothes by my appointed tailor in the City of Dublin? Whisper, boys... for a second... what about what yous talked of a being the probable end of me not so long ago? — Bankruptcy...?"

"What?"

"What?"

"Well, it's only the other day that I was reading in the papers where it was after happening to a Duke, and before him to an Earl, and before him again to six or seven plain Lords, and before them again to sixteen Sirs... You see, it's quite the thing and very swanky. 'A great soul,' they will say, 'and a grand business man entirely, but sure he had to put himself into a lot of expense when he found out that he was a Marquis.' And they'll have great respect for me as the man that done the world, and got the better of all my difficulties and settled my two childer well...

"'There's the Marquis of Garradrimna, a grand man,' they will say, when, in my retirement, I'll pass from my son-in-law's to my daughter-in-law's and poor Nancy'll be real contented at long last, and we'll be all doing well... And when I'm dead and gone, if they ever succeed in starting to make anything out of Garradrimna, which I don't believe they ever will, what better beginning can they make than by putting up a monument to myself? And there I will be for ever, as a grand encouragement to others, the Marquis himself, no less, in silk stockings and a sash and sword. For all time — "

" — The Marquis of Garradrimna," added Dickeen, in tones of genuine admiration.

" — The Marquis of Clunnen," added Bartle, in tones of flowery respect.

Yes, he had missed that life. It was queer, with the two children in it and all. They must be John Higgins's two children that had got themselves, that is, the reality of themselves, mixed up with his imagining. What a sarcastic business, too, all that of the Marquis? But it was strange, all the same, that, no matter what life he pictured, it always seemed to bring him back to where he was — until now. But now it was different. Ah, he was going to have his real life now!

So, by the time that Margo had returned from her excursion into the bye-ways of grandeur, her husband had, with the aid of her generous "treat" to him, succeeded in realising his good fortune only to this extent, that he could begin to make a real start in life now. He could *begin,* anyway, if he liked... But Garradrimna was always the same... There now, just passing on the street outside, was Bill the Savage, with his wind-blown rags and the sad smile upon his face, exactly as he had appeared in the workshop of Gilbert Gallagher in the "life" through which Marcus had just passed. The wind was rising this evening and, to-night, Bill would sleep in the shavings. He felt that he had a better understanding of the Savage now... But what would the Savage think of him who was, of a sudden, able to sit at his ease in the very busiest portion of the working day... thinking... thinking...? But there was the rub, like in Hamlet's play...

If one thought, letting cold reality into one's mind, instead of dreaming, one was likely to remember that, by hurriedly adopting a means of release from the life he had lived, he would be, in a way, confessing the failure of his life. He had not accomplished his twisting of Garradrimna into complete accordance with its own squint... And he was seeing now that it might not be so easy for a man to relinquish the dream of an ideal that has given him much anxiety, and into which he has put much earnest endeavour, even in the very presence of a certain way of relief from every trouble of the mind...

He was sorry now that he was situated somewhere about the end of the grim purpose of his life which had been the mainstay and the comfort of his latter years. Just when it had really begun to promise success even at the expense of his way of living... Maybe that poor devil, the Savage, going about with the evening wind shivering through him was still warmed by his dream, which he might never hope to achieve, but which he had not surrendered, however mad it might be.

CHAPTER XVIII

Margo swiftly rescued him from the depressed depths of his musing... The first signs of good fortune were upon her. Aye, good fortune according to Garradrimna's ignoble estimate of it, he thought gloomily, as she shook him by the coat-collar, with the words, "Wake up out of that, or is it asleep or only drunk you are, ye ould disgrace ye!" She flung him into the room to put on his Sunday clothes. She had bought him a grand purple tie which, she asserted, would make him look years younger, and she wanted his other apparel to be all of a piece with this before letting him at large through Garradrimna in his new guise as a man of fortune.

"Now, look it here! I don't want to put on any nonsensical airs all of a sudden, so I don't," and "Was there ever anything so foolish as a woman?" he said alternately, as he got reluctantly and laboriously into his best clothes, which were not much at their best... Well, all the same if he could afford to sit thus finely attired, purple tie and all, looking out without envy upon those who, heretofore, had spent so much of their valuable time looking in without envy upon him... But even the comfort that this thought seemed to bring for the moment was cut short by Margo, who was still impelled by the momentum of delight, as she moved about the shop kicking everything before her:

"I did a great evening's work, including speaking to Thomas Hardy about the modern bungalow that he has vacant at Cloneygapple."

"What's that?" he said, coming out to the room door, his hand suddenly going limp about his grand tie.

"The modern bungalow," she repeated with dancing eyes.

"Modern bungalow!" he repeated aghast, "is it what you'd want me to spend the remainder of my life in a yoke like that, just because my uncle Paul beyant in New Orleans did happen leave me a big skelp of money. To put me away out there near Cloneygapple. To cut me away from my natural surroundings in Garradrimna…"

"'Tis the bottles of stout that's talking now," thought Margo. "And musha let them have their say, but wait till you see when I have a proper go at him to-morrow."

They seemed to have no more to say, at least not for the present… But he gazed almost speechlessly down the long vista of strangeness that her words had opened up for him… The little he had been able to think, so far, of his money had not stood for abandonment of the little workshop with the squinting window… In failure triumphant or triumph defeated, he could only visualise himself there. But these sudden words of pride from the woman who was his wife desolated him with their dismal ring of reality…

It was nothing short of fearful to think of him being deprived of the background which would be of such assistance to the new personality he hoped to make for himself now. "The Millionaire Igoe," as they would certainly call him, might be a very disappointing figure if the appointments surrounding him were purely in keeping. The feeling he had hoped to create about himself, as of a man who had risen, like the burning bird, out of the ashes of his dreams, would be destroyed in all its splendid illusion if the ashes were not allowed to remain…

But one had only to look at the way that Margo was already adorning herself to see that she was bent upon accomplishing the airs and elegance almost of a Duchess. "The Duchess," they would call her, as sure as day... She would completely absorb the whole foreground by the dazzle of her showy personality. As a matter of fact she might become his future background too, immense and overshadowing, while he would appear before his native world, a very small, henpecked husband, albeit genteel and grand, yet an awful caricature of the original Marcus Igoe, who, for all his insufficiencies, had been a man who, one way or another, had come to personality with a determined purpose marking the concluding stages of his life.

He would have sold himself — for ten thousand pounds. But he would have sold himself, that was the point, and maybe the most worthless man in the world is worth more than ten thousand pounds. It was maddening to be feeling his good fortune this way. But what was he at the moment? Nothing — absolutely nothing! He was tossed like a bit of a feather between that thought and thought of the little shop with the squinting window, which so intimately surrounded all that his life had been, all its long-lost adventures, through whose very foolishness he had learned the grand comfort of meditation upon the nature of human destiny.

Even if it had only brought him in the end to thoughts of exquisite malevolence, he had had great experiences and much pleasure in his mind. Now it was to be only this... a future full of money and Margo and annoyance. This notion about the modern bungalow belonging to Thomas Hardy was a very fair sample of what he would have to contend with. He would have to assert himself!

"Now about getting this bungalow," he began.

"Aye, not another word about it. It's got," said Margo.

He laboriously brushed his hat in silence before going out to meet the full gaze of his fellow men.

CHAPTER XIX

SOON, returned to the almost obliterated self that he had become, he found it easier, for the sake and appearance of peace, to obey the mandates of Margo. But, strange to say, he found it hardest to obey what should have been the easiest of them, which was that he must wear his Sunday suit every day and walk in idleness through Garradrimna. They had already paid several visits to Castleconnor, driving over proudly in Wade's best hackney motor car. But, even the motor, with the taste of the speedy, splendid life that it imparted, still left him far from easy in his mind. Soon, the whole deluge of the fortune, less Charles Delamere's expenses and fees would be upon him, and then he fancied that he would not be happier either — only maybe worse. It would be farewell then, a long farewell to all he had hoped to do in the way of boots...

At last he expressed a curious wish to Margo. It was that she should permit him to bid good-bye to cobbling by making a most gorgeous pair of boots for himself, in which he might stand up, as befitted him, to receive, in a suitable manner, his legacy out of the hands of Charles Delamere, and then walk the ways of pride for evermore... She was all against the request at first, asking why wouldn't he think properly of himself, and get a civilised pair of boots at Connolly & Cooke's, The Gentlemen's "Feetwear Men" in Castleconnor...

Yet there was a touch of pathos in the request that softened her... although she could not help thinking that if only he had minded the boots in the beginning he might have remained a man of some standing and importance in Garradrimna, married her at the time she said she was going to America, and left her with less of a job to try to make something out of him now... She knew that this was only another example of his endless foolishness, but there were tears in his eyes, she thought, so let him have his way!

He may have been deliberately conscious of it, but it was destined that his late revengeful purpose was to have a touch of revenge upon him in its turn. His manual power had become so malaccomplished, through his mental twist, that he could not now make a pair of non-torturing boots, however hard he might try... For three reasons he dallied longer than the normal time over this pair. He liked the feel of the low stool once more, the hammer in his hand, and the last between his knees... This was to be his final effort in the boot-making direction... And he was earnestly trying to do a decent job for the first time in his cobbling life.

But his deepest desires were of no avail. The very dint of his effort succeeded only in accentuating the damnation of his performance... It frightened him, not a little, to realise that he had finally lost the "trade" to which he had served his time, but it was borne in upon him from the appearance of them that he had made a pair of boots that were really an enormity... He now attempted to delay the wearing of them, even as he had succeeded in delaying the making of them... saying to Margo, whenever she questioned him sharply, that mebbe now they looked just a little too grand in contrast with his Sunday clothes, which, through repeated wearing, had begun to put on the appearance almost of a week-day suit... She proceeded to counter this excuse by rushing him over to the Thompson "Emporium," in Mullaghowen, for an especially fine suit of clothes to be made immediately.

He did not fully realise the ferocious nature of the pair of boots he had made for himself until he put them on... He sat for a long time without moving... But he had promised Margo that he would wear them to-day. To-morrow he would be going over to Castleconnor for the balance of the ten thousand pounds, and his performance in his new boots to-day would be as a preliminary canter for that splendid gallop... But as he arose, after an appearance of long pondering of a subject far above his boots, and attempted to sally forth in them with a stride in keeping with his clothes, he realised that, after all, it was rather devilish that he had been unable to make himself a pair of boots in which decently to accomplish it. The other men of such trades as his had not failed him. Neither the Thompson experts who had made his suit, nor the people, with the curious name, in Austria who had made his velour hat, yet he had failed himself.

Margo did not know his mind at setting forth. Indeed, she felt inclined to compliment him on the creak of his new boots, a nice sound enough, that seemed calculated to the last fraction of a tone, as a means of attracting envious attention... She watched, indeed, with something akin to pride in him stirring her... until she thought she saw him give a little excruciating twist and then stop dead... She fancied the sound, too, of muttered profanity being borne backward upon the breeze. It fell, heavy and desolate, upon her rising hope in the gorgeous upliftment of her man...

A woman so schooled as she in the most intimate observation of her native place, was keen to observe every flicker that was capable of interpretation, and now, at some distance up the street, she detected a slight movement... the pulling aside of a frilly curtain, so that someone might have a good and complete look at her man, Marcus, and he marching by... Only he was not marching at all, only bending and twisting after a fashion that it was very sad to have to witness... No, never, she thought to herself! He would never be able to come up to the great expectations of the fortune!

CHAPTER XX

WHEN Marcus, after almost superhuman effort, had accomplished the end of the street, and passed some little distance out on the road to Mullaghowen, he fell, tortured beyond further endurance, into the rich, green grass by the wayside. He took off the boots and, hiding his stockinged feet under him, adopted quite a craftsmanlike air with regard to these latest products of his hands and brain...

People passing into Garradrimna and who saw him sitting there in his blue serge suit and black velour hat, said that, after all, second nature is stronger than most people imagine, and, even in spite of his great luck and he on the very threshold, as you might say, of a new, magnificent life, the call of the boots had brought him back to them again... They did not realise that, in this very moment he was further from boots than ever in his life before.

He was thinking of all the torture he had been the means of causing... and thoughts of atonement hurried swiftly into his mind... But he must get away from this particular and accursed pair of boots before he could think it out clearly... He would leave them here in this very ditch for the first unfortunate that might pass the way, and it was magnificent to realise that he could afford to leave them!

The final desertion of his calling, with all its implications, seemed to be symbolised in his abandonment of the grand pair of boots he had made for himself... He would turn over a new leaf now... This was to be the end of his bitterness against Garradrimna. Sure mebbe it wasn't Garradrimna at all, only himself. He crept home bootless by a secluded way at the back of the houses, cutting and bruising further his well-wounded feet, and irritating them with thorns, until he was an altogether woe-begone cripple when he presented himself before his wife at the back door...

She felt so thoroughly disgusted with him that the desire of her tongue was subdued for perhaps the first time within living memory. She hurried him into the room to take off his clothes immediately, and then set about dressing herself to go out... She simply must go out to keep from letting fall, at this early stage, the remarkable standing in Garradrimna that she had planned for both of them, and which she felt she was already beginning to accomplish. She would drive over to Castleconnor this very evening without waiting for to-morrow at all — just to show them! For the first time this evening since he had put on the pair of boots Marcus smiled... as he heard the sounds of her departure...

He began to feel a certain solace, even in his wounded and defeated condition, for he was quite certain that some of those who had witnessed his stately departure up the street had already laid bets with one another as to whether the manner of his return would be as splendid as the manner of his setting forth — or the reverse. It was a form of excitement that made him laugh outright, and helped almost completely to allay his recent pain and discomfiture, to be fancying how certain individuals had laid their bets...

And so, watching far into the evening because some of their money was at stake, the people of Garradrimna were ready to alight upon anything in the way of sensational news that might relieve their feelings.

It came, about nightfall, with the appearance of Bill the Savage wearing the identical, splendid pair of boots that Marcus had set forth in only such a short time before... The place outside the village where he had been last seen sitting with the pair of boots in his hand had already been trodden by anxious searchers, but not a trace of either the boots or Marcus could be found... It was surmised that, after the double deed, Bill had hidden himself in the woods until such time as, in his madness, he might consider it safe to appear. But it was the stylish creak of the now famous pair of boots that Sebastian Nedley's smart gosoon, Lala, recognised as Bill hurried, well-shod for the first time in his life, into the Marlay Arms, the house presently uppermost in Gar-radrimna.

Simon Seery, as befitted his importance as the present big man of Garradrimna, was all for caution. "No doubt," he said to one of the accustomed evening groups, "poor Marcus, the Lord 'a mercy on him! is after being done away with on account of his money and the boots. Sure, it was merely tempting Providence he was to go the road that way, mebbe with a big lump of money in his pocket and the gorgeous boots on his feet. It was too much for poor Bill anyway with the coards that he was trying to keep on the soles with cutting right into the flesh this long time. He'd nearly be able to stand anything that was a pair of boots at all, d'ye mind? But there's no use in lepping on top of the poor devil taking his pint there until we're as sure as day." Yet, despite this wise word, everyone was crowding into the bar to be ready for the pounce when the moment came...

It happened, just about this hour, that Marcus was struck by a remarkable notion, remarkable simply in that he had not long since thought of it, for it was simplicity itself, being nothing more than that he should go up to the Marlay Arms and stand himself a drink, and if he met any parties there maybe include them in the round. It was the way that men of Garradrimna had ever been accustomed to mark their little triumphs... Aye, there it was again... Garradrimna's conception of triumph! But, all the same, a man must do something. Yes, he would have a drink for himself, now that he could, and seeing that his wife was away from home this evening.

As he prepared to go out in his oldest and easiest pair of boots, it would almost seem as if he had contrived his whole life to the effort of this moment... There were almost moans of affright as he made his appearance upon the street for the second time this day, and, quite misunderstanding that the noise was about three parts sympathetic, he ground his teeth with fancying that there lingered in the cry of each old woman so vigilant behind her window, a kind of echo of the screech of torment that, at his other setting forth, he had suppressed with such cost to his immortal soul.

They were devils right enough, and he might never hope to have satisfaction over them according to any decent standard. But he would be magnanimous all the same. He would be desperately magnanimous this evening, in fact, quite un-Garradrimnian. He would stand a drink to the whole of his native place and then see what effect that would have... He hurried in the direction of the Marlay Arms, and was not at all surprised, such was his present mood, to find nearly the whole population of Garradrimna, almost to a man, assembled there before him. How well they had guessed what was in his mind!

Rather loftily, as if to impress them with a sense of his present importance in their midst, he yawned the loud yawn of idleness, as he stepped into the bar. Everyone turning, surprised upon the sound, from intense contemplation of Bill the Savage, saw what they took to be the already murdered man walking into the bar and heard him actually saying:

"What'll yous all have, boys?"

CHAPTER XXI

A REMARKABLE feature of the mind of Marcus Igoe was its mutability. It could suddenly stop moving in one direction to begin moving in quite a contrary way without, as it appeared, the least effort in the world. It was well that this was so, for he felt he needed this quality on the morning that he prepared to emerge from the office of Charles Delamere with a deposit receipt for an amount something over eight thousand pounds in his pocket. (The estate in New Orleans had not quite realised all that had been expected of it.) The expenses had been very heavy, as Charles Delamere explained, somewhat, as Marcus thought, to the disadvantage of his American agents... some sort of a fly, too, had gone and eaten up some of the property. Those wooden houses, you know, in America, and those mosquitoes or insects...

The portion of the fortune that Marcus had already striven, according to his lights, to enjoy, the taste of the money, as he now described it with admirable sarcasm to his solicitor, had been more of an irritation and an annoyance than anything else... But here was comfort and good fortune surely... It gave one a kind of glow all over like very good whisky, only this was a permanent sensation likely to increase rather than diminish. He could not explain exactly how it felt to be a man of wealth, he said, when Charles Delamere inquired of him, unless it was that he imagined himself to be feeling a kind of funny with everything around him having a most gorgeous colour... and everyone as pleased with themselves and laughing like anything.

Mr. Delamere who, no doubt, had some reason also to be well pleased, was easily overflowing with delightful words. He solemnly affirmed that he had never, in the whole course of his experience, and it was a long and much varied experience, saw a man to behave with such suitable realisation of a great moment. And, as an accompaniment to the subsequent extended hand-shake, he made mention of the words "dignity" and "restraint." But the mind of Marcus, even in its present mood of change, was not to be outdone by soft flattery like this, for he seemed to see the whole performance in satirical relation to himself. Addressing Mr. Delamere with deliberation, he said:

"I'd like you to make a note of that, sir, for, when my monument is put up in the very middle of Garradrimna, as it is most likely to be put up after my regretted demise some years hence, I want nothing flamboyant that might remind anyone of incidents of my past lives, that is to say, if you are still in charge of my affairs after I am gone, but the figure of Marcus Igoe, as he used to be and always was, with the last between his knees and the sole of the boot uppermost with a half finished track of nails around it; in my left hand, between the forefinger and the thumb, a little nail held over its appointed place in the track, and in my right the hammer upraised to drive it home; my head bent like my mind inside upon my business that was never anybody else's business, and a fierce, determined expression upon my face... So, good morning now, Mr. Delamere, and thanks, thanks very much for all you have done *to* me!"

Having said which, and leaving Mr. Delamere once more wordless and bewildered, he hurried, as fast as the delicate state of his feet would permit, to join Margo who, becoming rapidly disgusted with his flush of eloquence, had moved through the hall towards the outer door... It was not until they were both well outside the solicitor's big brass-knobbed entrance that he was recalled to the reality of Margo. As the last few moments had shown, it might have been possible, with the gift of sarcasm that had come to him almost as a compensation for the resignation of his malignant purpose in life, to express himself forcibly in any circumstance, but this other soul to which he had allied his after it had gone through so many adventures, although theirs was probably the only real adventure of them all, had, of course, altogether different feelings and intuitions that were maybe all for his good — if he could only see it.

And so it was, that even now, full of satisfaction because of his triumph of manner over that of Charles Delamere, he knew that she was bound to say something that would soon reduce him to himself again, although all that remained of the fiasco of yesterday was rather more in his feet than upon her tongue. Indeed, she was just presently looking down at the movement of his feet, as it were, in quiet admiration. They seemed to remind her rather forcibly of the gouty extremities of the Hon. Reginald Moore lately arrived from one of his wanderings in foreign parts with the Hon. Benjamin Rand... It was very satisfactory, indeed, that her man had been able to put an aristocratic appearance upon himself at such small cost, as it were, and without going outside the confines of his native place...

It was, perhaps, only because Marcus, at the same moment, was having a similar thought that she had a notion that his head, at the other end of him, was uplifted in an aloofness, a kind of difference from those around him which corresponded perfectly to the grand manner of his feet. Maybe she would make a man out of him yet according to every single one of her own notions, in spite of the way he had once forsaken her and made a show of himself, one way or another, before the whole country. Look at how he had consented, after all his big talk, to take, at exorbitant rent, the modern bungalow belonging to Thomas Hardy! To-day, she did not want to be severe on him, but she simply had to speak of the new car she intended to make him buy at once. She drew up to the matter swiftly by, strangely, upon this day of all days in their lives, complaining about expense.

"That fellow, Wade," she said, "has us near robbed with the price he charges for his ould hurdy-gurdy of a car... a holy show of a thing... and our lives in danger nearly every time we go in it."

He knew what she meant exactly... He saw... But, amongst other anticipations, he had already resigned himself to it as something that could not be long delayed. A car of their own now, the Lord save us!

CHAPTER XXII

ALTHOUGH he was not at all inclined to admit it to her, Marcus was soon compelled to realise to himself that the two sweeping things that his wife had already made him do, the renting of Thomas Hardy's bungalow and the purchase of the luxurious saloon car, had done more suddenly to uplift him in the eyes of Garradrimna, to make him a triumphant figure, than anything he could even dream of doing on his own initiative... Maybe Margo had a big enough way of grasping things — in a certain way.

He heard himself being addressed on all sides as "Sir," and found people hanging respectfully upon his words, and it was a long time since that had happened to him before. This, he felt, surely stood for the condition known as "respectability," and he had never of late, even in the wildest flights of his imagination, had ambitions to be considered "respectable." Indeed so much was this still the case now that, in dark moments, when he felt the encroachment of the condition upon him, he would make a sudden, impulsive attempt to defeat it.

In the course of his daily walk through and around Garradrimna he would catch an old acquaintance by the arm, and, to the great surprise of the man, whom he might have looked upon, heretofore, most peevishly, as an enemy, hurry him into the Marlay Arms for entertainment. It was an action in keeping with the later portion of his life and in accordance with the codes that had then dominated him. But maybe it was a newer Marcus Igoe, too, one who had already subtly triumphed over himself, and his deplorable conception of the pageant of cripples going the rounds of his native place... He did not seem to remember at all that, even to the extent of possibly gaining a sweeter, kindlier outlook, he was still as the merest putty in the hands of Margo, because, no matter how considerate for his welfare she might appear, she was fully convinced that she had married, for all her silent devotion to him down through the years, a middling poor specimen of a man.

He had already consented, because he must, to two of the swift and surprising means which she had chosen with the aim of re-arranging the manner of their lives. And as with the telling of the first lie, he found that, to retain the original purpose and meaning of it, he must consent to one after another of her whims... He was somewhat troubled in his mind as to where it was all going to end.

To go into Garradrimna every day was a duty which he began seriously to feel that he must do to keep himself still something like himself in spite of the weight of the money with its consequent "grandeur" that was being forced upon him. Surely it was not unreasonable to think that all he wanted now was to be let move quietly about all the humble ways that had known him in his different days, his mind free of care, a new meerschaum pipe in his mouth, plenty of tobacco in his coat pocket, and plenty of money in his trouser's pocket, and a most gorgeous ease upon his every movement.

The most prosperous men who had ever sprung up around Garradrimna, he thought, what else had they done but move like this through all their sunny days about the places that had best known them when they were young and poor? But he had been flung by Margo into strange ways, a grand house, a motor car with chauffeur complete — a "cheff" he called him — and a crowd of impertinent-looking servants — whipsters he called them — always addressing him as "Sir," whereas, because the sense of his earlier ways had long since departed from him and become submerged by the dismal experiences of his later period, all he seemed ever to have wanted in the way of attendance was the person, whomsoever it might be, to hand him his drink, an ordinary pint for preference, in nice condition across the counter.

Where was the real Marcus Igoe now? Aye, where was he indeed? He would often set out, as it were, to find his own lost self, wherever it was gone to in Garradrimna, going farther even than the Marlay Arms, going into the house of Mrs. Ursula Wyse, for instance, that was now beginning to be called, for a curious reason, "The Picture Gallery." He seemed to recover some of himself in the presence of the satire it had begun to embody. It amused him mightily to contemplate the nature of the Picture Gallery. Surely he must have had something to do with creating the illusion that it was. The son that he had never had had not married Mrs. Wyse, and he himself had never been the Marquis of Garradrimna. But now was the thing happening, although in a different sort of way, all over again… It was a joy to contemplate it. He could see all the flaws in Mrs. Wyse's *second* attempt to be a great woman in Garradrimna.

CHAPTER XXIII

OF all places on earth, Garradrimna seemed the very last where one might go in quest of pictures, for the village was not sufficiently populous to justify the erection of a "cinema." But pictures of beautiful women, if these were the notion, indeed, works of art! Could one even think of the like, one's own mind would attempt to settle the matter by prompting the answer in a phrase of Garradrimna: "Well, it's not the one way everyone goes mad!" Of course there was the well-known sign of the man drinking a pint which had been put up by Gilbert Gallagher — no one to this day knowing the real artist — Gilbert or his co-adjutor, as they still called him, "Bill the Savage." Excepting that there was a smirk of a smile about the face of the man in the picture at certain angles... which reminded one curiously of the face of Bill himself.

It was seldom, of course, that anyone standing beneath it lingered long enough to gaze up and make certain, for that would have disclosed him as about to perform the action it depicted... which would never do... although if one, in passing the Marlay Arms at any conceivable hour of the day, looked up at the sign and then entered the public bar one could see any number of excellent imitations, all sincerely flattering, of the gesture and the action of the man in the painting. Yes, this *was* a picture no doubt, and certainly in its way was the work of Bill the Savage — if he could be really guilty of it, even as the work of an Old Master.

There was something in the idea of a Picture Gallery, after all, seeing that Garradrimna was held thus, as if for evermore, by the spell of one perfect performance by a master hand. This invited. This compelled. This conquered, although its author, always supposing that he could be its author, was, for the present, forbidden the precincts of the bar since the bare-faced incident of the boots of Marcus... But no matter for that; it was not so impossible after all to think that Garradrimna could go much further in the matter of pictures — if it liked — and that it should already, in a sense, possess a Picture Gallery, possibly very shortly, the ruins of a Picture Gallery that had been famous in its day exerting a rather wonderful influence upon the life around it.

Yet at no time, although many had gone looking for it eagerly, was the Picture Gallery, literally speaking, for all its wide fame, easy to be found. One might pass all the way from the old Castle of the De Lacys to the Chapel Gate, looking as long and hopefully as one might, even passing down narrow alleyways to peer more closely, and yet fail to see anything even remotely resembling the shape of a Picture Gallery. Nevertheless, in the vicinity of Garradrimna, it was possible for one to hear such a question and such an answer as the following:

"Musha, where are you in such a pucker of a hurry to this evening, my dear man?"

"Begorra, where am I going is it? Well, then I'm going straight into the Picture Gallery and, if the pictures aren't looking too lovely this evening, mebbe it's what I'll go on a bit further."

From hearing the stray fall of words like these, it was possible, unfortunately, for anyone who did not know Garradrimna so well as Marcus Igoe to form a wholly extravagant estimate of the amenities of the village. It was still, amongst the inhabitants, perpetual food for laughter to remember that a certain unfortunate traveller who, in writing a book about this part of the world and having been thus misled had expressed somewhere in print "that the enthusiasm for pictures in Dublin was already extending its influence to rural Ireland."

He went on to say that, "with the general adoption of a system of local galleries, possibly on the lines of the rural libraries, if not actually co-operating with them, we are bound to see in Ireland, as in Italy long ago, the uprise of schools of provincial painting which must give to the Island of Saints and Scholars a new title to fame... A very flourishing Gallery has been established at Garradrimna, in the Midlands." But the writer regretted that his passage through this particular district had been so hurried as to preclude examination of the Picture Gallery in Garradrimna. His words bore fruit in the appearance of some of those who had read them to inquire about the marvellous existence of a Picture Gallery in such a place... Yet they never saw it either, and always said, if asked by others, that their passage through this particular district had been so etc., etc.

A remarkable, indeed an almost inexplicable, feature of the Picture Gallery was the fact that although one might reasonably hope to discover it after inquiring for it in the right way, and enter in the hope of finding some rich entertainment of the soul, one could never quite succeed in seeing any pictures at all... If one went on to inquire from the Curators, as it were, two faded ladies of uncertain age even most politely: "Is this, please, the Picture Gallery?" the reply would be a very vacant "What?" or "What's that you're saying?" as if they did not seem to understand... The beginning of one's own doubts of the real existence of the whole thing, would be hurried into deeper disbelief by the light in their eyes, which had been, of a sudden, darkened and depressed by that querulous, disillusioned, "What?" or "What's that you're saying?" repeated by one or other of them. Yet, to think of the Picture Gallery being something in the nature of a practical joke

113

would not have been an altogether just conception. The fundamentals of art were here. If it came to real pictures, there were the potentialities of Bill the Savage.

CHAPTER XXIV

MARCUS IGOE had observed, in the course of his period behind the squinting window, the ups and downs in the life of Mrs. Wyse... He had said, with everyone else, that it would be a hard struggle for the widow if she didn't marry again. If even only the girls were a bit older, everyone, including himself, had said that they might have been made to serve as "a kind of decoy ducks for the purpose of enticing young foolish fellows into the shop to spend their money towards the building up of the business. But a hungry-looking pack of lanky girleens, none of them terrible good-looking, and with no prospects in the way of fortunes to make them any better-looking — what could a woman do with them? But even if they were grown up itself, and extraordinary good-looking into the bargain, it would be the devil's own expensive job to dress them all and keep them from tearing the eyes out of one another, they said, about fellows."

The presence of so many growing females in the house, effectively forbade what might have become a solution of the widow Wyse's difficulties. She was a fine, marriageable woman still, and the good business in addition would have made a safe bargain for any man wanting to settle himself well, only for the crowd of daughters that went to complete the amount of trouble he would have to take on his shoulders.

As Marcus, in the days of his leisure, calmly pondered her case in its later stages, he was always struck by the strangeness of the notion that his son — if he had been in it — that it would have been a terrible thing to have even dreamt of letting him in for a thing like this? It would have denied himself, too, the comic scrutiny of the situation that he now so much enjoyed... He observed, with the keenest interest, the working of Mrs. Wyse's brilliant plan to settle all her daughters one by one.

The first of them to arrive at an age sufficiently advanced as to warrant the application of the plan was Josephine. Her mother, by a great effort in the way of manipulation of her slender means, duly arrayed her eldest daughter for the attempt to capture, and she was given charge of the bar. But it was the misfortune of Josephine, as well as being the eldest, to be the most hopelessly plain-looking of all the girls, yet even this weakness Mrs. Wyse bravely attempted to counter by causing the perhaps none too captivating looks of the other girls to be made even less disquieting by the appearance they were constrained to present by the side of Josephine. The result, for various reasons, was not quite so successful as both Josephine and her mother had anxiously expected... Little flaws began to appear almost immediately in the excellence of the plan.

"Well, you're absolutely a picture," said Mrs. Wyse to Josephine in the presence of all the sisters on the morning that the offensive had been begun on behalf of the eldest daughter. The momentous announcement was variously received by the others — the youngest, Philomena, anxiously inquiring: "When am I going to be made a picture, mother? I'm twice as nice as Josephine, so I am, and it wouldn't have cost half as much to dress me up grand."

It was strange, yet perhaps not so strange, when one thought of the immense importance of little things in the curiously twisted scheme of Garradrimna, that the word "picture," dropped merely in casual extravagance by Mrs. Wyse, was destined in the end to bring fame to Garradrimna, and to make a certain reality out of nothing. For, immediately, the word went abroad that Josephine was after being set up as a picture to try to bring custom to the house. The report became elaborated crudely, satirically. The nickname of "the Picture" was securely labelled upon Josephine, who could not, by any stretch of the imagination, be thought of as a genuine picture at all.

"And, musha, who served you with the pint this morning?" one man of Garradrimna would say to another as he emerged from Mrs. Wyse's, the brown beads of the porter like dew upon his dark moustache.

"Who served me, is it? Who else only 'the picture'?"

"And how is it looking this morning?"

"Ah, poorly, just only middling, as you might say: the colours is getting to be a bit cracked or something, and it'll soon want to be re-varnished it it's the intention of the widow to keep it much longer on exhibition."

From all of which it might easily be gathered that the satirical mind of Garradrimna was equal to the most involved and difficult metaphor, and that the first "picture" hung in the "Gallery" was scarcely a success. Of course there were people in Garradrimna who always expressed themselves quite plainly, and these were forced to say, after a year or two, that Mrs. Wyse would be hard set to get e'er a man at all for Josephine. Even Marcus Igoe, from the very beginning of the thing, had said it, many a time through a mouthful of rivets — as if it mattered to him, but he could not afford to be behind-hand in talk of that kind.

Mrs. Wyse, calmly realising the gathering force of this sound opinion, and being a woman not likely to be daunted in her desires, began to have notions of replacing Josephine by Charlotte, the second eldest, and then waiting patiently to see what she would see by way of a turn in her fortunes.

117

CHAPTER XXV

THE setting up of Charlotte as an attraction did not stand for a complete withdrawal of Josephine. Rather, on the contrary, was Josephine put to a new and, her fond mother fancied, a better purpose. Somewhat declined from importance, she was reduced to a merely secondary position, that of a means of contrast by the side of her more promising sister. It was arranged that, for the present at least, the light should not fall upon Josephine, and whether, as a result of this last shrewd touch by her anxious mother, or through sheer strength of the native graces of Charlotte, the second picture, as they called her immediately, began to promise certain success. She looked fine, anyway they said, by the side of Josephine, and, by degrees, new customers began to struggle into the bar. Dribble by dribble, these were reinforced by others until the result was quite a crowd.

Naturally, those who stuck to their accustomed haunts, the elderly or quite disillusioned men who had no interest in "pictures," began to feel lonely, and, the lost appeal of the other houses finally fading, they were driven to join the crowd. Even Simon Seery, the proprietor of the one-time all powerful Marlay Arms, felt the brunt of Mrs. Wyse's carefully nurtured scheme, and was obliged to employ Gilbert Gallagher to repaint the famous sign of the man drinking a pint. It was said that, confused into a condition almost of lunacy by the loss of all his best customers, and the continuous use of the word "picture" in connection with the Widow Wyse's, he thought, blindly, that in his "picture" lay a complete solution of all his difficulties.

Marcus observed Gilbert, assisted by Bill the Savage, taking down the sign one morning, and he went up the street in the hope of discovering what he had always suspected. Impelled by all the curiosity of Garradrimna, he waited to see if, side by side, the portrait would prove to be that of "the Savage" himself and none other. There was nothing but silence... The artists evidently resented his presence at this juncture, and the dark look upon the face of "the Savage" grew almost into a black mist before his eyes... He looked long at the picture. It might be "the Savage" for it might, quite easily, be anybody, including himself... That gave him a little bit of an unquiet feeling... They might do it to him. It was very like a thing they would do. A few touches here and there, while they were re-painting it and it would be Marcus Igoe, his image to swing in the wind for evermore. It was like hanging a man or beheading him... And although few might recognise it, for the reasons already realised... it would be an awful thing to have on one's mind all the same.

And it happened — at least he was nearly certain it was himself when it came to be hung above the door of Simon Seery... But no one seemed to notice. Simon was satisfied that the colours had become almost audible through power of the process through which it had passed while in the workshop of Gilbert Gallagher... But, had he been gifted with any artistic instincts, he would have realised that something must have happened to it... But all he saw was, sadly, that it had ceased, at least quite definitely for the time being, to exercise any supersession of glamour over Mrs. Wyse's or any powerful compulsion, so far as his turnover was concerned, to the action it so vividly helped to portray. The rival house seemed to flourish and increase itself. It was said now that Charlotte could have the refusal of every desirable man in the place, from Edgar Linnart, the patriot, to John Reginald Cully, the reporter for the *North Leinster Gazette,* both of whom moved almost continuously in and out of the shop, finding all sorts of excuses to do bits of business there at all hours of the day.

But Charlotte herself quite suddenly put an end to all speculation as to whom she would "take" by marrying Thomas Vandaleur, the cattle-dealer, who was about "the solidest match" they said, "in the seven parishes." A powerful man entirely!

For a considerable time before this splendid result had been achieved, Mrs. Wyse had found it necessary to introduce, in addition to Josephine, her remaining three daughters into the shop. But this she had done with the artistic discrimination that had already distinguished all her dealings and doings upon their behalf. She had subdued them, as it were, to the captivating effect she had desired of Charlotte until they might well be considered as meagre of attraction as Josephine, who had quite failed as a "picture."

But, all the while, the younger girls had been wildly rebellious in their own minds, and this was a contingency for which Mrs. Wyse, with all her calculations, had made no allowance. She did not fully realise the strength of this feeling until just after the marriage of Charlotte, when, immediately, all three of them, Rebecca, Agnes, and even little Philomena, were wild to take their sister's place. But Mrs. Wyse still ruled strongly her own household. With a swift, strong hand she quelled her rebellious daughters. And then she set about her own way of teaching them sense.

Josephine re-appeared behind the bar re-adorned for conquest. This was more than Rebecca, the third eldest, who was at least as attractive as Charlotte, could reasonably stand, so she ran away to Mrs. Thomas Vandaleur's, where she proposed to stay until her mother had come to a better frame of mind regarding the whole extraordinary arrangement. She had not long to wait, for the second attempt of Mrs. Wyse to get Josephine off her hands by foisting her upon an unwilling public, was a more dismal failure than even the first. Not even the severest subjugation of Agnes and Philomena could effect anything like an approach to the miracle, and her mother, alarmed by the sudden dwindling of her customers, was forced to send for the errant Rebecca, who returned with some of the splendour of Mrs. Thomas Vandaleur upon her to increase her value as a public exhibition.

CHAPTER XXVI

IF Simon Seery, out of the anxiety of his position, had foolishly fancied that the temporary return of some of his customers stood for a return as well of its ancient magic to the sign of the man drinking a pint, his hope was swiftly demolished. Something had gone wrong with that sign anyway! For Rebecca Wyse was proving by far the most attractive "picture" that her mother had yet set up. The business was suddenly flourishing to an extent that exceeded the wildest dreams she had had at the inception of her plan.

But Rebecca, as her heartscald, continued the wilful, disobedient way of which she had already given promise. It became increasingly doubtful whether she would settle herself now in accordance with the plan of her mother, but it was evident that marry she would, undoubtedly, and perhaps sooner than might be altogether wise from a business point of view. It was clear that a marriage with Edgar Linnart could be easily arranged, and he no bad match either only for the "patriotism." But Rebecca herself seemed to fancy John Reginald Cully who had nothing, not even convictions, unless he was after the fortune that he might be expecting out of the now flourishing business... But Rebecca suddenly settled the matter by eloping with John Reginald Cully.

As soon as her mother had recovered from the first heavy fall of her tears, she spoke wisely:

"Well, let her! The devil a penny he'll get out of this, anyway, in case it might interfere with the fortune that her other little sisters may want still. Sure she's off my hands, anyway, and he'll have to keep her with his fountain-pen and his shorthand, and his polished leggings!"

Edgar Linnart, as might be expected of him, put on the mood of one disappointed in love. He came daily to the "pictures" to confuse his sorrow with the sorrow of Ireland. It was said by everyone that, as sure as day, he would marry the next best thing to Rebecca, namely, one of her sisters, one of the other pictures, and with this end in view Mrs. Wyse placed daily before him her first "picture," Josephine, for his solace and delight. But, somehow, the magic failed to fall... and his prospective mother-in-law, always moving shrewdly about the shop, was keen to observe that his broken heart was not beginning to be repaired, and so, before the combined disaster of Edgar's destruction and the loss of more customers could happen, Agnes, the second last of the pictures, suitably "framed," must be put up in the shop to bring him back to himself again.

Her never-failing wisdom was again rewarded, for the wound in the heart of the patriot began almost immediately to close. Leaning across the counter on the very first day of Agnes' installation in the bar, he said to this new, faint touch of beauty:

"Miss Wyse, I say, Miss Wyse, in the words of the old profession, in fact one of the oldest professions, that of auctioneer, I'm going, going... gone, yah know..."

The eyes of Agnes brimmed with the quiet, shining tear, and her mother, overhearing the grand confession, said quietly to herself: "Imagine him getting 'gone' like that so soon," so, knowing that all was again well, and, being pretty cautious, she called now for the third time the subdued Josephine out of the bar and left the rest to Agnes.

CHAPTER XXVII

AFTER the marriage of Agnes to Edgar Linnart, a kind of scruple began to stir in the mind of Mrs. Wyse regarding her daughter Philomena, the last of the "pictures," who had watched the whole performance of her sisters with anxious eyes. It will be remembered that it was she who was exceedingly jealous and tearful when she had not been put forward as the very first of the pictures, and, later, to be the second, after the marriage of Charlotte. "Musha, the Lord save us, and you only a child," her mother said on both occasions, when, in her wisdom, she had proceeded to decree otherwise.

There could be no doubt at all as to the wisdom of her mother's plan for, so far as Philomena was concerned, she was, by reason of the endowments of nature, the best of all the pictures, and, besides, the easy circumstances into which the family had rapidly moved through the success of the bar and the respective marriages of Charlotte and Agnes to Thomas Vandaleur and Edgar Linnart enabled her easily to achieve fascination. And, in addition, there was the fact that the accumulated fortunes which Mrs. Wyse had not given her other married daughters might make a very respectable dowry for Philomena...

Consequently, Mrs. Wyse's scruples took the form of saying that Philomena could afford to wait. And there may have been, at the back of her mind all the time, the faint, lingering notion that she might yet get Josephine off her hands. It was the one thing that had beaten her, but she was a persevering woman, and might yet succeed. As well as all these little determining circumstances, there was the fact of Philomena's own obvious eagerness, and that it was as well she should be kept in her place, in case she should turn out to be a self-willed hussy and marry foolishly like Rebecca, so, with wisdom, she thought that Josephine might be given another little chance... just once more... you know, you never could tell.

Now, all this time that Mrs. Wyse had been displaying such anxiety to get the girls off her hands, the people of Garradrimna had often wondered why she, herself, seemed never to have thought of marrying, seeing that she was still a better-looking woman than any of her daughters, married or unmarried... They did not know what Marcus Igoe knew about that... They did not know that he was the man, above all in Garradrimna, who had seen into her mind... through something that had never happened, yet maybe through no fault of hers... There was, in a sense, something of actual correspondence between certain things that might have happened once and something that had begun actually to happen now... For the wonderment of Simon Seery that she had not married began to take a practical turn, seeing that he was compelled to witness, from day to day, the gradual ruin of his own magnificent business beneath Mrs. Wyse's widespreading, successful influence... From thinking deeply upon the sadness which all this occasioned to his single state was an easy step to having thoughts of the widow herself. It was a way out of his difficulties, and, perhaps, the only way.

It was not until the people of Garradrimna, Marcus Igoe in particular, saw the proprietor of the Marlay Arms walk into the Widow Wyse's one fine evening that they fully realised how successful the widow had been. A publican driven to patronise another publican in the same village signified something akin to disaster. Nor did Mrs. Wyse realise her amazing success until the very same moment. And it so excited her that a brilliant notion for its consolidation and extension came hurriedly to her mind. She, of a sudden, was dazzled by marvelling that she had not thought of it long ago.

The two men who observed its happening, Marcus Igoe and Bill the Savage were silent, Marcus because of the sense of comedy with which the ease of his life had now invested him, Bill with a quiet sense of his power although he had nothing, but he had known how to kill the magic that had rested aforetime in the famous sign of the man drinking a pint... Each of the three felt that the others did not know what was in his mind... Bill that Marcus did not know that he had deliberately depicted him on the sign, Marcus that Bill did not recognise that he had done so, and, Simon, that neither of the other two guessed that the failure of the sign had driven him to his present purpose... And then there was Mrs. Wyse herself, with only one thought in her mind — Simon Seery, the Marlay Arms and the whole trade of Garradrimna within her grasp now!

As the visits of Simon Seery continued, she began to be very anxious that the vast possibilities he represented should not elude her. He was very nice to her, of course, but one could not afford to be too romantic with a man in the position in which he presently was.

It was unfortunate that, just then, on account of her persistent attempts to impose the first picture upon them, her magnificent custom should again have begun to dwindle. It must be quite apparent to even the presently romantic eyes of Simon Seery since not a few of the very best customers had begun to creep back to the Marlay Arms. There was no use in being too head-strong where it might result in the loss of the splendid chance that was now placed before her. Therefore Josephine was again withdrawn and Philomena put up in her stead. The result of the "new" picture was again instantaneous — a crowded house and no one at all in the Marlay Arms. So there was no use in Simon Seery having any belated notions of a revival of the business. Nor did he appear to have any. Nor did he seem to care. It looked as if he might be about to go to the bad.

And yet, at the same time, he appeared the happiest man in Garradrimna. He came regularly every night for a chat with the widow, and to take his drink like those around, and with as much interest as anyone else in Philomena.

It would be as well, thought Mrs. Wyse, to finish him while one was at it. There was no use in having this danger always hovering near. She would keep Philomena before them until Simon Seery had finally committed himself by asking herself to marry him, seeing that there was nothing else to be done, and he after going through nearly all he had left before her very eyes in her own house. She could be terribly unscrupulous when she had set her mind on a thing. And Josephine was not yet married. It went against her grain to be having Philomena, and she so young, so much in the bar watching Simon Seery make such a fool of himself, having to talk to him so much and be nice to him while she herself was waiting for the opportune moment when she should pounce securely upon her prey.

Nothing of the kind had ever been kept so secret in Garradrimna... The whole comedy of it going on, or at least he fancied so, in the mind of Marcus Igoe. A thing like that seemed to take on reality only through very depth of the vision with which it was observed. Thus far, he had merely observed life spasmodically, and in a way that made his undoubted gift of perception and criticism merely of secondary importance, but now he realised, for the first time, that he had the power to create illusions of life in certain directions by the very strength of his concentration. He felt that he could make things happen, even as the squinting windows had, aforetime, made things happen. This was a vast power, surely, and the feeling that he possessed it sometimes frightened him. He would have to be very careful that he did not permit himself to use it lightly. He was troubled in a way about this poor woman, this Mrs. Wyse...

But Simon Seery went and got married to Philomena one fine morning, ran away, quite unaccountably, with the last of the pictures under his arm, as you might say... Everyone but Marcus Igoe, the detached observer, who seemed to see a little further than any of them, said that wasn't the mother, the Lord save us, a wonderful woman the way she was after engineering the settlement of the whole four daughters? They did not see the two black sides to her defeat that Marcus Igoe saw, even as she herself saw them, for he knew that she was still too wise to let people see that she did.

But it was terrible... terrible... Poor little Philomena gone off with him, with him, imagine, of whom, dimly now, she began to feel that she had been fond, for all the fierce battle they had fought down through all the years.

And her famous wisdom, where was it now?... But her heart fluttered into a little quiet when she thought, when she remembered that they must still be thinking Mrs. Wyse... wiser than ever... That was it... wiser than ever... to her own mind now, only too wise. She had gone beyond herself. She had most sadly overreached her wisdom.

CHAPTER XXVIII

AS part of its celebrated power to inflict pain and punishment, Garradrimna possessed two dominant qualities. It could cause a most ludicrously satirical situation to be raised up around a house or a person, while the house or the person remained blissfully unconscious of it all the while. And, perhaps directly by reason of this, it could iniflict the heaviest of lashes while pretending to remain largely unconscious of what it was doing. It will be easily seen, therefore, that Garradrimna was quite capable of producing the most mortifying situations within the confines of itself.

The case of "the Picture Gallery" was a notable example. It was very strange, yet perfectly true, that all the time that Mrs. Wyse had been engaged in the laudable pursuit of getting her daughters off her hands, she had remained as perfectly unaware as they that her daughters were being termed "pictures" inclusively and one by one. In her wildest dreams, for sake of their future, she had never once thought of them as pictures of beautiful girls, nor did Garradrimna ever really think of them that way at all.

Consequently, when it came to be established further afield, she remained as blissfully ignorant as the most remote stranger concerning where "the Picture Gallery" could be situated in Garradrimna... And, this being the final, exquisite touch of Garradrimna's irony, it did not come to be thus fully established until there were no more "pictures" for exhibition. Hence the

129

"What?" or the "What's that you're saying?" of either of the two faded ladies of uncertain age, when one inquired, even most politely: "Is this, please, the Picture Gallery?" The querulousness of their answers and their accents of disillusionment required a little fuller explanation.

After the marriage of Philomena, two hopes fled finally from the breast of Mrs. Wyse, hope of getting Josephine settled and hope of ever re-building the business again after the next time it might begin to decline. She had no more "pictures," or rather, daughters as she thought of them. Josephine was still Josephine, business was business, and she herself, after all her amazing success, was a grievously disappointed woman. If only they knew the full extent of it. But she would never let them see, that... She was so anxious to say a comforting word of this kind to herself that she must have a feeling really that it was being seen by one or two people, at least, by Marcus Igoe as he stood often by her counter now, a man of leisure, quietly contemplating Bill the Savage, as he stood there pondering his pint.

It was said in Garradrimna that Bill the Savage saw queer things in the drink, and that, from moment to moment, his face gave token of the adventures of his eyes among the dreams that came to him out of the glass. It was on these flickering changes that the mind of Marcus Igoe was almost wholly employed; they were, in a sense, all the real joy that his money had yet brought him. This and a certain pleasure in thinking about such pieces of folly as that of Simon Seery in running away with little Philomena. He was safe from that, anyway, safe as houses, although, sometimes, he would have a queer feeling that Bill the Savage was looking at all his "lives" in the Crystal that was native to Garradrimna... making, perhaps, some new life for him out of the bits that he saw. The minds of all three of them would pass into a sort of movement around this notion that was enforced upon them for the moment, perhaps, merely by the power of Mrs. Wyse's own disappointment... Why, she would never forget it. The cheek of it, and the base ingratitude, from the two of them, from Simon Seery and her daughter Philomena!

It was thus and thus... her mind would occupy itself... But as time went on, and as she continued to see her frustration in those who came into her shop, particularly in the kind of mirror that Marcus Igoe and "the Savage" made for her, she was compelled to think of it as a more practical disaster. Under the spell of Philomena, picture that she was, people now saw something in the picture on the sign, and business at the Marlay Arms increased wonderfully, indeed to such an extent that the Picture Gallery itself was left with only a little dribble of customers. But this was not such a calamity, such a nemesis altogether as it might have been in other circumstances in Garradrimna. Of course she was not to be pitied now, as she had certainly deserved to be at the beginning of her struggle. One way or another her daughters had all become permanently fixed in life. They had made a success of themselves, all save Rebecca, but she had good "back" always, they said, in her sister, Mrs. Thomas Vandaleur... And, sure, about Josephine, wouldn't she have been lonesome, anyway, without one of them to keep her company?

Yet the deeper eye of comedy, the vision that arose out of seeing Bill the Savage and Marcus Igoe looking at one another, could see that she was a pity all the same, yet only maybe to the extent that all of us are a pity at the end even when our plans have achieved success in spite of ourselves. Mrs. Wyse remained, somehow, in the mind as one who had had in life one purpose only... in which she had succeeded and in his most serious moments Marcus was given to think... that if only he had been allowed to continue successful to the end...

131

Yes, most assuredly, it was a pity of Mrs. Wyse, two faded women standing always in a poorly patronised bar, a mother, more widowed and oldish now, and her eldest daughter, nearly all as one as herself, and both scarcely knowing why they spent so much of the day richly adorning themselves to no purpose at all. For nothing at all, it would seem, only to be thinking, the daughter, that she might have married well only for the mother — think of all the times she had been taken down to give a chance to one of the other sisters! And the mother — if only she had waited and waited, using every stratagem to get Josephine married, she might have re-married well and banged out the whole lot of them anyhow! And then, parties always coming in inquiring was this the Picture Gallery...? And other parties always making most cutting allusions to "pictures." What pictures? It must be this Marcus Igoe they meant or the other fellow! The two of them always looking at one another... A nice pair of pictures, them two! She would send *them* hopping about their business anyway... So, there and then, she told them what she thought of them.

Whenever Marcus experienced a rebuff of this kind, even in spite of his money... maybe only because of it... some sense of his inadequate quality would reassert itself, and he would feel driven to say to himself:

"D'ye know what it is? I'm watered down, to all intents and purposes, so I am, by money and grandeur and comfort and ease and the continuous necessity of doing nothing, and the motor car and the bungalow and them damn servants until I'm only about the consistency of the worst whisky in Garradrimna whenever I endeavour to discover a splink of my original self. I was stopped by the money in what I was going to do, and, as sure as you're there if I don't do something terrific they'll soon begin to look down on me again, as of yore, if not in a way far worse, for what will I be only the Honourable, as it were, Mrs. Igoe's husband, with no manhood or meaning attached to me, good, bad or indifferent."

CHAPTER XXIX

Hoping that she might relent, out of pity for him, Marcus deliberately tried his best to cultivate this feeling. For example, after any determined essay in pride on the part of Margo, any ascent, by even a single round, upon the social ladder through great effort and lavish expense, he would appear about Garradrimna next day, as one depressed and drooped in spirit...

If only, she would point out to him again and again, he could recover the famous politeness that was supposed to have been so large a part of his past... But that side of him was lost... Vanished, too, was the romantic side, either of his early or his late period... Gone, also, was the ludicrous possibilities of association with Bartle Boyhan and Dickeen Crosbie, for Margo firmly forbade him their company... He might patronise Bill the Savage, who was, in her view, a madman and a villain past recall, but the others would try determinedly to put themselves on the same level with her husband and she was not going to have that!

Every way you looked at it, he was knocked out of gear... However hard he would sometimes try to simulate his ancient feeling with regard to Garradrimna, there was something which effectively forbade its accomplishment, although it gave him at the same time a sense of the power he had half realised through contemplation of the case of Mrs. Wyse—if only he could rise to it. And what was this something? His money, what else? It was, continuously, the protection which made him proof against any calamity that they could bring down upon his head, and so the chance of life was gone, the adventurous regard of events... If he had no money again... Ah, then... But if he had no money, what use would he be at all now? An elderly man who had become suddenly spoiled by a belated re-introduction to the ways of softness. But, at the rate that Margo was getting through it... there was a chance that... There was just a little taste of excitement in this... if it could be taken as a means of comfort...

Margo herself was far from happy. A constant effort, never quite resulting in success, could scarcely be calculated to improve the temper of one who had been baulked all her life. Of course she had swung, at mere mention of the fortune, far above the set that she had known in Garradrimna... the begrudgeful crew!... The way they had looked down on her... when she had married Marcus near the end of his variegated career, with everything gone that she might have minded so well for him from the beginning...

When she dashed past them now with the car, in grand style, they did not appear at all as inhabitants of the same planet, and so any relation such as envy on the one hand, or scorn on the other, was, in a sense, non-existent between them. It was the people above her who bore most strongly upon her consciousness, for it was the way with them that they in turn regarded her as someone who was inhabitant of another sphere... And to think that Marcus had once gone around after that crowd... made a show of himself with Olive Fetherstonhaugh, while she had been faithful to him all the time, waiting for him in the house of his father...

But she could not turn back now, or even attempt the slightest change in her performance, else she would be a living slur upon herself for all time in Garradrimna... She worried so much over it that Marcus found people beginning to condole with him on the "appearance of the Missus." The word, falling around him with such frequency, affected him curiously. It made him think of the amount of wisdom, commonly called sense, he must have, after all, when one considered the deplorable lack of it that Margo was presently exhibiting...

Then, before ever he realised the disaster that was overtaking her, she died leaving him a lone man.

Thus, suddenly, was presented to him the possibility of another new life. He had not wished for it, only wanting Margo to do the things that might have preserved her to him. But she had yearned to produce another life out of the money for herself and him, and all that had really happened was that this had come to him in another way, but it was going to be as different as different without her.

It was not until she had been some weeks interred that the full sense of it smote him powerfully, and that he truly realised the weight of his loss. It was quite natural that he should feel this way, for had she not been a reliable support upon which he had leaned for years, despite the well-fought dissimilarity of their minds? He was lonely and afflicted, thinking how he might use the money to solace him for his definite break with the past, before he could enter into the new life whatever it might be.

He thought, out of deep respect for her, of the most likely kind of means by which she might have wished to be remembered in this world, if she had not been whipped off to the next before ever she had resigned herself to going, in which case she must surely have made some kind of provision for her immortality here below. He began to occupy his mind with thoughts of a most gorgeous tombstone, a sort of monument by the side of which all the other tombstones that ever were in Garradrimna must certainly look nothing at all, and no fit company for anything so fine and upstanding.

It was as he leaned over the Churchyard wall one day that he pondered this aspect of the matter... He almost jumped and danced and "Ha! Ha'd!" in amazement as he now saw so clearly what had never before appeared to him. The Churchyard itself was an exact reproduction of Garradrimna! If only he were any sort of humorist or author at all, he would fittingly express the splendid realisation. But, even as he was, the spectacle now presented to the eye of his fancy was not wholly lost upon him. Indeed, in a way, it was most extraordinary to think of the general effect of Garradrimna being so faithfully reproduced. One had only to peer through the narrow aisles of the tombstones to perceive the native quality of his native village, the slant of the houses, the numerous combined irregularities which produced the squint of the windows...

Ah well... to think that it was here he contemplated putting up the monument to Margo, to place her again in the very middle of the situation from which she had retreated to the grandeur of the bungalow... Margo had never, even at her most irritating, treated him so badly that he should do a thing like this to her, and she gone further now from Garradrimna than even the bungalow... Of course the very beginning of his thought had not embodied this consideration at all, yet it had entered, very important and significant, by the back door of his consciousness. No, it would not be fair to Margo, he thought finally, even though it was a definite abandonment of much consideration of the matter upon which he had already employed himself. For it had been his intention to make this no common tombstone, but something sublime and imposing, like some of the statues he had seen in Dublin, whither he had gone with Margo, for the first time in many years, upon one of the last of her proud expeditions in the car.

But those, he had noticed, were all statues of great men. Why was it there were no statues of great women in the public streets of Ireland? And there must have been great women, just as there had been great men down the long course of his country's chequered history. Margo, for instance, had been a great woman; "great" in her constancy as she had watched him making a fool of himself for so many years; "great" when, as the better half of him in the first state, she had earned fame in Garradrimna by her fine, wifely solicitude in causing him to make a living out of the boots; "great" when, in the days of their good fortune, she had devoted every effort and every stratagem towards the making of something out of him, as it were, who was nothing. And even if she had not succeeded it was, maybe, only because she had died, the poor unfortunate woman!

CHAPTER XXX

As the only apparent result of all the trouble of his mind about it, he caused to be erected by an undistinguished Midland sculptor a quite plain tombstone in the churchyard of Garradrimna. They said it was very stingy of him, but there was more in it than met their eyes. He had pondered it down into this monastic simplicity through consideration of the empty glories with which Margo had filled her latter end... Where was the use in bringing ostentation here, when he had hated so thoroughly that unfortunate foible of Margo's? Nevertheless, in spite of his continuous effort to comfort himself by thinking this way, a sense of the insufficiency of what he had done drove him often to spend an hour in contemplation by the churchyard wall... He began to discover now that all the idle time it enabled him to have was really a greater burden than the money itself... "Thinking is bad wit," was Savage Bill's only known contribution to philosophy, (perhaps merely because he so seldom spoke at all), but the saying had throbbed the insistence of its truth into his mind. He was doing nothing now only thinking—the most foolish thing of all... Life passed him curiously. He saw it partly as bits of something happening around him now, partly as bits of life that he had experienced in the past.

He saw a day in winter:

He saw the meet of the Hounds in Garradrimna. Eleven was the hour at which they were to move off from the Marlay Arms. From half-past ten the ladies and gentlemen of Meath, on their sleek strong hunters, had been moving towards the scene... And to think that he had once been one of them... Ah me!... those days, and, looking at the Hunt now, he seemed to glance back and see a part of himself that was no more... The narrow street of Garradrimna looked forlorn and bedraggled after the heavy rains of early November. It seemed almost as if the day had not long dawned... But, in a weak burst of sunlight, the village made an effort to put on its best appearance. On both sides of the street, almost to a man—and woman, the shopkeepers stood in their doorways commenting on the companies of equestrians as they arrived.

He had never done this in his days in the little shop, never raised his eyes from his boots even... About the door of the Marlay Arms the motor was in evidence... They would invent some sort of a motor yoke to run over the fields shortly... Those sportsmen who had come a long distance had travelled in this way. Their grooms stood beside their horses, fellows with hard, clean-shaven faces... The hunting people now walked out of the Hotel and sprang into the saddles. The sound of laughter mingled with happy salutations above the sound of the champing bits and the pawing, impatient horses. Bartle Boyhan and Dickeen Crosbie and a few of the less distinguished corner boys stood upon the outskirts of the hunting throng. A shilling or so for holding a horse, or opening a gate, or tightening a saddle girth meant another sort of hunt for them.

The velvet-capped huntsmen—those sportsmen who were also professionals—kept the eager pack of hounds in order. The Master of the Hounds displayed a vast responsibility. By eleven the Hunt had completely collected. There was an order from the M.F.H. and they passed in review down the street... Imagine, he had actually passed thus down this very street once with Olive

Fetherstonhaugh, after having given five shillings apiece to Bartle and Dickeen who had started the game young...

One almost unconsciously picked out the contrasting types. There was the born gentleman, there the real lady!... No great shakes either when you had spent a fortune nearly in getting to know them, but they looked well, all the same, in their neat, well-tailored clothes. With a good deal more of self-invested importance and a good deal more of self-consciousness, came the shopkeepers and the larger farmers, the men whom he himself had just been like once. It was a big ambition in many a Meath family to have one of their own ride to hounds. Some of them sat most uneasily in their saddles, the poor devils! He realised that they were more to be pitied than laughed at. There was the kind of lad that he knew so well, the "horsey" man who had a hunter to sell, and who now tried to show him off to the best advantage. The grooms had dropped behind. They rode their horses well, but they still retained the manners of the stable, a dirty pack of blackguards!

There were men who followed on foot—just as he was going to do now. Among them one might discover some of the very oldest enthusiasts of the hunting game. Some of them had owned horses once but, one way or another, they had become dispossessed, and there were others, horseless all their lives, who, even still, would think nothing of running for miles after the Hunt across the wet fields.

"There is some kind of an element in it, don't you know," said one of these old men to Marcus.

Some of the big farmers and shopkeepers of the place, too wide of girth to seat a hunter, jogged along in traps. The motor followed respectfully behind the horse, for here the horse was still superior.

They had passed through the grand gates of The Hon. Reginald Moore's demesne. The horn of the huntsman rang out through the quiet woods and a touch of gladness seemed to creep into the dying trees. The brilliant coats and shining headgear were in bright contrast to the wintry desolation of the fields. Some turned, thus soon, towards the Castle for refreshment and the noble host came out upon the steps to welcome his guests... Marcus had not gone so near this noble person for many a long day... Momentarily, he wondered what the devil had happened to the Hon. Benjamin Rand... The horses waiting and the people crowding the steps, the whole colour of the gathering against the background of the lofty Norman castle seemed to make a suitable picture to hang in an old country house... He had had pictures like it once in his place at Harbourstown...

The note of the chase was sounded, and, suddenly, all was wild excitement. The horn rang out again, the dogs yelped madly on the trail and the men hallooed... The little pageant passed across an open field and, as the woods re-echoed to the sound of the galloping, one began to feel "the element," the thing that gets into the blood—one wanted to be running with the rest of them after the horses and the dogs and the swiftly passing moment of joy...

The run was of short duration for this demesne was too plentifully wooded. The sound of the dogs breaking through the undergrowth told that the fox had gone to ground... The covert was made difficult of negotiation by thick clumps of laurels... the professional huntsmen were re-inforced by Bartle Boyhan with a spade... The dogs were soon in a shapeless, clay-besmeared mass about the hole. Marcus saw it all, even to the half-crown from the Master, which Bartle spat upon for luck to the Hunt before he put it in his pocket... He did not want to see the slaughter of the fox... They were away again... He saw the pathetic figure of the old sportsman... listening for the sound of the horn that was already distant music... Soon he would have to hobble home, too tired to go any further... "Fine dogs, fine men, I knew them well," he muttered, as Marcus left him standing mournfully by the mound of freshly-turned clay.

Marcus felt himself wandering far into the country... after the sound of the Hunt... But the day was dying and he knew the chase had ended in the distance... He realised that he had walked a fearful length... too far altogether. He turned homeward towards Garradrimna. Soon he heard stamping and pattering behind him. The huntsmen with their hounds went slipping past him along the wet, dark road towards the place of kennelling...

He saw a day in summer:

Ah, yes, he could remember many a brave day in summer, but none lovelier, perhaps, than the days when the Circus came to Garradrimna by the old stage-coach road from Ballydrumcree or Castleconnor. The certain promise of the Circus had been foretold by large posters in blue and red which had, for a week past, adorned the piers of the Court-House gates.

Those who were arrested by these magical warnings never quite believed the wonderful things the posters told, and yet they never quite succeeded in escaping the spell which the announcement of its coming cast over Garradrimna. The visit of the Circus was like an annual dream, which might yet come true, but although, in a sense, it was disappointing always, one never awoke from it to complete disillusionment. One had dreamt, one's soul had wandered far, and a feeling had emerged to become, even for a time, a part of the consciousness... That one might pass some time with the white tents, and the green and golden wagons, into a most happy land.

Buzzanno's Circus! The name was, in a way, as intimate as the name over any shop door in the place. But wonder and music and beauty, all went to colour this merchandise when the elaborate caravans of Buzzanno's Circus had rested here.

And yet, for all the amazing difference that existed between these splendid things, which possessed the freedom of the windy roads, and the little dark nooks of shops that they knew so well, there were many who followed the fortunes of the Circus with an interest as intimate and personal as if it were the property of a couple of the neighbours. The very sight of the posters, fresh upon the piers, awoke in them many memories...

Even on occasions of the kind Bartle Boyhan and Dickeen Crosbie would discard some of their satiric quality and be reminiscent and sentimental. They agreed to consider the Circus as beyond them, and so also did Marcus Igoe. An attitude of reverence had always been his way when it came.

"Again, begad, and we not dead yet or a ha'porth."

Marcus had said this to his colleagues and contemporaries as they stood before one of the posters on the eve of the Circus, and while gladness began to splash into their eyes.

"The Lord save us! D'ye remember when we were gosoons?"

"Aye, d'ye remember." And of course Marcus remembered a little more... The summer evening he had gone shyly with Mary Margaret Caherlane, and they had seen the wonders together almost as with the one pair of eyes, although he had been too timid, too much afraid of his father, really, to sit by her side... With the reading of the circus bill all was young and romantic again. Here was something that had not changed anyhow:

"THE BROTHERS BUZZANNO, The Lightning Equilibrists."

"MONS. FRANCOIS McCORMACK, Ventriloquist."

"SWEENEY AND TODD, The Most Laughable Comedians in Christendom."

144

"MDLLE. GENEVIEVE, the World's Most Beautiful Woman, who will, as usual, put her lovely head in the Lion's Mouth at the Imminent Peril of her Life, as already performed before all the Crowned Heads of Europe."

"DE NOVO, Conjuror and Mesmerist."

There were, in addition, all the other amazing people who did all the other wonderful things. Momentarily, it would appear past belief to the old men, that they, great fellows and all as they undoubtedly were, could go on doing them still. Pretending to be deeply puzzled by this, Bartle Boyhan would sometimes feel inclined to speak his mind:

"It's most extraordinary that the Brothers Buzzanno, for instance, is able to be at it still. D'ye know, they must be middling ould men now, and it's damn curious to imagine them being still so active on the feet. To think that they were at it just the very same when we were gosoons, and they're still young fellows, and we're nearly ould men... and how d'ye make that out?"

"Arrah, Bartle," Dickeen Crosbie would say, "you're only foolish to let it bother your head. Sure fellows like them never age at all, with the travelling and enjoyment, and the gorgeous women and the grand life."

And there, the ageing men would stand before the poster wondering why they were getting so old... While the people of Buzzanno's Circus could have remained so young as to perform still all the feats of youth... But, seeing only the magical side of the Circus, it was not given them to know that, although the names which had won wide rural fame remained the same, the actors in the "parts" that were so wondrously named had been changed almost year by year, just as the hands might be changed in any shop of Garradrimna. Yet, so it was in the course of nature. Even the Lion of the Forest, "A Veritable Emperor as well as King of Beasts," as he was described on the bills, often grew neurasthenic and died, of that or of an insufficiency of horseflesh, which was the occasion always of "Enormous Expense" to Buzzanno's Circus in his replacement.

But, all the same, the Circus and all it held was a constant symbol of youth that never faded. They were never more certain of this than when they listened to the jokes of the clowns, and surely thought that because these were nearly the same jokes still, they must be the same men who made them... And so, for those who were not young, as well as for those who were still young, the Circus was a thing that helped to lighten the years. It was the shining days of their youth that they had again when they saw the procession of the ponies and gilded chariots at mid-day, the loud trumpeters and the be-ribboned drummer. They did not see the decrepitude of the ponies, the tawdriness of some of the chariots from which the gilt had fallen, the utter "seediness" of the Bacchanalian bandsmen.

At night, the flaring petroleum lamps cast a glamour that made everything rich with colour, bright and joyous. And, even to the older men, including Marcus Igoe, who sat amongst the young lads, all this was dazzling and marvellous, for they felt in their bones that the Circus always made them young again... It was as if some magic dust had been thrown in their eyes...

But where was the good in that, to be going back over the past, to be dying that way; why not do something? Why not invent another life for himself like the way Margo had tried to invent a life for him? He was continually remembering, too, without much pride in himself, his attempts to dissuade her.

"Good God, Margo, is it what you'd want to hike me off to that damn place again in the car, and I near dead still after the last journey, such cursed foolishness!"

"Of course you're too ignorant and too old-fashioned to understand, and, musha, it's nearly too much to expect of you, to know what being social means now, although, don't you remember, you were a great fellow at it one time?"

"Social, well begad then I'm not, after my years of hard labour at the last in Garradrimna. Thanks be to God, I'm no socialist, so I'm not, I'm what they call a capitalist, thanks to my uncle Paul that was so thoughtful of me and he dying beyant in New Orleans."

He was sorry now for all his deliberate attempt to misunderstand her, his mere quibbling with words… It made him nearly cry to think about it. He was following the custom of the place and going daily to the Marlay Arms. It seemed in vain that Simon Seery besought him to pull himself together. At length the proprietor of the Marlay Arms was driven quite to disgust with him from seeing the wan, dreepy smile that had so affected Margo on the oft-remembered day of Mr. Charles Delamere's visit about the money.

CHAPTER XXXI

The feeling, present constantly between Marcus and Garradrimna in the old days, had declined to such an extent that he
now held no meaning for the village nor did the village hold any
meaning for him. It would certainly take some very extraordinary
combination of circumstances to flash them back into their original relation to one another. And it seemed that, through all this
period of personal hiatus stretching between the death of Margo
and the present, his soul had been groping towards some kind of
recovery of itself, towards some fine or startling thing that he yet
might attempt to make himself Marcus Igoe once more. But, in
spite of all he could do to banish it, the compulsion of his thought
by the Churchyard wall, his frequently recurrent mood wherein
he tried to recover lost bits of himself, was still strong upon him.

He suddenly went away upon a visit to Dublin to solace
himself thoroughly by, maybe, lashing some of the money upon
a bit of foolishness, as everyone thought, but none of them could
have guessed the exact purpose of this trip, which was one of
business rather than of pleasure... yet it was a most curious kind
of business. It was based upon a conception of its own, and might,
therefore, easily be interpreted as a sort of mad fancy that was
also a kind of fun. For, upon beholding the unusual thing, they
always said in Garradrimna: "Well, be the Holy Farmer, that bates
hell!" They might have said this had they been permitted to see
him setting out from the Marabel Hotel on the Quays on any

148

morning of his visit to proceed with an extended examination of the public monuments of Dublin.

He had begun with Parnell, standing with all the solidity of a connoisseur in a picture gallery before the Memorial to the Chief, walking all around it and looking up at it, now with one eye, now with the other and saying: "Am—um—um... Not bad... middling, smartly done, even to the fine beard and the fierce expression on the handsome countenance. Look at him, however, Parnell, imagine! a man whose greatness was beyond the most noble conceptions of Garradrimna, with his right hand, as it is represented in the statue, not attempting to set bounds to the march of a nation, a thing that he once said no man had a right to do, but pointing straight into the biggest public-house in Parnell Street! Had they no consideration at all for the man's memory, where they put him? It would be damnably sarcastic, wouldn't it, if anyone put up a certain statue in Garradrimna, with himself portrayed in the act of legging it straight into the Marlay Arms!"

The lesser statues in O'Connell Street, those to Father Matthew and Sir John Dwyer Gray and Smith O'Brien on the Bridge, did not appeal to him. "Too small," he said, "altogether too dwarfed. Mere things of nothing; not worth putting up!"

But he spent much of his time hovering in delight around Nelson's Pillar. He took notice of its imposing appearance and the fact that it seemed to draw people around it like a magnet. He walked about it excitedly exclaiming to himself from time to time "Nelson's Pillar!" "Igoe's Pillar!" alternately and continuously. He paid the price of admission and climbed up the steps on the inside of it. A great idea, that! You never saw yourself going up. And then, on the top, the whole city of Dublin burst upon your view. He had a momentary vision of a life beyond Garradrimna. All the people down there, he thought, could not possibly be knowing what was in one another's mind, about any subject under the sun... He felt released and uplifted, until he looked behind him at the statue on the tip top. The blind eye of Nelson, as he stood there in loneliness, passively viewing the scene below, smote him with a sense of Garradrimna, a sense of squint, and he felt like being a little satirical of Dublin.

If you knew it well enough, Dublin might easily come to be a second Garradrimna. If he lived here, he would begin by making a village of it bit by bit. He would make a village of the street he lived in, first of all, and then he would turn his attention to other places... Names of streets through which he had wandered since the beginning of his visit suggested themselves— Dame Street, Fleet Street, Duke Street, Abbey Street, round where the Abbey Theatre was. He looked up once more at the silent figure of Nelson before descending the steps. On the street again, he smiled as he hurried on to view O'Connell properly. "Very nice," he said, "and the angels is lovely, but it would never do to put so many angels round me in Garradrimna. Big Dan anyway, the Big Beggarman! Didn't they do him well with his heart in Rome and his bones in Ireland?"

The effigy of Tom Moore was rather overpowering. "Begad, it's massive looking anyway," he said. He thought of the statues of Burke and Goldsmith at the entrance of Trinity College as badly in need of cleaning, and not at all the kind of thing upon which he had his mind set. Henry Grattan, with his hand up in the gesture of eloquence, he thought fairly good, but more suited to a former Chairman of Garradrimna Guardians than to himself. The horse under the effigy of King Billy, a little further up Dame Street, he thought extraordinary in its way, and it drew from him a word of sarcastic commendation. "Great legs," he said, "powerful great legs! No wonder he tramped the life nearly out of King James at the Battle of the Boyne!"

As he stood there gazing he was accosted by a tall, pale-faced man with a black moustache and a black hat.

"If it's statues you're after, old man, our most peculiar examples are in another quarter of the town. You should see the one to Dargan and he warming himself in front of the National Gallery, or the one to Victoria opposite Leinster House. There's weight in them, I'd give you my word, weight!"

So Marcus got a jaunting car and reaching Merrion Street, got off and looked through the railings of Leinster Lawn at Dargan.

"Damn like one of the ould farmers round Garradrimna done up into a statue. Mebbe he was some sort of a great man, but ordinary, common ordinary, with them thick bushy whiskers of his. You'd want to have some sort of an appearance for a statue."

Then he drove round to Kildare Street and looked at Victoria. He remained longer gazing here, taking unconsciously the pose which had become customary with him, as he leaned over the Churchyard wall in Garradrimna, for the Victoria Memorial caused him tearfully to remember Margo, seeing that here, at last, was a statue to the memory of a woman, and what you might call a fine lump of a statue too, and Victoria, mind you, not at all unlike Margo...

"There's more enormous statyas in the Park," said the jarvey hopefully, but Marcus did not seem to hear. He was still thinking deeply of Margo... At last, taking the hint, and to relieve his mind, he thought that he might just as well take a drive to the Phœnix Park. The jarvey encouraged it on the instant by jumping upon the car and slapping the cushions for Marcus.

As they reached the great gates, after a perilous drive up the Quays, and sped up the main road, the Wellington Memorial in the near distance drew from him an almost breathless "Begad!" of amazement and admiration. Whisking past the Gough Statue, he said to the jarvey: "Now that *is* something like a horse, anyway, not like the fierce-looking yoke that they put anunder King Billy in College Green."

"'Tis curious," said the jarvey, "that there's nothing in this great wide, open space only about three statyas, when they're tripping you up and endangering your life and holding up the traffic down in the City. But believe you me, they'll soon walk all those boyos off the streets and march them out here, where they'll have plenty of fresh air, and d'ye know what it is, there's about fifteen thousand acres in this place, for it's the finest public park in Europe, and if great men start rising up in Dublin, at the rate they're going at present, and if they see their way at length to adopt my schame, you'll see this whole place dotted, actually dotted, with statyas some day yet, so that the poor young lads won't have room to play football or hurling, or cricket or tennis or the other English imported games. That's what you'll see, and then there'll be an agitation against it for destroying the Park."

They were already at the Phœnix monument looking clear-cut in the evening light, with the wide green space around it.

"I always thought myself that that must be some English Pagan trick," said the jarvey, "putting up a statya to a bird! Now that wasn't playing the game, and the place below actually crawling with fit subjects for monuments only waiting to be recognised for the purpose. That yoke should be kicked down some night and the bird beheaded and the whole bloody thing substituted by something rale Irish and Christian, the dirty ruffians!"

There was a touch about the Phœnix monument that lifted the imagination of Marcus, the fluted column, the Phœnix rising from its ashes on the top.

"The lovely little burning bird!" he muttered to himself, as they drove back down the road.

"Would you like to see a monument where there is no monument?" said the jarvey.

"Is that so?" said Marcus.

"I'll show you then, so hell for leather to Stephen's Green!"

As they drove down the Quays again, a link with Garradrimna arose... Guinness's barges were on the river at their own wharf, with gigantic cargoes of barrels destined for England and maybe other foreign lands... He thought of the sign of the man drinking a pint above the Marlay Arms... But he was now going to see a monument where there was no monument...

As they drove on, the mind of Marcus was filled by a great emptiness, an aching void that could only be suitably filled by some fine and imposing thing! Some sort of composite arrangement of all the monuments of Dublin, a gigantic erection that should put even a combination of Wellington and Nelson and Victoria to shame, and that should be loftily distinguished, above all, by a noble inspiration caught from the lovely little burning bird... After the clatter of cobble stones, the hack was moving at a sudden wild pace up the smooth surface of Grafton Street.

"We've landed now," said the jarvey. "There's where the Loyalists and Freemasons put up an arch to the unfortunate poor divils of Dublin Fusiliers that were killed in the Boer War, and there's where there is nothing, where the Fenians hung a bit of an ould wreath between two lamp posts in memory of Wolfe Tone."

As Marcus stood gazing the jarvey whispered:

"I'll lave it to yourself, sir!"

Marcus was recalled to reality by these old words, and, putting his hand in his pocket, presented the man with a whole fistful of silver.

"Good-bye to your honour now," said the jarvey, rounding off the period of their acquaintance with the most suitable words, and in the recognised manner of earlier Irish fiction.

As he stood once more alone and saddened by the anti-climax of the monuments, Marcus saw the man who had spoken to him in College Green, and who had helped him to extend his knowledge of the monuments of Dublin, now slightly swaying in the wind like a slender stalk in a deserted garden in autumn winds. The man was muttering to himself: "Roughly speaking... Roughly speaking... Now what did that mean, the poor fellow! Roughly speaking?" Then the man addressed him.

"You bear the most astonishing resemblance to Anthony Trollope that I have ever seen... ashsthonishing."

"Trollope? I never knew him."

"No, you wouldn't... Beef to the heels!"

Marcus stirred in recognition.

"Beef to the heels like a Mullingar heifer!" It was a saying of Garradrimna and the Midlands... They were already acquainted.

"Come in and have a drink, sir," said Marcus.

"Not so much of that now! Are you aware you're speaking to a Poet of the Irish Literary Renaissance?"

"I never heard of them," said Marcus, "but come on and have a drink anyway."

"Andy Delahunt's?"

"Right y'are."

They walked a little way down the street before moving down a quiet entry that led to the back door of Andy Delahunt's.

"Never go in by the front door; that betrays indelicacy. It's only done by transport experts and experts on mineralogy and high-power systems."

At the end of the passage they entered the back room of Andy's... and came upon a loud hub-bub. Men in the big coats and big hats of cattle-dealers of Meath were all around.

"Is it a fair day or what in the village?" said Marcus.

"No, they're poets, mostly, and their admirers... talking about their poems... Their pockets are full of poems... absolutely full of poems. Dark men labouring at their rhymes. Joe Campbell, ya know."

"I am afraid I thought they were selling cattle."

"I'm afraid you are not equal to this group... At every word a reputation dies... There's that resemblance to Anthony Trollope, however. It should see you through."

The drinks were before them.

At a neighbouring table a young man was developing a thesis.

"No damn good... They don't want novelists in Ireland. What can you do, when every old woman and every harness-maker and every cobbler is a better novelist than we are? There's a better novel in every one of these than we could ever do. What's wrong with them in the villages is dint of literary energy. Each one tries to get his novel over on the other, and they're continually trying to talk down one another with their unwritten novels. That's how they play hell, and the real reason why we novelists ourselves scarcely ever write anything at all."

"There's something in what you say," said the Poet, "but if only you could talk as well as you write."

"This," thought Marcus, "was what was called intellectual conversation, quare stuff." Around him bits of it came to his ear from little groups...

The Poet for the moment seemed remote from it, unhearing, yet, at the same time, it seemed to be making him think...

"I know what you are at now," he said to Marcus, "you are thinking that if someone wrote down all this, just as you are hearing it, it would look absolute drivel, like James Joyce, but recite it aloud in a Dublin accent and you would get the pure

155

native quality of Dublin. This is how 'Ulysses' was written for Joyce."

"What'll you have now, sir?"

"But you have made me lose my 'bus. I must get my 'bus; meeting Mulligan to-night, but then, of course, you don't know Mulligan... or I mean to say Mulligan wouldn't... ya know..."

At a push of the bell, the white curate had hurried forward. The drinks were again before them.

"But I mustn't miss my 'bus," said the Poet, leaving Marcus and going to another group to open the conversation with "I absolutely mustn't miss my 'bus."

Then, out of the maze of talk came the same expression continuously, while the Poet remained longer and longer in spite of his continuous declaration of hurry. But Marcus was not left alone. He had been accosted by two men, by Peader and Padna, the one a Gaelic, and the other a pseudo-Gaelic writer, but he did not think much of them for a start. He had already thought of himself as a novelist here in this company. For, as he argued it, if they spend so much of their time here, how can they have any time to write the books they're always talking about any more than the people below in Garradrimna...? Didn't that lad say there now that all the good novelists were below in the villages? Wasn't he just as well able to think high, imaginative thoughts as those around him?

"The lovely little burning bird," he muttered aloud, causing the Poet to stagger momentarily in admiration, and give a queer, half-admiring, half-sarcastic smile.

But, already well into the company of the two Gaelic writers, Peadar and Padna, he was a kind of, as he felt, upon his native heath. The Poet had been more or less aloof with his polished accent, but here were men who talked and looked exactly like himself. They might not be real writers, but they looked more like people of Garradrimna, and maybe that was all for the best. It was as easy to be a writer, after all, as to walk into Andy Delahunt's. He could invent a story about a man just as well as any of them. But he wished to God, here and now, that he could write down the book he had in his mind about Garradrimna. If only he gave his idea to one of these fellows. Maybe he would write it down for him, and let him put his name to it—The... something of the something—by Marcus Igoe...

He got up when the white curate called "Now time, gentlemen, please!" at ten o'clock, and left the place with a fine feeling of elation... Passing Trinity College he looked at the statues of Burke and Goldsmith, both with books in their hands, and then he thought of his line about the little burning bird that had lifted him almost at one bound into authorship. He had an appointment for to-morrow with the lad who had spoken so well about the village novelists, and he would put it to him straight. He liked him better than either of the Gaelic writers who did not appear to have much in them at all, don't you know.

Next day he made a grand tour of the places which he had pieced together from the farewells that he had heard spoken on the previous evening... The Bodega, Bowes, the Palace, the Scotch House, Davys... He had a real notion now that one might come to make a village of Dublin quite easily. He saw a good many of the same faces in each place. He saw Peadar with Padna and avoided them. He saw the dark Poet in the middle of a commending crowd. He got salutes, and was permitted to stand drinks in the most unexpected companies. But he felt a bit remote to-day... He was thinking out the arrangement he was going to propose to the Novelist at five o'clock.

They had arranged to meet at Andy's, and, when he arrived, there, sure enough, was the Novelist looking very like Rodolphus Keeling in his big coat and hat. He wondered the fellow was not a farmer, and pitied him accordingly... But he had a chance of the means of getting a bit of a farm if he took on the notion of this unwritten book by Marcus Igoe.

"No, not that way," said the Novelist just as soon as Marcus had put the proposition before him... They would recognise my style. You know I'm labelled this long time, almost patented. I can never write but of the one thing always, and in exactly the same way. That's what the critics who never read my books say, anyhow. But now that you have asked me, I think I'll do a book about you all the same. In fact I have been writing about you for the past few years."

"About me?"

"Yes, I had you imagined as a suitable County Meath character. That has often happened. I project a creation out of nothing, and then the actual character himself comes up from Garradrimna to meet me. Did you never read any of my short stories in the magazines?"

"No, I never read stories."

"Did you never read my story of 'The Comedian'?"

"Never."

"Well, that was all about you... I'll give you a copy of it to read now if you like."

The Novelist heaved up his bulging *attaché* case and fished out a magazine.

"It's in that," he said, "the comical story of yourself and your father."

"My father was never very comical."

"But, he is, rather, in the story, you had a comical sort of wife too. Indeed, you had a most extraordinary life in Garradrimna."

"I had, but tell me, do you tell fortunes?"

"No, I'm a creative artist."

"So am I too. I'll make something out of you some day, if you'll only listen to what I have to say!"

"Oh, will you! But, read that, anyhow, and tell me how you like my depiction of you. You're a retired draper, aren't you?"

"Aye, but I'm so long retired that you nearly might say I was never at it at all. It was my father... "

"Of course, but you began that way... of course... and your father had a son right enough. He turned out something exactly like what you are now..."

"This fellow is a walking devil," thought Marcus. "It's of myself he's talking. So I was the son?"

"I suppose you thought you were going to get away with that interesting life of yours, but I caught you."

"I see, but how the hell did you know me?"

"Well, I may tell you later. I have an appointment with Somebody at the Palace, and you can read the thing while I am away... Back in about half an hour... You'll wait?"

"I'll wait, to be sure, and read about myself while you're away."

The door slammed, and the Novelist was gone.

It was the hour when the evening forgathering in Andy's generally began, and soon the arriving groups saw the elderly figure of the man who had already a double claim to recognition in their eyes. He had invented a line of poetry which their leader had already commended and envied, and he bore a distinct resemblance to Anthony Trollope, the novelist, who had once lived in Donnybrook and worked in the G.P.O. There he sat reading intently something in a magazine. In the course of two days he had progressed thus far into the mannerisms of the place. That was what they thought as they saw, for only the second time, the figure of the ex-cobbler from Garradrimna in the Midlands, now hovering perilously upon the verge of literature... actually falling into it from moment to moment... as he sat there reading the story of himself.

CHAPTER XXXII

AS one paused before the spectacle of Garradrimna sitting there in the morning sunlight, one always felt that its life, not altogether comedy, was not without a sense of drama, for, somehow, a thought of the immortal performances at Athens always hurried in to take its place by the side of one's inevitably dwindling thought of Garradrimna, and to lend one's whole regard of the place a sudden and fine difference. As one contemplated the trees which made up the woods belonging to the Hon. Reginald Moore, circling down, tier under tier, to the Altar of Dionysus, or, in other words, the Main Street, one had a notion, that was not any sort of blasphemy, of all the Ironic gods sometimes sitting there upon their high, windy seats to witness a performance upon the little stage that was Garradrimna.

But that word "stage," suddenly shouting all through one's thought to hound one out of the coloured world of the classics into the drab world of to-day! Yet, this had to be, for, assuredly, the men going out leisurely from the village into the fields, enveloped in fresh fogs of smoke, were no hinds of Ithaca; the broad blacksmith, appearing almost to recline against the dark and smoky background of his shop, would never make a set of shoes for the Wooden Horse of Troy. (Not bad that, for a start, as a description of Willy Cullen, thought Marcus.)

One had a swift vision of a performance by the Garradrimna Dramatic Class (A grand looking lot of devils!) remembering

161

clearly, beyond all the other stage furnishing, the "proscenium" by Gilbert Gallagher, its two pillars of support, painted, or rather "faked," upon a flat board, with the shadows all the wrong way, and having hung, as it were, upon this another obvious "fake," two masks of, respectively, the Tragic and the Comic Muse, the whole surmounted, or held erect, by a strip of canvas which sagged most inelegantly in the middle, and upon which was painted, with the most curious elaboration, the much abused quotation from Shakespeare: *"To hold as 'twere the Mirror up to Nature."*

One closed one's eyes and took another look, this time inwardly. Instead of the pillars, with no light upon them that ever was on land or sea, and the masks of the Tragic and the Comic Muse, one saw two strange realities of Earth, making, in a way, the proscenium of a larger stage, on one side the police-barracks with the round, comical-looking faces of the peelers, and, on the other, the mouldering Norman Castle with all its associations of tragic history. The arch that hung between them in one's imagination was the flag that the fighting men of Garradrimna had thought of hanging up provocatively down each succeeding generation from the barracks to the Castle.

One's heart beat higher with this tragi-comic realisation, and, opening one's outward-seeing eyes, one saw, with a new clearness, the houses down the street. These had almost the artificial look of "property" houses in the morning light, and might be regarded as the "wings" from which people had strutted out down all the years to enact the heroic farce of life in Garradrimna.

Quite naturally, it would seem, because "all the world's a stage and all the men and women merely players," Garradrimna had dramatised itself. The play that it made had its inevitable blending of the tragic and the comic elements, and in such well-measured proportions as to be an acceptable performance to the Ironic gods among the high, windy trees. It was a fairly equal battle always between these two elements, with its resulting sense of proportion, or else the general quality of life in Garradrimna might easily have become heavy, important and self-sufficient. Thus, although Garradrimna had produced more than a few "great" men, but "great" in a purely local or tricky business sense, the adjective being used with an extravagance that bordered on the satirical, it was the reason why Garradrimna had produced no really great man in the line, for instance, of world commerce, all the elements of which were here in embryo. ("Do you know," Marcus said to himself, "that's a damn smart fellow. Look at the way he got anunder them there by putting it just that way!")

The nearest approach it had ever made to such an achievement was in the person of Denis Igoe, (Oh, ho, what is he going to say now?) the proprietor of the well-known drapery and boot shop, whose window, exhibiting some of the suitable merchandise to be had within at different seasons, lent a touch of variety that was pleasing amid the unchanging fronts of the other houses. This was, inevitably, one's feeling until one entered the shop and came face to face with Denis Igoe himself, that distinguished-looking man, when one became saddened immediately by the feeling that here surely was the face of one whose proper destiny had been denied him by residence here. For this was the face of a man who might have been anything—a Bismarck, a Clemenceau, or a Mussolini. In fact, even in the course of the shortest interview with him, one felt inclined to think of Gray's Elegy and of him as "some Cromwell guiltless of his country's blood." (Very hard on the old man, that!) For, upon a thorough examination one realised that it was a funereal face, after all, never varied by emotion, even as the windows of the shop varied emotionally with the changes of the seasons, yet, it was this face, the tremendous impassiveness of this countenance, that had made the fortune of Denis Igoe. Somehow, you had to accept it, as well as anything its proprietor might say or do to you in the course of any business transaction. He was a man of few words, but of much quiet, incisive commercial action. He got into you, anyway, they used to say, and got the money out of you, and what more could ever be said of the trickiest-tongued man in Garradrimna?

(Oh, now d'ye know the *De mortuis nil nisi bonum* rule should be applied to this fellow, but it's good stuff all the same!)

It was said, rather maliciously of both, perhaps, that Gilbert Gallagher or Bill the Savage had used his face as a model for the mask of the Tragic Muse upon the "proscenium" of the stage, yet this small thing which might, at its inception, have been really a pure invention, grew to hold a certain periodic excitement for Garradrimna.

At performances of plays, some of the most tragic plays of Ireland, as well as "powerful" English plays like *Maria Martin or the Murder in the Red Barn,* there was always an uneasy feeling amongst the audience that it was the strong but gloomy personality of Denis Igoe that influenced the nature of the performance, and they were all more or less tired of tragedy. Thus it was that they began to look hopefully towards the mask of the Comic Muse, as if the genius of Gilbert Gallagher or the other fellow must at length be completely fulfilled, and that out of the womb of Time must come the one who was destined to make them laugh.

CHAPTER XXXIII

DENIS IGOE was a widower (well, he was decent enough to leave my mother out of it, anyway!) with an only son named Marcus, who, while his fond father had been assiduously engaged in selling everything in the soft goods line from a yard of flannelette to a blue serge suit length, was presently mixing, towards the achievement of social polish, with the sons of some of the most notable Irishmen of his time, at an expensive college near Dublin. The son had the ponderous head of the father, although the facial expression had always been somewhat different, and he was now displaying his undoubted possession of brains, but after a most peculiar fashion.

It was in a play by Boucicault, and with other young men playing the female parts, that Marcus made a successful first appearance, as a comedian. It was a proud moment for his father, specially invited up for the performance, when another proud father sitting behind leaned across the chair backs, after one of the great bursts of laughter in tribute to the genius of Boucicault or that of Marcus, and said: "D'ye know I believe there's a great future before that young fellow?" Somehow, perhaps merely because of his exceeding fondness, he was all inclined to confuse the idea of a future for his son with the quality of his own present, which was so successful and fine...

Not even what some of the heads of the college told him after the performance had the effect of averting the disastrous

165

intention that already threatened his mind, not even the seductive picture they drew, of a most successful orator, emerging after a little more amateur stage experience in the person of young Marcus Igoe, succeeded in outshining the only vision he had ever had, that of himself as he endeavoured perpetually to appear in the similitude of a heavy bronze statue to the memory of himself in the very middle of Garradrimna. And, when he was dead and gone, his son in the shop behind him making a great future for himself out of the business that his father had so securely built. So there and then, he resolved to commit the grievous mistake of considering the education of his son already finished, and that it was high time to take him away from the hard labour of study to the enjoyment of business in Garradrimna.

Marcus, still flushed with the glamour of his recent stage success, signalised his return home by organising the Garradrimna Dramatic Class. ("I never did! I never had anything to do with them! That's a lie for him!" He exclaimed thus excitedly until he suddenly cooled on realising that he was merely reading a story which looked shockingly like the truth, all the same—in places.)

And it soon became apparent that this little endeavour was destined to make the Dramatic Class loom higher as a background to his personality, than the shop of his father. (Maybe it did all the same in some queer, unknown kind of way.)

His father was inclined at first to regard all this as merely an exhibition of youthful wildness that the lad would grow out of, but the rather intimate association with certain parties in Garradrimna that it necessitated was anything but pleasant to have to put up with, and when, after one or two uproariously successful performances of different plays, the nickname of "The Comedian" came to be bestowed upon Marcus, it appeared sadly, to Denis Igoe, as if a dangerous-looking cloud, which had been at first no bigger than a man's hand, was descending upon his life. Great goodness! And he himself, so almost tragically respectable-looking. A comedian, a comic, a playboy, a gallivanter! His only son!

Perhaps it was not so strange, when one considered the essential personal drama of every turn of human life, that, as "The Comedian" sprang towards the bulk and breadth of manhood, the two men were obviously symbolic of the temperamental clash which had occurred in the household. For, all through the business portion of the day in the shop, the father might now be seen looking as saturnine as Sir Henry Irving in the part of *Eugene Aram*, the son beginning rapidly to suggest what a good Falstaff should look like in a laughable farce. Of course it was impossible for two principals, the "heavy" and the "light" to carry a whole play upon their backs, but, very soon, it also became apparent that they would not be obliged to do so. Characters would spring out of life to assist the play to its end, and of course there were the people of Garradrimna always standing near to make of themselves a Greek chorus upon the slightest provocation, thus helping at once to lift the conflict into the plane of Attic Drama.

For of course Garradrimna was vastly interested in all the circumstances of this unique clash. Besides, Marcus had made of himself one of the most popular young men in the village, "a lad you could be laughing at, not like the ould fellow with his important face that nearly everybody in the place was more than sick of." (Marcus felt himself laughing in a queer sort of way at this.) But the genuine appeal was not lost on them of the father striving his hardest to maintain the balance towards business seriousness of the house of Igoe. In addition to what had been his habitual look, he now wore the cloud of worry upon his face of one who has divined that it would be an easy step from laughing at his son upon the stage to laughing at him in reality, and that this might readily come to mean the end of all Marcus's comicality. And indeed there were signs upon the matter that it bade fair to be so, for was he not following, after his own peculiar fashion, in the footsteps of all the other only sons of Garradrimna who had tried their very best to make prodigals out of themselves by spending the substance of their loving fathers upon such things as horses and hounds?

He had bought a whole library of plays and spent most of his time delving through them, searching for such as might be suitable for the Dramatic Class, and which, at the same time, would give "fat" parts to himself, for he was not without the natural, vain afflictions of the stage-struck young man. He would go off expensively to Dublin to see a play, just as any of the other prodigals had ever gone to any of the Metropolitan race meetings, with this essential difference between the two ways of futility, that one might back a winner an odd time at the races, and thus temporarily recoup oneself for a little of what was lost, but the money spent on seeing plays was gone past all hope of ever seeing any of it again. (Marcus paused for a moment wondering had the writing business turned the fellow's brain altogether that he had flung a man who had never anything to do with plays into this kind of connection.)

CHAPTER XXXIV

THE only compensation was the delight of Garradrimna, sometimes expressed in ways that were not altogether pleasant. For,
whenever after the performance of a play, the whole population
seemed to glance humorously in the direction of Denis Igoe, he
felt some affront to his power and personality being thus exer-
cised, felt in fact, being quite swept off his feet, for this was a
method of regard which, formerly, had been alien to him, and
which so disconcerted him now that he did not see it for what it
really was—a genuine tribute to him as the father of such a son.

It was indeed pleasant for any stranger to come into Garradrimna now and to behold the delight, as it were, upon its whole
face, even from afar off. It would almost seem to the stranger with
an inquiring mind, as if a National Movement for the propagation
of laughter had been inaugurated in Garradrimna. For Marcus
Igoe had begun to extend his comic activities to the neighbouring
villages, and even in remote parts of the Midlands, where mention
of his name had blown in, a dramatic performance without him
appeared as impossible as a performance of *Hamlet* without the
Prince. It came to be said at length that he was really only wasting
his time in Garradrimna, and that the larger world of the stage
should claim him. It was the persistent rumour of all this, with its
element of paternal flattery, that he was not slow to feel, which
drove Denis Igoe at length to endorse the dramatic activities of

his son, but when once a man begins, even reluctantly, to endure there are no limits to what may be put upon him.

Marcus had begun to develop the habit of meeting pals of "The Profession," the travelling showmen who came frequently enough to Garradrimna, and who were all known vaguely to the inhabitants as "circus people." (Well, I did like circuses an odd time all right, but I had never much to say to t'other class of characters.)

It was scarcely to the taste of a man with the face that Denis Igoe had to be having to answer the inquiries of all sorts of strange-looking gentry who came into the shop looking for Marcus. (I never remember any of them coming!) But worse was still to ensue. One night that "McCormack and Jones's Great Galaxy of Talent" were performing in a very battered-looking booth on the fair green, the leading comedian, Mr. Charles Biglow, owing to "sudden and unforeseen circumstances" which had really happened, as everybody knew, in the bar of the "Marlay Arms," was unable to appear, and as the show was packed out this particular night there was nothing for the proprietors to do but make a pathetic appeal to Marcus to replace, even for the one night, the incapacitated comedian. He did not think twice about it, for he had never been able to refuse any request to go on the stage, and in less than half an hour, he was "bringing down the house" in some part in which he was well practised.

In fact for a whole week he succeeded in "bringing down the house" in each succeeding play of the "Galaxy of Talent's" repertoire, for the management were not slow to discover that it was to their benefit to keep Mr. Charles Biglow temporarily incapacitated. And, each night, he dallied longer and longer by the door of the lodgings of the "leading lady," Miss Georgina Frances Dixon, as he gallantly left her home from "The Theatre." Of course the people of Garradrimna were not surprised to behold this perfectly human conduct on the part of Marcus, seeing that he had already induced Jane Jennings, the assistant in his father's shop, to become leading lady of the Garradrimna Dramatic Class, and had always accompanied her to her door on the nights of performances and rehearsals. But, somehow, this present extension of his consuming love for the stage, with every little incident connected with it, seemed to have imparted a little necessary drama into the comedy of the Igoes.

There could be no question about its effect upon Denis Igoe. To see the face of him now! It began to be said that little girls sent on messages and mothers of families were frightened out of their wits nearly by the pure sadness of his countenance, the wan, desolate droop of his ragged, grey moustache, the subdued note in his voice, for, strangely, it was at an inauspicious moment of his career that he chose to break his long and powerful silence. There was something that made one laugh, although a little gruesomely, in the fact of a man who had hitherto relied upon his face, now having to call his tongue to his aid, and at a time when, through the intensification of his native quality by comic circumstances, his business had begun to decline. The sense of contrast between the father and the son appeared almost to possess the automatic compensation of a dramatic contrivance. And the Greek Chorus of Garradrimna had now four characters to entwine its tongue around instead of two.

It seemed, in spite of everything, that Marcus was about to fulfil the dream of his great future that his father had had, but, of course, after the fashion that was peculiar to his own joyous personality. His absences from Garradrimna were now more regular and business-like, if one could think of him so crudely as having any connection with business at all. For one reason or another the "unforeseen circumstances" surrounding the person of Mr. Charles Biglow would seem to have become chronic, because Marcus was now receiving the most urgent calls to take his place in other towns of the "Galaxy of Talent's" tour. Cattle-men from around Garradrimna back from distant fairs used to tell the most fabulous stories of Marcus's performances in towns they had visited. (Gorra's, it was a great way of getting away from Garradrimna all the same!)

It was said that he would never stop till he finished up on the stage of some real theatre, and, as well, that it would "mebbe be a big lump of an actress he would be bringing in on the flure to his poor father before ever the ould fellow felt." There were two glum faces in the shop now, the face of Jane Jennings so sadly changed by the desertion of Marcus, and the face of Denis Igoe himself. Both seemed afraid or ashamed to meet the gigantic, constant smile of Garradrimna which betokened the general enjoyment of the comedy that Marcus was now so successfully building up about his life, so they were firmly resolved to do something with him next time he came home within reach of them! But, as the atmosphere of the shop became daily more and more oppressive, with the continued loss of good customers, the proprietor and his assistant found themselves moving into such gloomy sympathy with one another as they had never before experienced. The bond born of a common persecution, which might so easily become something grander, was between them.

CHAPTER XXXV

THE element of dramatic surprise entered largely into the next home-coming of Marcus... (here even Marcus himself was surprised) for he came home married to Miss Georgina Frances Dixon. (If he had, what would poor Mary Margaret Caherlane have done? Why, cry her eyes out, and sure you could not blame her, there never was anything between himself and Jane at all.)

It was the real stuff of comedy this, and its full value was not lost upon Garradrimna, so well trained by Marcus to appreciation of such situations upon the stage. The laughter was loud and prolonged. It appeared that Marcus was now definitely and finally committed to the stage, and the father would have to bow with all the grace he might be able to accomplish, to what should always have appeared as the inevitable if he had had the grace to see it.

Then the laughter seemed to ease for a bit before the obligatory scene of the comedy which, everyone felt, must soon appear. But when the visit of Marcus and his theatrical wife became, as all Garradrimna thought, unduly extended, a sense, almost of fatality, seemed to hover over the house. Jane Jennings gave notice, and left the employment of the father of Marcus. This in itself seemed to continue the action, although the "leading lady" of the Garradrimna Dramatic Class was no Igoe, in spite of the fact that there was once some notion that she might have been. But, so far as the essential action was concerned, there seemed now to be a mysterious pause, as if the actors had missed their cues or forgotten their lines, or something like that...

This awkward moment Garradrimna hurried anxiously to fill after a fashion that was essentially in agreement with what might possibly bring the fortunes of the house to a fine farce-like conclusion. The rumour was rapidly established that the call of "the circus" in the blood of Marcus's wife had out, and that her father-in-law had erected in the backyard of his premises a brand new polished steel wire for walking on as in a circus, "just to keep her in practice for the work."

The result of this identification of the severe-looking man with what he had always considered a blackguardly way of living was something more swift and surprising than anyone had expected. It was nothing less than the purchase of Miss Donlon's little newsagency and fancy goods shop at the end of the street by Denis Igoe and the putting of Marcus and his wife into it. It was said that the old fellow had taken the bit between his teeth at long last and that he was going to knock some of the comicality out of Marcus. (D'ye know now that novel-writing fellow has some sort of a proper imaginary hang of things all the same?)

Soon another most unlooked-for thing happened, and this was the sudden discovery by Garradrimna that Mrs. Marcus, far from being disappointed, actually found the new life to her liking, for she had had enough of the stage, and was strongly of opinion that Marcus had had enough of it too. Yet, everyone felt that the climax of the comedy was still to come. So filled with expectations were they that they could not even be fully satisfied when the news went round that Jane Jennings had filed an action for breach of promise against Marcus. (Oh, the Law again! The Four Courts and that scurrilous blackguard of a Counsel! But mebbe she did not go on with it!) In fact there hurried in with this for the first time, a general inclination not to laugh at Marcus. Men who were married and men who were not felt that it was not such a very pleasant thing for a newly-married couple to have to endure this tremendous reminder of the earlier lady in "the man's" life. (She never was it. "That's a damn lie for him anyway!") They could see, too, that the face of Marcus was beginning rapidly to assume an expression that was not a bit funny-looking.

On the morning that he got Mr. Charles Delamere, the solicitor's, letter, apprising him of the fact of the proposed action he hurried up the street to his father's with the news, and he was not laughing either as he went. (Imagine, Delamere was agin me that time, but sure he always was, even when he was with me itself!) But his father laughed, and heartily enough too, as he read the letter. People passing the door at the time, and taking a casual glance in, as was the custom of the place, could scarcely believe what they saw, and hurried back again past the door to confirm the sight of their eyes. But, beyond all doubt it was a fact—Denis Igoe with most of his dreepy expression gone most miraculously out of his face and he laughing as at some great joke; his son Marcus, the quondam comedian, with the most woe-begone expression overcasting his once bright face...

CHAPTER XXXVI

WHEN Denis Igoe married Jane Jennings, out of pure love, as some said, or by way of making a better adjustment between her and his son than by spending another big skelp of money upon the folly of Marcus, as the uncharitable said, Garradrimna was left breathless with excitement at the extraordinary turn that the comedy had taken. They thought that surely it could go no further than this. But they were destined to be given another laugh before the whole play finally subsided into the long, low chuckles which would remain as a memory of its run in Garradrimna.

A remarkable contrast was soon manifest between the respective wives of the father and the son. Marcus's wife had developed into an excellent business woman, (more or less like what Margo had turned into, he thought), and she had already succeeded in making the best of the opportunity that had been given her, the best even of Marcus, who had passed, as everyone thought, beyond this possibility. He was dutiful and obedient about the place (I suppose he had to be, the poor fellow!) but anything even remotely related to the stage was marked strictly "out of bounds" for him. He was not permitted even to go to the little performances by the Dramatic Class in the Hall, now so sadly declined since his palmy days.

Sometimes, as he stood in his own, or his wife's, door way, some of the companions of his dramatic youth would stop in passing to have a chat with him, and the talk turning back to the past he would mutter sad words about himself, "A mute inglorious comedian, that's what I am!" This often, too, even as two very important inhabitants of his native village passed down of an evening to a rehearsal or a performance at the Hall. These would be Denis Igoe and his wife, for even with her marriage, and she could now so well afford it, Jane had not lost the love of the stage that had been so well implanted in her by Marcus. Furthermore, she had, in fact, induced her husband to take it up as a harmless hobby to brighten his declining years.

("I'd never have stuck it, nor Mary Margaret either. She'd have had that one's life for trying on that game with my poor ould father!")

And now, perhaps as the most fitting close to the comedy, the frequent spectacle was to be seen of Denis Igoe, at the behest of his wife, putting himself up on the stage for the amusement of Garradrimna. Perhaps it was merely the ridiculous quality of his attempt that made them all laugh so loudly but, at any rate, they all laughed as heartily as of yore. They laughed so much, in fact, that he was always cast for the part of the comedian, while Jane was always, as in the days of Marcus, the heroine. And, besides, it was so interesting of itself, as a novel experience, to see a father following in the footsteps of a son. (Was it indeed?) People used to say that, hadn't the face of him, after all, changed most remarkably for the better, seeing that it was now nearly all as one as the "painting" entitled "Comedy" on the right side of the stage, while the other one, the "painting" entitled "Tragedy" upon the left side would remind you nearly of the face of poor Marcus, as it appeared now? (Indeed!)

The genius of Gilbert Gallagher, or was it that of Bill the Savage, had won to a strange fulfilment.

Garradrimna liked to draw its own peculiar moral always, even from a comedy. For one of its favourite observations, after the most tragic or the most comic performances had put the most desperate or the most ridiculous character on the stage, would be:

"I declare to goodness, you'd sometimes nearly see people like that in real life."

Now it would look upon Marcus for ever as an example to every other only son.

But, apart altogether from any such banal consideration as this, the Greek Chorus of Garradrimna was satisfied, for it had at last produced a perfect piece of irony. And all through that most memorable season of the Dramatic Class when Denis Igoe established himself as a comedian in succession to his son Marcus, retired from the stage, the gods rocked with laughter in their high windy seats until the last leaf was gone...

CHAPTER XXXVII

So that was the story of "The Comedian," of himself, of Marcus Igoe belonging to Garradrimna. There was a touch of him in it all right, a suggestion of things he had done, things he might yet do, but there was far too much satisfaction to Garradrimna in it altogether and he, Marcus Igoe, had, in some queer way, always risen superior to Garradrimna, so he had, always, and always would rise superior to it!

The door had opened with a great clatter... The Novelist had come in with a swish out of the wet night.

"The Poet has almost given me the bird on account of you," he said, peering a little unsteadily at Marcus.

"The lovely little burning bird," said someone at another table, which witticism, possibly more nearly epigram in the dialect of the place, was loudly guffawed all down the length of the room and even out into the shop where the rougher hangers-on of Literature were forgathered.

"The bird," said Marcus bewildered, "what bird?"

"Another theatrical term, I suppose, only I meant to say that he nearly cut the face off me on account of you... said it was bad enough for James Joyce to have got away with it, and created Davy Byrne's out of nothing. 'But when you start bringing up your characters from Garradrimna' says he, 'and go around drinking with them, I think it is about time that I got off—'"

"The 'bus," said Marcus, whereat there was another but much louder guffaw that rang all over the place, causing Andy Delahunt himself to come in on his rubber heels to see what new spark had arisen... "Mebbe another James Joyce," he said to himself as he came, "you'd never know the hell."

"Not so much of that," said the Novelist. "I'm serious. The Poet was furious... 'Your damned cattlemen from the Meath of the pastures,' he said to me... 'Your blasted characters.'"

"I never was a cattleman, and I'm not a blasted character... That's myself, more or less, I suppose, that you have in this story here."

"Of course it is. And if it isn't exactly you, it'll have to be. Therefore, don't you see that you'd better leave your whole self to me. There's nothing about you, the whole inside and outside of you, that I'm not going to set down now. I'll beat Joyce at his own game! I'll demolish the jibe about the County Meath Pirandello and his seven sleek publicans in search of the author! I'll do a different thing, only I'll do in my characters all the same! I'll do a bigger thing now than any of them have ever thought of doing!"

Then in a less argumentative, indeed a quite meek tone, he added, more directly addressing Marcus: "But I am very grateful to you, sir, for the big conception you have given me to-night," and Marcus winced at this compliment from a man who appeared so important in these surroundings.

"How would it strike you," said Marcus, "if someone was to put up a monument somewhere in Ireland to a man that was supposed to write a book that was never written?"

"Gorgeous," said someone, a tall pale young man in spectacles and riding breeches who had just come in.

"There's the very man for you," said the Novelist to Marcus, and then, addressing the new-comer: "Here's a chance for you at last. How many commissions for the erection of monuments to famous men all over Ireland have you got and refused when it came to the point?"

"Thousands," said the Sculptor, pushing the bell. "Such bloody things as the Committee always wanted me to do. Great big fellows, lump of fellows with pikes in their hands."

"Of course you never did them. But here now is a man who wants something after your own heart, something that will leave you as free as air and never interfere, to the slightest extent, with the genius that is in you... Are you capable of bodying forth a character of mine with an unique notion at the back of his head?"

"What I said about the book there now?" ventured Marcus.

"It will be the first monument to a book, not only in Ireland but in the world. You have a bigger chance than ever Epstein got... He'll tell you what he wants..."

"What *he* wants? Is this more '98 Memorial Commemoration stuff?" said the Sculptor, suddenly indignant.

"No, I mean he'll communicate almost miraculously to you what you yourself want, just as he has done to me... He has just given me the idea for a book about as long as *The Forsyte Saga*... Only to compare me with Galsworthy is a bit, as the Poet would say, yah know."

They managed most wonderfully there to withdraw from the hum and hubbub and clatter around them ... and remained for a time talking in low tones, looking almost as conspirators.

At ten the Novelist and the Sculptor, the men who were going to lift Marcus beyond life, saw him to the Marabel Hotel, where he insisted that they should come in and have more drinks, which they did willingly, for they had talked a lot... They talked more, and Marcus, as he at last ascended the stairs by the help of the night porter about two in the morning, felt that he had made a big success of his Dublin visit. It was like what you would read about in a story all right, how the place had engulfed him, then brought him glittering to the surface, to rise almost as a new life out of the waves. That's what a place like Dublin could do for a man where they had proper appreciation and brains... Them two young lads now... The lovely little burning bird ...

He fell into slumber, half dreaming of the two biggest and happiest days in his life. In fact he had almost passed into another life. It was smart of the lad to give him the story to read, so that he could have proper appreciation of the extraordinary versatility of which he himself was really capable...

CHAPTER XXXVIII

ALTHOUGH he was just a little uncertain of things in the morning, he knew that he had definitely committed himself to a great idea, which would not only perpetuate himself but would also perpetuate others more worthy than he. Look at the success he had been in Dublin! If only he could be the same thing in his native place, where they knew, where they viewed him, not wholly with disrespect but not with the proper respect, only with a regard which reduced him always in his most pleasant dreams, reduced him, even now, in the thought of it, from his new conception of himself.

But all the way down in the train to Aarboy he felt the not unpleasant excitement of thinking that what he intended to do must certainly revive to a blaze the ancient rage between Garradrimna and himself... As people with ordinary human feelings, no matter how otherwise he might seem inclined to think of them at times, he felt quite certain that they would never be able to stand it. It would be altogether too much for them, this brilliant notion of putting up a monument to himself, even to one aspect of himself that they might never be able to realise. A most gorgeous monument at that, before he was dead or a ha'porth! And musha, why not? Couldn't he spend his money any way he liked? It was his own, wasn't it. He could get rid of the modern bungalow with all its chattels, including the motor and everything for more money than they had originally cost him. And, besides, thought of the interest on it accumulating from moment to moment had the effect of causing the fortune to appear as big as ever to his mind. Indeed there was nothing in the wide world standing between him and the statue to himself.

He mentioned the matter next morning to Simon Seery, who, after a fair amount of "sizing up," began shrewdly to commend it. He said it would give tremendous employment to labour, anyway, and that someone was bound to come near making a fortune out of drawing the sand and the stones. This rather disconcerted Marcus for a moment. It held a hint that he was really about to confer a benefit upon Garradrimna, instead of doing something that should mightily offend it for ever more. But he had his satisfaction a moment later, when Simon, with tentative directness, inquired which of the local contractors he was going to make up by giving him the job... This was said with such a roguish lift of the left eyelid as irritated Marcus beyond measure.

"Whethen I'm not going to give my grand job to any local botch, but to some genius or another that'll know his business and be able to accomplish the plans and specifications and drawings and dimensions that at the very moment are being prepared by one of the smartest fellows that Ireland has ever produced. Talk about brains! If it's going to take a big whip of money out of me itself, it'll be for something worth while. And as for the labour I'll be employing, it'll mebbe be foreign labour. Indian coolies, mebbe, or hardy niggers from the heart of Africa."

The expansive face of Simon Seery fell into a broad grin as Marcus went out the door with what he evidently took to be a sense of triumph in his very strut... The Dublin visit had left the ex-cobbler unchanged... There was salvation in him still from Simon's point of view, for Garradrimna remained his obsession as it always had been.

As for Marcus, he went marching down the street, excited, manful, bellicose... He had again a purpose in life, as wonderful as when he had been sitting behind his own little window in the middle of the street—the accomplishment of a gorgeous memorial to himself before he died ... or would it be only a part of himself, or which side of him would be uppermost when the thing was done? That was the riddle which waited excitedly for an answer... While the chances of answer were maybe more problematic than ever now.

And more and more problematic did they grow as Marcus, with a clearer appreciation of everything since his return from Dublin, discovered evidence of a remarkable phenomenon, an exhibition of beauty, that gave him a new but still highly dangerous impression of Garradrimna. It seemed as if all the old women, with the long tongues that would always be making an unseemly clatter, were being replaced by comely maidens, in most cases with their hair hanging down, at least such of them as were not beginning to get barbered in the new fashion.

There was scarcely a family or a house in the place that had not imported just such a vestal virgin to light his lonely way. And, perhaps not at all wondrous to relate, they all appeared to be falling over one another to be nice to him. Ah, ha, he thought, so that was what they were after now! Setting traps for him, now that he seemed at last to be in a position to be able to compliment himself upon having thought out a scheme to put Garradrimna completely in the shade. Yet not even the gathering rumour of his startling scheme for the final magnification of himself appeared in the least to deter them... It only made them appear to him as if endeavouring to be doubly fascinating—trying to catch him, he fancied, before he could fling away all his money.

Instead of an old woman squinting at him, there was a lovely young girl smiling at him from every window... Girls had been brought from Cork and over from Glasgow and back from America to explore his present possibilities. Even Simon Seery himself had not been behind-hand in his endeavours, for his new barmaid, Rosalind Briody, was an impudent-looking second cousin of his wife's...

"Now weren't they devils entirely to think of countering his every attempt to triumph over them in a noble-minded sort of way?"

CHAPTER XXXIX

THE ostentatious visit to Marcus of the Sculptor from Dublin, accompanied by the Novelist, was a remarkable occasion. He had been waiting for them for hours when, at last they drew up, with belated speed, to the Marlay Arms. "We're a bit late," said the Novelist, "but the lad here wanted to have a drink in County Meath, and I was glad of the opportunity to revive old acquaintances... characters of mine... We stopped at Blanchardstown, Mulhuddert, Clonea, Dunboyne, Summerhill, Rathmolyon, Trim, Aarboy and here we are! We had a great day."

"Yous are damn late anyway."

"He came down armed with several sets of drawings," said the Novelist, "but he has already another lepping through his mind."

"I'll consider them all," said Marcus. "Come up to the coffee-room... I suppose yous are dry since Aarboy. But yous could have made another stop at Higginstown."

"Not alone had we to go through towns and villages, but we had to go through whole novels. I thought some of my characters would bate us, — the dirty ones, but they were all very nice."

"I wonder what'll they do for yous at all when yous. have done for me?"

"You'll have made us immortal."

"Be hell, let me see the plans anyway!"

In the coffee-room, specially engaged as private for the occasion, the drawings were produced.

The first, which the Sculptor himself evidently favoured, was that of Marcus himself hewn out shapelessly from a great block of marble bent over the last with a battered brogue in his hand.

"I see ... ," said Marcus, ... "let me see another one..."

"An earlier one," said the Novelist promptly. "Let us go back a bit."

"Well number two is the equestrian figure, Marcus himself, side-whiskered, top-hatted, and ready for hounds."

It was a polite, Victorian-looking statue and would, no doubt, have given tone to Garradrimna.

"A big contrast there anyway. Again?"

The third might do for a statue of a prosperous-looking merchant with full beard like a civic dignitary in an English provincial town.

"I don't like the beard," said Marcus.

"He doesn't like the beard. Let him see another."

The fourth was that of a portly gentleman in court dress, on an enormous scale like the Earl of Eglinton and Winton in St. Stephen's Green Park, with silk stockings, a sash and a sword.

"Too flashy," said Marcus. "They'd never believe that I ever wanted to look like that. Show me *the* one ... you know the one that'll most likely suit."

It was shown and there was Marcus as he might be at the moment, yet satirised as if a sense of earlier defeat might be detected beneath this portrayal of his present easy and prosperous appearance.

It might have the book in the hand.

"Well, it's not going to!"

"Show him another one, the one where Tragedy and Comedy are combined, 'The Comedian.'"

And there was a huge face with the conceptions Tragedy and Comedy intermingled, the whole growing as it were, out of a block of marble, which, upon close examination, was a huge book that appeared to open its pages behind.

"You will notice," said the Novelist, "how, rather marvellously the likeness to Anthony Trollope, that being your own likeness, sir, is preserved."

"I see..." And then, Marcus thought... "It's sculpture out of Andy Delahunt's. That damn fellow James Joyce, or whatever you call him that made the place. They'll never be able to get away from him! Now for the little burning bird!"

"So you guessed I was keeping that for the last."

"But it's the real Epstein," said the Novelist.

This exquisite little drawing showed a bird in flames, and if one looked long enough one saw a curious resemblance to Marcus, rising from the ashes of a book. There were grinning, leering faces below the book... Faces of people in Garradrimna.

"How the hell did you get them all in so well?"

"Well, if a man is a genius," said the Novelist, with a most hopeless gesture by way of explanation...

"It is, but the bird isn't a bird exactly."

"Of course not, that's your soul."

"Me poor ould sowl ... is that so? Is that it?"

"But what about the other one, the one you have in your mind?"

"It goes beyond anything he has yet conceived. It would be too terrible for Garradrimna. Too bloody awful for words. It would demolish the place..."

"Would it? Sure that's what I want!"

It was an unlucky stroke for the Novelist to have spoken of the imaginary conception... They had to do now with a man on his native heath, with a character whom the Novelist had really endowed with too much life.

"Didn't you say something about a statue to a book that was never written? Wouldn't it be a great notion now, never to put up a statue, that was never designed, to a book that was never written by a man that never lived...?"

He noticed their looks of dismay, of defeat... They would not beat him, Dublin smarties though they were!... But he added:

"Leave the yokes with me for a week or so until I decide... I'm all flummoxed as to one aspect of the matter, whether it should be an enormous flop of a thing all on the ground like Victoria or a commanding figure above in the clouds like Nelson on the tip top of a high pillar."

"These are only the drawings, but I'm sending you down a lorry-load of clay models on Monday," said the Sculptor.

"And you'll have to pay for them, too," said the Novelist, "whether you use any of them or not. We'll stop at nothing if you don't!"

"Well, I suppose I may as well have some sort of sport out of my money while I'm in it."

The two young men seemed not a little sorry for themselves, but they partook of his entertainment, the best that the Marlay Arms could provide for the occasion, and then they went down into the public bar for a final drink. It being Saturday night, the bar was crowded. There was an eloquent hum of talk.

"That's as good as Dublin any day only better. Isn't that fifty times more lively than Andy Delahunt's? There's a man," said Marcus, indicating Bill the Savage. "If he would only speak he could say things, things that would simply cut the hide off that

Poet of yours with the sarcastic manner above in Dublin... If he would only speak... If he would only write..."

They looked at the face of Bill the Savage, and were soon as men who had fallen into something from which they could not escape, something which clutched their minds and hearts and all their consciousness...

Now was the gaze of Marcus Igoe meeting the gaze of Bill, the whole of him in that gaze, and there was a crowding in of characters whom Marcus bad, in a sense, made through the course of his various "lives." Bartle Boyhan and Dickeen Crosbie were there... But even those who were not there were there in spirit ... a great crowd of interest all about them making the scene. The Sculptor and the Novelist felt warm imaginations stir in them. Marcus Igoe had certainly surrounded himself with the capacity for remembrance in Garradrimna.

CHAPTER XL

THE days that followed were the most peculiar that yet appeared in the whole chequered career of Marcus Igoe... Now, how could a man be expected to make a choice, surrounded as he was by so many excellent and well-meant efforts towards his magnification...? He seemed to grow outside them a bit as he made consideration... He would have to pay the fellow from Dublin nearly a fabulous sum for all this stuff for the means of annoyance, for the means, imagine, whereby he was daily driven an inch or two nearer the asylum... The finest effort of his mind, had, after all, succeeded only in putting him in this position. Sometimes, as he chatted, almost forlornly in the intervals of his deep pondering, with Simon Seery's new barmaid, he had wild hopes that, perhaps, out of the bright young mind of Rosalind Briody would flash a noble solution of his difficulties. But it would not come, no matter how much he talked to her, at least not in the way of any connection with his thought of the moment.

Although much against the grain, he was again driven to speak of the matter to Simon Seery, or at least to beat about the bush in the hope of receiving some suggestion that might enable him to make a choice between the designs, so that he might get on with the monument, for he was really burning with eagerness to be at it.

"Musha, sure I'm after been thinking a lot about the whole thing this long time," said Simon, crouching his bald and shiny head down between his hands in an attitude of tremendous concentration, "and I have come to the conclusion that no matter whatsomever monument you put up to yourself, this is the most odious wise thing you could do with your money. We often, God forgive us for our ignorance, used to wonder the devil what you could mean by running up and down the street, and in here and out again and over to the churchyard wall, and back to the bungalow... But of course we see it now, as plain as anything. Your poor mind was labouring all the while to give birth to a great idea, to an absolutely huge idea for the upliftment of your native place... "

"But the devil saise the penny anyone here is going to make out of me. Didn't I tell you that already?"

"Not directly, of course. See that now ... sure that only further proves the fine wisdom you are showing over the whole thing. It might remain a purely local affair, making for a whole lot of jealousy, and in spite of all the money you'd be after spending you'd go down, as the bard says, 'unwept, unhonoured and unsung,' but for the fine foresight you have shown that it was better, in the interests of Garradrimna, to let the name of it go out into the world by importing architects and designers and madmen from Dublin, and intending, as you are, to import foreign labour and other forms of genius, but of course you're only striving to make a cod either of yourself or of us if you don't see that the money you'll scatter on the wages of these decorators, no matter where they're from'll be spent in the village. Look at the condition of these fellows leaving the other night! That'll be the start. The few tramps' lodging-houses we have outside this place of my own'll be turned into hotels with the pure dint of the prosperity, and people like myself'll have to be hugely enlarging our premises. That'll go on for years and years for those 'sculptures' or architects or contractors are great for wangling out a job of this kind to the last... But then, sure, you'll have your revenge when you think of the great day of the unveiling, with contingents arriving from all parts of Ireland or America, mebbe, with bands and banners, for you'll be after proving yourself a National benefactor.

"Special trains to Castleconnor and Aarboy, and motor cars and side cars and common cars drawing them out here, and they leaving a big skelp of money in the place and they going away. Then the railways all over England advertising the thing as a perpetual attraction like the 'Vale of Avoca' or the 'Lakes of Killarney,' and a constant stream of tourists coming over here. As a natural result of all this, Garradrimna beginning to develop and expand. All sorts of new business places springing up. The village, your native village, becoming a town first and then mebbe a city. Round your own statue to yourself, around 'Igoe's Pillar,' as we'll mebbe be calling it, like Nelson's Pillar above in Dublin. It'll attract American capital to Garradrimna and that's as sure as you're there. Big, stout men with horn-rimmed glasses and long cigars coming right in here and saying to me:

"'Say, where's the wise guy that put the G in Garradrimna, meaning the famous, Marcus Igoe, mister?'

"Of course, then your photograph'll be published all over the world on the front pages of newspapers and you'll be given as an example in books on how young fellows can attain success—by reading the books. The simplest word out of your mouth, things you never even meant at all'll be noted, the same as if multi-millionaires like Carnegie or Rockefeller or Ford were after saying them... Why, you'll be absolutely unique. You'll have done a thing, a simple enough thing, but since no one ever thought of it before, you'll reap the benefit—the idea of a man laying the foundation stone of it first of all, with a little silver trowel suitably inscribed, and then, after a great whip of money being spent putting it up, unveiling, with an eloquent speech, a monument to himself..."

The eyelids of Simon Seery flickered anxiously. Marcus was cowering before all this elaborate sarcasm... He saw, with glee, the rich man hurrying out of his house, heard him saying: "I'll be back later on."

This speech... had clinched it... He could not get over that. The light, cynical way, an addition to his personality, that he had achieved through his Dublin visit, and which, no doubt, he might have maintained in suitable company... was being attacked and might be destroyed if he did not take measures to save himself... That was what Glarradrimna could do with a man, that was its native power.

He reached the bungalow and stood over the table upon which were set out the designs and the models. He thought of other moments when the plans of his life had been broken bits of his other "lives." Here they were before him now, accusative, complete enough in their delineation... He began to smash the models one by one and quite deliberately, until, after a little while, nothing remained on the table but a shapeless mass of brown clay. Above it, the figure of Marcus himself rising not without some resemblance to "the lovely little burning bird." "Ashes to ashes and dust to dust," he muttered, remembering, from some funeral, this bit of the Protestant burial service.

He spent the evening in Simon Seery's... It was as if what he had once thought out of his contemplation of the case of Mrs. Wyse had come to a different form of realisation, a case in which he was going to be the defeated one. They had a saying in Garradrimna, perhaps somewhat more than a saying, a belief, that, if great misfortune happened to a man, he had been "overlooked." Was that the game now? Was that what Simon Seery was at? Trying to "overlook" him. Making him do things with his life even to his destruction, as he himself had once fancied he could have done with Mrs. Wyse, only he did not believe he had done it. But maybe he could do it yet and, most certainly, Simon Seery would be the subject this time... Although he might have to call in the help of Bill the Savage. Had not that unfortunate creature influenced all his thought in the Picture Gallery?

This evening he seemed to find that Rosalind Briody was extraordinarily fascinating, and, at a chosen moment, Simon, still anxious for the success of his plan, hurried from the shop, but stopped to listen anxiously outside the door. He almost danced for very triumph at what he heard after a long silence that had been filled with heavy sighs:

"Begad, that's a lovely little bit of a ribbon you have in your hair this evening, Miss Briody," Marcus had said to Rosalind.

Chapter XLI

THE rumour of the capture of Marcus by Rosalind, as was only natural, created something of a stir in Garradrimna. It is not every day that a small village in the Irish Midlands sees itself missing the opportunity of becoming a far-famed place of pilgrimage. It was compelled to save its face by accepting the thing with as fine a pretence of a calmness as it could well be expected to produce in spite of all its innermost and uppermost feelings. The changing moods of the village seemed to be all at the mercy of the wild whim of a man who held Garradrimna in the hollow of his hand, did he but see it ... did he succeed in escaping the continuous, burning thought that Garradrimna held great power, to his detriment over him... But he could not see that—ever, because of his faithfulness to the memory of Margo.

The mistake was that he had not married Margo in the very beginning. They had a bit of philosophy in Garradrimna to the effect that the best tribute to the departed wife was to take on another one... And that, simply, was all he was apparently thinking of doing.

Yet it seemed possible that maybe the Seerys and the Briodys were counting a little too much on marriage as a means of conquering the unconquerable Marcus Igoe, with his great background or personality now making a sudden effulgence of power.

They were not so happy at all on account of something he had recently said to Simon Seery:

"Begad, this marrying would be a devil of a big venture, especially for your second time and to a young lassie. A fellow'll have to be very careful and saving, for you never could tell how long he might live, nor what terrific expense herself might bring down on him one way or another. He'd have to be most damnably careful, but believe you, me, Simon, there's nothing like putting a little wad in the ould stocking for a rainy day."

This declaration left Simon, as he said, "a kind of wake all over." For he had been already calculating various means of uprise to himself and his family through this possible alliance with Marcus Igoe.

He was further daunted when Marcus said that there was no use in rushing into the affair too soon. He had the bungalow to get rid of and the gorgeous car and the servants and any amount of personal belongings, the riddance of himself from which would all the better enable him properly and absolutely to resign himself to married life once more... He had already instructed the auctioneers...

A few mornings later he rushed into Simon Seery to request that he would give a really good show to the bills of the auction all round the shop. Amongst the articles mentioned was, sufficiently emphasised, *"a gentleman's complete wardrobe."* Even to the very last vestige did he mean to dispose of "the costumes," as he thought of them, which had been forced on him, "to disguise him as a gentleman." He was going to make a most determined beginning—at the very beginning of a certain course of action that might, eventually, mark his ultimate triumph over Garradrimna. It would be a memorial, an enshrinement in one strange action, the like of which had never been known before in Garradrimna.

He was going to return to the little workshop with, including one thing and another, (and particularly the fact upon which he built securely that people spend about twice as much on things at auctions as they could buy them for in a shop), about as much money as he had had when leaving it. The bungalow, too, because of its occupancy by a rich man, had increased in attraction. He calculated on nearly doubling the price he had paid Thomas Hardy when Margo had made him purchase it outright, instead of, as she said, merely wasting money renting it. The car, too, which he had scarcely used since the death of Margo, would be snapped up by people possibly who could not afford it but who would regard it as definite asset in the way of advancement. *And there would be no more nonsense.* He was firmly resolved on that.

Those who were compelled, by reason of their failure to "catch him," to be at first antagonistic, were now so amused, so comforted, so thoroughly delighted that they almost felt inclined to applaud Marcus for the way he was managing the whole business… Therefore he seemed to move in what should be the beginning of a moment of victory for him, again defeated. He passed in a sense commended by all the envious laughing eyes of Garradrimna. Ha! Ha!! Look at that now! He was popular. But they weren't finished with him yet by a long way. If only they knew… If only they had the least inkling of what was in his mind, they might not be so readily inclined to think that it must be pure meanness on the one hand and pure madness upon the other, that had driven him to his present "figario."

Yet there were moments when he, with others, saw that it was an extraordinary way of beginning to do honour to his future wife, this deliberate resignation of all the comfort and grandeur which made up the greater part of the reason why she was anxious to marry him. But, nevertheless, he stuck to his intention, and nearly disgraced himself at the auction of his effects by following

199

after the auctioneer all through the sale to see that he did not knock down anything too cheaply. Simon Seery, watching shrewdly, was forced, in a way, to commend the peculiar humour of Marcus. It was plain that he was going to be careful of the money for the little girl anyway. Simon said this to himself in spite of all the quizzical looks around him, which seemed to say that the wise proprietor of the Marlay Arms had not made such a great bargain after all in getting hold of a miser, and they had always an idea, so they had, of that being the way that Marcus would finally turn... There were always at least two ways of looking at everything in Garradrimna.

CHAPTER XLII

SUDDENLY Marcus saw himself married to Rosalind. The wedding had just taken place, and certainly a more undistinguished wedding Garradrimna had never seen. The very poorest person in the place would have succeeded in effecting a better show of style. And it was all of a piece with his meanness that he had merely suggested going up to Dublin for a few days' honeymoon, instead of to London, or Paris itself, which easily might have been expected of him. And the way he put even the idea of the meagre honeymoon: "Sure, I suppose we'll have to gallop up to Dublin, anyway, to have our photographs taken?"

The most important feature of the honeymoon was the end of it... the little bit of a dance that was held to celebrate their home-coming. This, as befitted Marcus's present state of mind and intention, was a rather poor affair, too, being confined to relatives of "the corpse," which was a facetious way they had in Garradrimna of referring to the "happy pair." Garradrimna had its own way, too, of being complimentary to the merry-makers. That night it pulled down the blinds or put up the shutters early upon all the squinting windows, as if to obliterate itself before the curious joy that had come into its midst.

The only window in the whole place that showed any illumination was that of Marcus Igoe, the window of his little workshop where he had chosen, most suitably he thought, to hold the celebration. Yet, even now, among the few nicely chosen guests, it was noticed that he did not look well at all, while "herself" looked lovely and young. It was seen that he stole often to the door, and, as the dawn began to break, stood longer and longer looking at the young summer trees... By the morning his guests had almost forgotten him... and even when they remembered him he was nowhere to be seen...

They came upon him in the back room anxiously engaged upon some task which they fancied must be the counting of money... until they really saw... He was simply comparing two photographs, the one he had just got taken, and the one that had been done of himself and Margo, the comical-looking one in discharge for a small cobbling debt by Professor Banvard, the tramp photographer, a great many years before. As the wedding guests crowded around the door they wondered what on earth he could be thinking of... But it was sadly clear to himself that he was thinking... of his monument... Was this to be his memorial now? Did it mean that he was finished?

Despite his elaborate preparations and his extraordinary plan for a new mode of life, it was soon painfully apparent that, not only was he married to Rosalind, but he was married to the whole family belonging to Rosalind, not even excluding Simon Seery. Of course his new wife had dropped various hints to which, at that moment of their falling with light thuds upon him, he had appeared to remain grandly oblivious. But now, suddenly, he swept away Rosalind's worry by saying:

"I suppose, don't you know, I may as well begin doing for the whole family at once; them two brothers of yours for instance, grand pups they are! George Whelehan, whose house I could never bear the sight of before my two eyes, is thinking of selling out, and I'm of opinion that we could manage to get it for them by private treaty. He'll want a big whip of money out of me, I being who I am, but I'll effect a slight saving, by buying it privately. However, it's not the first of the houses I mean to purchase for your people, who are now all my people, thanks be to God, and it won't be the last."

It was very satisfying to see Peter and Dan Briody, the two formerly penniless brothers of Rosalind, so well set up in the village. It was whispered around, in spite of the secrecy with which the deal had been effected, that Marcus had given a huge price for Whelehan's little brat of a place.

There were other members of the Briody family, and there were other places... The thought had come to him again, as if out of some far back life, of enforcing ultimate peace and understanding between himself and Garradrimna by buying up the squint of the windows ... while the householders of Garradrimna, baulked in their ambitions of him through the monument, were only too glad to let him have his way—at a price, but a good one necessarily, seeing that they had had to wait a little longer than they once expected for a bit of his money.

There arose, all around him, rumours of people thinking of selling out, and thus for the first time, became dimly apparent a possibility of the ultimate fusion, impossible though it had seemed, of the dearest desire of the hearts of Marcus Igoe and the people of Garradrimna which were, in short, that he should beat them and then they should beat him—at one and the same time. But then, of course, everything was possible through the exercise of a little transcendental brilliance gathered in the course of the various "lives" of one man.

This came to appear nearer realisation when, after the purchase of Miss Megann's little drapery place for Elizabeth and Christina, the two sisters of Rosalind, he proposed to purchase Brogan's newspaper and tobacco shop in the hope of giving Alexander Briody, old Briody himself, a soft way of living as well as the rest of them... Sure he could be reading all the English weekly periodicals and novels, and, in his spare time, selling an odd one of them as well as an ounce of tobacco or a package of cigarettes to the young lads, the poor unfortunate ould fellow...

When he blithely proposed, further, to purchase everything in the shape of a house that might be put up for auction, something like a genuine feeling of alarm suddenly arose in the family. So long as the purchasing, wild as it looked, had been proceeding to their advantage, it was all very well, but when he went, for no reason that anyone could well see, and gave £400 for the tumble-down shanty of Michael Chadwick, the retired harness-maker, Simon Seery began to detect that the madness of Marcus had taken a new turn, and one which might be to his own advantage eventually as the owner of a house, one of the biggest houses in Garradrimna.

Look at the way several parties were after manœuvring to get nearly enough to buy farms out of useless bits of places in which they had never done any business! The idea, so to speak, of Garradrimna taking up its bed and walking out into the fields was almost an accomplished fact. And, besides that, sure his own wife's people, the Briodys, would soon, in spite of everything, be the owners, as it were, of Garradrimna, and some sort of arrangement was bound to emerge whereby he would be sure of his position again, a sort of Co-operative Commonwealth, like what you'd see talked about in the newspapers. Each for all and all for each, in which all would get their proper share, or more than their proper share, as the case might be, or as they fondly hoped it might be. So, while the less perfect order of things lasted, it might be as well to have his welt out of Marcus while there was yet time. It appeared a shocking kind of a thing to do, but Marcus was a shocking kind of a man. So Simon sent for Joseph Cogan, the auctioneer, and put the place up for auction at once.

Great joy sprung into the soul of Marcus as he read the posters, fresh upon the piers of the Court House gates, a few mornings later. Simon Seery's was a big skelp of a house occupying a biggish portion of Garradrimna, and it would be a great gap in his plan if he were unable to buy it. It seemed suddenly gorgeous to him even in the descriptions of it on the bills. The auctioneer had cleverly illustrated the announcement by a photograph of the house, at what appeared to Marcus a very "squinting" angle. This would be the finest effort of his life, the purchase of the place from which a great deal of his annoyance had sprung. But it would cost a tremendous whip of money, and, for a certainty, Simon Seery would use every stratagem to make it as big as he could. It might indeed finish all his money, but this would finish Garradrimna...

And, so it was that, just at this moment, the interrelation of these two facts bore down enormously upon the mind of Marcus Igoe. For even at this late stage he was compelled to admit that all his previous efforts must have been failures, seeing that he was still making efforts. And it was as good to finish it definitely. Finish what? He scarcely seemed to know when he asked himself the question, yet whatever IT was it would take all the money he had left. But he would have fully purchased the squint of Garradrimna.

He could never be sneered at any more, for the simple reason that there would be no Garradrimna to sneer at him, and the Briodys and the whole jing bang lot of them, including Simon Seery, would have been beaten, too, for he would have spent all his money, and there would be nothing more they could get out of him ... so it might come to appear, after a while, to any of them who could think it out properly that it might have been just as well if they had left the marrying of him alone. Not, of course, that he did not deeply love Rosalind and pay her all the high respect that was her due, but he felt, unquestionably, that there should be some reciprocation of respect, no matter what happened, and why could not even a fine, beautiful-looking girl, such as she was, have great respect and love for her husband, even though he had not a penny? Then there was the thought, hiding some jubilation, of Simon Seery and his business in Garradrimna, which resembled that of the spider and the fly. If Simon retired from the shop, which held for him all the properties of a cobweb, he would be as a very fat and useless retired spider with all the villainy gone out of him and all sorts of debility setting in.

Marcus licked his lips upon it as he thought of and muttered over slowly to himself, a very fine-looking word, that was always being used by fellows in newspapers, namely the word "Pyrrhic" as an adjective qualifying the word "victory." It was exactly what Simon Seery would have won, a Pyrrhic victory, and that kind of triumph was not of much use to the winner.

However, he did not become fully convinced of the tremendous nature of the difficulties before him until the auction was right in on top of him... For a few days it almost seemed as if Simon Seery's sneer at his ultimate influence upon the life of Garradrimna was about to be realised, and that his native village might yet be famous above all the villages in Ireland—for a strange reason, and in a most curious way, because he was compelled now to witness the sight, through the days that were rapidly leading up to the great one of the auction, of men coming into Garradrimna from all parts of Ireland to see the grand place preparatory to buying it.

It was said that Simon was giving heavy and expensive luncheons to prospective buyers, and that the bar of the Marlay Arms was continually thronged with men drinking alone and looking very fierce at one another, each thinking, possibly, that every single one of the others was going to out-bid him or, in some underhand, backstairs way, do him out of the lovely place that his heart was set upon... The stage management seemed to increase in invention as the day of the auction drew nearer. In the face of what was so obvious to them, the people of Garradrimna were moved by the problem of choosing between two loyalties—loyalty to Garradrimna or loyalty to the man who had done his very best to make himself a walking devil of a pest nearly ever since he had got the money.

If they told him of their deep and well grounded suspicions that the whole thing was simply a carefully laid plan of Simon's to bid up the place to the uttermost limit and rob Marcus entirely... If they told him that they felt right well that the sensible thing would be to leave the auction severely alone, or else to just drop out of the bidding, if he could manage it, when the highest point would obviously have been reached and beyond which none of the imported buyers would be likely to bid... since Simon Seery would have told them how far exactly they might venture... All that would be a magnificent defeat of Simon's plan and well worth a whole cycle of life in Garradrimna to have the pleasure of seeing his face when it happened...

It would be the very finest expression of loyalty to Marcus and the best means of giving pleasure to themselves... but they were still in their hearts utterly Garradrimnian, and could not see their way to do it. Ah, yes, in spite of every better instinct, it must be so, for this was loyalty to the spirit of Garradrimna and the loving tradition of Garradrimna and the ultimate hope of Garradrimna in its final defeat of Marcus Igoe. Sure it would be the grandest thing in the world to see him without a single penny again! He wouldn't be so funny then, with his going back to the cobbler's shop! Sure he had been making a living show of himself all his life anyway and you never could know what the hell to make of him.

CHAPTER XLIII

ALL of the manœuvring around the auction was not confined to Simon Seery. Marcus had paid several momentous visits to his solicitor, Charles Delamere, in Castleconnor, and there had been serious and anxious consultations between them in the inner chamber of the office... The clerks in the outer room had distinctly heard loud words, but considered that these were no more explosive than might be expected when two "cute" men had taken it into their heads to disagree upon some point of tactics. It was little they knew, these simple poor fellows, the nature of the proceeding that was happening within, the completion, the last stitches, as it were, in the extraordinary piece of cobbling that Marcus Igoe was doing with his life.

Nor was it given them to see that their reserved and remarkable employer looked just a little bent and worried as he took the journey a day or two later to the auction in Garradrimna.

On the contrary, Marcus, as he walked up the stone staircase to the auction in the Courthouse, never before looked half so sure of himself in the eyes of Garradrimna. Perhaps it was because of the more or less defeated figure of his solicitor walking by his side. But there was a dangerous glint in his eye that gave one the disquieting notion that he might yet have a surprise up his sleeve for them.

Big as Simon Seery's place undoubtedly was in comparison with the other places in Garradrimna, a thousand pounds would have been, at this stage in the world's history, a "shocking" price to pay for it in any event, but the bidding started almost at this figure or was there or thereabouts in a few minutes.

Some of the strangers were absolutely fierce with their bidding from the very start. When it had reached £1,200 Marcus gave his solicitor a nudge and Charles Delamere gave an immediate jump to £1,400. This only appeared to encourage the friends of Simon, for Joseph Cogan, the auctioneer, was immediately overpowered by an absolute deluge of bids ... until a breathing space was reached when the figure stood at £3,500. Joseph Cogan looked hard at Mr. Charles Delamere, who was gradually realising the ignominious position in which he found himself placed... The usually so staid solicitor, capable of distinguishing himself in almost every emergency, felt anything but his usual self here amid this mob of ruffians belonging to Simon Seery.

It was certainly most demeaning for a man of his standing, and he felt it keenly. The whole performance was going to lessen his esteem in the eyes of the community. Here he was publicly identified with the flinging away of a client's money on a mad whim. He had never met with such a case in the whole course of his legal experience, and he felt scandalised, affronted, mortified. He was exactly in such a situation as demanded that he must descend to a deeper damnation if he was still to maintain himself at all in any show of relation to his reputation ... so he now ... with as extraordinary a display of coolness as he could summon in the circumstances, resolved to frighten Marcus and, possibly, the other bidders by jumping as much as £500 at a single hop...

Marcus gave a start, then smiled grimly as he leant across and whispered into his solicitor's ear:

"That'll do, Mr. Delamere, thanks! You have overstepped your instructions, do you hear, and, consequently, you are no capable manager of my affairs any more. You're suspended, and, if you don't look sharp, I'll fire you altogether! I'll make the next bid myself!"

Although they had not heard what had passed, Simon Seery and some of the others guessed what it was... and they divined, too, the possible cause of the smile of resignation upon the face of Charles Delamere. Maybe, after all, he was after having enough of the madman, in the face of what he was doing with his money. What good could he be any more to any solicitor outside heaven? No wonder that there fell a dreepy sort of look upon the poor man's face now and he saying something to Marcus. But what was going to happen now? It was certainly the most remarkable situation that had yet been produced in the life of Marcus Igoe or in the annals of Garradrimna... Suddenly they saw Marcus struggling on to the platform upon which the auctioneer was seated.

"I want to stop this business," he shouted. "I want to make a speech that'll stop it, and damn quick too. I have a proposition to make now, which should, in a way, relieve all our harassed and excited feelings. I'm prepared in the interests of humanity, for this thing has already gone nearly too far, to do something that everyone here'll consider very magnanimous of me. I'm prepared to exchange all my recently purchased property in Garradrimna, for I still hold the title deeds, although other parties presently occupy my houses, for this house now at auction to the highest bidder. That may appear a quare sort of bid and not the highest bid at all that might be got, but when you consider it fairly, and apart from the wholly extravagant nature of the financial situation here at the moment, it's a fine exchange, and, if Simon Seery wants to get rid of the Marlay Arms at all he should jump at it, actually jump at it. In fact I have a little slip of paper here in my hand showing my expenditure in houses in Garradrimna, and, looking at the figures to date, I should say that it exceeds by some pounds at least the amount that the Marlay Arms is really worth.

"And if it is not accepted..." a pause, but no sound from Simon Seery. "No... my offer is not going to be accepted, I can see that. Then I'll tell you in a nutshell what I'm going to do as an alternative. It has just struck me, after a hurried consultation with my solicitor, that I could easily expend my money to better advantage upon a new first-class public-house or hotel that could be erected to stand in a most distinguished position all by itself at the other end of Garradrimna—something that'll have a different atmosphere altogether in the place and, sure, no matter what I might have paid for it, I'd never have been able to get rid of the more or less objectionable atmosphere of Simon Seery's. As I have said, it will be erected at the other end of the village, for one of the big lessons I learned, one of the most acute observations I made while I was living in the very middle of you all was that a great many people had no strong liking for walking up the whole length of the main street for their little sup, that it was nothing short of a hardship on a great many when I used to see the poor chaps trying to take the look of the windows off themselves by taking a good look in at me ... struck no doubt by recollection of some of the more renowned exploits of the many-sided life amongst you ... the things I did, what I dreamt of doing, and then all I didn't do, in short the whole conglomeration that you call myself, the curious character known to the world as Marcus Igoe. Was it any wonder that, thus, the defenceless one, as I was of yore, intimidated after such a fashion as this, I made crooked boots that went a long way to misshape the native population of the whole place from the soles of their feet upward.

"But I have thought it all out so clearly and made such judicious purchases of the very worst of the squinting houses and I have such a brilliant plan of what I am going to do with myself now, that such occasions of mutual torture as between myself and my neighbours are not likely further to arise.

"I'm going to call the new establishment 'The Marcus Igoe Memorial Hotel,' and you may take this as my unveiling speech since it is maybe my last public utterance in Garradrimna, for I do not foresee any further need of words after this effort. I was dissuaded from my idea of a memorial in the ordinary common and accepted sense by the undoubtedly fine but merely sarcastic opposition of Simon Seery. Still a memorial of some sort it had to be, a kind of sweeping gesture near the end that might stay behind me, as of more permanent account than my money or my wife or the numerous and distinguished family she has brought me either. The torment of what to do in this direction has preyed long and deeply upon my mind, but I think that now I have arrived at a fairly satisfactory solution. It will, of course, successfully demolish all that remains of my money. Heretofore, the problem was left largely to my imagination and that was a great mistake, but the issue is now no longer in doubt. Think of the spell of prosperity that will suddenly accrue to tradesmen of every de-nomination, a fortune alone in the drawing of the sand and the stones ..." (He looked at Simon as he said this, but the eyes of the proprietor of the Marlay Arms had become glassy, his face expressionless...) "And of course I'm not forgetting, for how could I, the young artistic fellow in Dublin, the Sculptor, who supplied me with the plans and specifications of myself for the great monument that, magnanimously, I did not use, as well as the young Novelist fellow, who had something more than a mere hand in making me appear as I have appeared from time to time. It's not often, I suppose, that a couple like them get the job of doing a pub, although I'd say when they'd get the chance they'd prove to be experts in that line. There'll have to be one room in it like the Scotch House and one like Davy Byrne's and one like

The Palace, and one like Mooney's and one like the Bodega and I'm going to superintend them and watch them and incite them until the whole thing'll wear the complexion, nearly, of some gorgeous ecclesiastical building, all responsibility for it being a perfectly natural and suitable conclusion in Ireland to a man with the character of me."

With such vehemence had he addressed them thus far, that they had listened spellbound. Simon Seery, for whose particular benefit it was all said, did not feel himself addressed in particular until the very end, but the cumulative effect of Marcus's words bore down upon him now and cut him to the quick. Surely, Marcus could not possibly mean his words for anyone but him... There now he was mentioning his name:

"And if Mr. Seery, in anticipation of the valuelessness of his great place by the time that all these arrangements are made, feels inclined to sell to me now I'll consider the offer at my own price. It never dawned on me until I heard some of you here putting up such ferocious bids, how extraordinarily valuable a pub better than this one could be. Looking at it my own way, and, that is to say, if I live long enough, it'll be a fortune I'll mebbe be making out of it yet, for that's the way with money, when you haven't it, you haven't it, but when you have it it's continually breaking out and enlarging itself into more."

This was the final touch required to "put wheels under them" as Marcus thought of it, and, immediately, they were beginning to slink out of the auction room. Charles Delamere lifted his eyes in admiration over his glasses at Marcus... He had indeed nothing but admiration for the way the situation had been turned... Joseph Cogan, with a knowledge of the twists and turns of human nature comparable only with that of Charles Delamere, merely smiled.

CHAPTER XLIV

THE eye of Bill the Savage was upon Marcus as he stood there by the counter crystal-gazing into his pint. He knew of the rumour that had already gone abroad of the attraction of Marcus by Rosalind... The number of times he had been seen coming in with Bartle Boyhan and Dickeen Crosbie and they only egging him on... It would seem that Bill had just now compelled the wise man to see what would have become of his life if he had married Rosalind... Marcus lifted up his head as it seemed with a great sigh of relief that a certain thing had not befallen him, as one might think at the end of a dream when the desperate and dangerous thing so clearly experienced had not really happened at all. No, it had not happened... It was a dream surely... dream in the glass, dream in the eyes of Bill the Savage... There was Rosalind looking young and lovely still with the ribbon in her hair... And he had not destroyed her or anything by marrying her...

It filled him with a sense of relief, of escape, of thankfulness, and about his mouth there played a grey smile of understanding. There was certainly much that could be learned from the dream... the idea of selling out for instance... Now there was a lot in that only he would never think of coming back to the shop with the little squinting window... He owned it still, of course, and a vague notion struck him of making a present of it to Rosalind... To Rosalind and Bill the Savage, for it appeared to him of a sudden that a glorious love affair was happening just beside him...

He had recently strayed into Gilbert Gallagher's shop and there found Bill the Savage painting ... painting a portrait of a girl. "Signboard for an Unknown House," he was going to call it, he said, when the words were at last dragged out of him, and what grander thing, thought Marcus, could be than that the face of the prettiest girl Ireland had ever seen should swing in the soft wind above the door of the shop that had, in a sense, made his life.

It would be nice, he thought, to present the house to Bill the Savage and his bride, to let them make of it what they would. Then this picture might be made a symbol, a symbol of loveliness here in the very middle of Garradrimna, to suggest the beauty that Marcus Igoe had sought all his life and, signally, had failed to find. They could say then, past all their jokes about picture houses, that here surely was the House of the Beautiful Woman. It was something that sinned against all the codes of Garradrimna, the giving of something for absolutely nothing, but if only it could happen now it would salve his conscience; it would be the best adjustment before he went.

He felt himself at length drawing up to the matter almost as a matchmaker might ... beating about the bush, suggesting the possibilities of a succession to himself in Bill the Savage, now that he was going to leave Garradrimna, as he said, at first lightly, jocularly. Sensing Bill as a man of imagination and having due thought of the things he might yet do for the upliftment of the place, the imaginative, splendid things like some which he himself had translated into action, for look at him even now thinking of Bill the Savage in an imaginative light, seeing the side to him that no one else could possibly see in Garradrimna, the desire the poor fellow might have and should have, since it was no wrong, for this lovely girl!

He became bold as he toyed with the thought, the most extraordinary that he had yet had. Rosalind knew full well that it was on his mind now to be saying momentous things ... and she was listening eagerly... But there fell a blankness upon her face at the declaration of Marcus, made at length in all seriousness now, that he was about to leave Garradrimna and that, before he went, he had something to say to her... Of course he had, she thought... but then he said it... after a good deal of preliminary flourishing, that he had a nice little fortune for her just as a present, if she would take it into her lovely little head to marry Bill the Savage...

He meant it, long afterwards telling the story, he said that he had meant every word of it, with its eloquent and grand opening which sounded nearly like the beginning of a written constitution: "It has appeared well to us..." Now could any man blame him? A lovely young girl like her had no business to be thinking about him ... when she could have a life's purpose before her in being an inspiration to Bill the Savage, doing something with him that should be a lesson for ever to any hussy who might take it into her head to turn the head of a poor fellow in a public-house. And it was plain that the head of poor Bill had been turned by all the girls he had seen in all these places...

Why was it that he had changed from the manner of his early masterpiece, his extraordinarily fine work that had as its subject the man drinking a pint, to paint this portrait of a young girl that had for its model all the girls who ever served him with pints in Garradrimna... But the finished work was a perfect portrait of Rosalind... Yet Marcus realised before he had gone very far that he was talking to the air ... he heard her crying ... he saw Simon Seery coming in. He felt himself being flung out ... and then the rumour hurrying through Garradrimna, upon swift wings, that he was after, in company or collusion or conspiracy with Bill the

216

Savage, insulting the poor, lovely little girl above in the Marlay Arms...

They would regard him, doubtless, as one to be excused and he would go unscathed... He had money and it would cause him to remain immune. But it might not be so safe for Bill. A little later that evening he thought of going to see Bill the Savage in case anything might have happened to him...

As he went down towards the workshop of Gilbert Gallagher about nine in the evening, he heard an unusual commotion. He heard men shouting and talking angrily as he approached the place. He heard wild laughter inside. It was unusual in this silent, almost tomblike, place where Bill scarcely ever said a word to Gilbert. He went into the unwonted scene, and there saw a terrible sight. Men armed with paint brushes and paint pots were at work upon the body of a naked man, the body of Bill, while others danced around with guttering candles in their hands yelling: "Paint him!" "We'll see now what he'll be like when he's painted himself; the infernal cheek of the ruffian anyway, painting the grand little girl!" "But what he done to her is in bits there on my ground now, we med fliggits of it and tore it and cut ribbons out of it!"

The whole performance seemed to smite Marcus with a feeling of grim terror. This was life asserting itself over him. He had been playing with Garradrimna so far, himself and the monument and all the rest of it! But Bill the Savage had never played with it; he had always realised it and thought deeply and sadly about it. He had suffered for it, and here now he was being punished. If the paint did not poison him through the cuts and bruises he would be lucky... Marcus turned on them and, cowed of a sudden by the rich man's appearance amongst them, they slunk away murmuring and shaking their fists. What would he do now? That was the thought in their minds. Simon Seery had inflamed them with some of his free drink... He drove them out of the workshop and, assisting him tenderly, went with the painted Bill, now looking more than ever "the Savage," to the Market Square...

The whole population of Garradrimna seemed to be crowding around. He was making a speech... A speech of leave-taking, as he wildly thought of a sudden... A memorable pronouncement which would be a greater effort than the one at the auction, and which would leave its mark for ever upon the life of Garradrimna, a gigantic effort... But, not a sound of interruption... They were agreeing with him, absolutely...

Endorsement, full and complete, besmeared, as it were, their sweating, drunken faces... He was going from them, as he said, and they were simply grinning at him because he was going, enjoying it. He, the sometime potential benefactor of the village, the man who felt so sure of his immortality here that he had thought of erecting a monument to himself! If he had declared his intention of leaving them heretofore, public deputations must surely have been organised to beseech him to remain, but now, when he was making his gesture, standing there by his broken and bleeding friend, telling them he was going, they were roaring and cheering him ... glad that he was leaving Garradrimna!

"I'd like to do for the whole of you," he shouted. "Leave you without the candle going to bed at night before I stop!"

That, momentarily, seemed to give them pause for, deep in their consciousness, was the sense of the circumstances under which the saying had once been once used. It was the prophecy that had been here once quoted from Jeremiah, by a holy man, in utter denunciation of Garradrimna:

"Moreover I will take from them the voice of mirth, and the voice of gladness, the voice of the bridegroom, and the voice of the bride, the sound of the millstones, *and the light of the candle.*"

218

It was the sense of final desolation in the last words that had survived as a tradition in Garradrimna. The words "light of the candle" smote them apparently with a feeling of terror, but only for a moment. Their sense of derision once more uprose to strengthen them in their onslaught. They yelled and tore up clods of earth and stones from the grass-grown cobbles of the Market Square, and Marcus, almost carrying Bill in his arms, had to retreat before them. He escaped by a side lane, and in the tumble-down shanty of Michael Chadwick, the retired harness maker, he bolted himself in and succoured the wounded man.

As he remained there through the lonely watches of the night with nearly a dead man in his arms, the poor "Savage" now painted by savages in similitude of the thing he had been nick-named, he realised that maybe he had gone too far with Garradrimna... There were some things, you know... But he had had to break with it somehow, and if that nice little girl, Rosalind Briody, was involved a bit in the smash, sure it could not have been helped.

CHAPTER XLV

HE had thought it all out. After selling all he had, and as soon as poor Bill was quite recovered, he would go to the quiet townland of Harbourstown, quieter now than it had been in the old days, ah, quieter by far. It was now the townland of the old men, of the old age pensioners, and the old schoolmasters, and the various other kinds of superannuated men. It had come to be, in short, the very thing that it had been called.

Sometimes, that part of County Meath looked like an inlet of the sea; when the autumn mist was upon it, and when, in all the cottages on the slopes of the gently hilly fields, the lamps were lighted. Yet it was always somewhat of a puzzle to the wayfarer as to why the little cluster of lights, behind a collection of small shops and cottages at a very ordinary kind of cross-roads should be called Harbourstown. Harbourstown... Harbourstown...? It seemed a strange name for any place so far from the sea, for at noontide, one remembered, looking down the valley, that one was standing somewhere about the very middle of Ireland. Men surely had lived long lives here without having ever seen the sea... It was quiet always almost in every place that lay deep in the fields of Meath, but quieter in Harbourstown than in any other townland. There was a stillness upon the very movements of the people who lived here...

For the most part, there was no movement at all only the quiet talk of old men recounting their lives in little houses or by the roadside... Men who, although they had not seen the sea, had felt the tides of life and time surge round them ... although some had never gone farther across life than the distance to some nearby village... Bytimes there would be real wanderers, men who had travelled far, old sailors who had seen every country on earth, and they would talk of other harbours which knew the great business of shipping. But now they were here, where nothing was ever done only quietly remembering... The place had a definite association with memories... with reminiscences... It was its quality... The inhabitants would seem to have been purposely built to suit the surroundings of their home and their harbour now from the waves of the world.

And to think that this was the place to which Marcus Igoe was returning, one who had had, as it were, many voyages coming back to harbour, on a broken sail, when the night was falling. But he had passed through much since he had gone out from this place; he had lived... It had been so quiet and lovely here in the old days, when, at the behest of his poor mother, he had tried to make a gentleman out of himself. His personality had flourished in this quietness, so deeply unlike the rough and tumble of Garradrimna. It was not so far from Garradrimna, to be sure, and the grievous voice of the village sometimes reached Harbourstown. But there were so many old men that few here had such consuming interest in the things that were happening now... They were always thinking of the things that had happened... And would he be like that, an old and merely retired man with memories, remembering only instead of being himself still, of virile personality and going on ...? It would be a great experiment, anyhow, this return to Harbourstown. Out of view of the fine place he had once lived in, he would take a little house and live quietly here.

He had not been long in Harbourstown when, one day, a strange thing happened. He had gone walking upon a windy hillside. It was a day in spring and Thomas Gillan, one of his new neighbours, was sowing corn. He saw the sower magnified against the great wideness of the sky. He thought he felt words of poems coming into his mind—"And Thomas Gillan scattered corn, along the winding slopes of morn." It was like something that John Cassidy, the schoolmaster's son, the poet of Harbourstown, might have written. Was this, he felt, the Phœnix rising in him again...? And here he was free, here was release for the soul. Here he could be thinking any lovely thought he liked.

But what was that figure standing gaunt against the hillside of Mulroo roaring himself out to the four winds? It was "the Trojan" Burke, the man who had retired years ago from Garradrimna. It was, in a sense, himself, and so, across the young green field he went, as it were, to meet himself. But even as he went forward the one he wished to meet swayed and staggered and then his voice was dumb, the great voice that had, aforetime, boomed over all Mulroo and Harbourstown in noble denunciation of Garradrimna. It was a momentous happening for which the very clouds in the heavens seemed to stand still. Marcus Igoe had wanted above all to meet this man and to have a talk with him, and here the thing, or man, had fallen and maybe died before his very eyes...

He was now like one walking into the shadow of himself, or else a ghost going forth to inhabit clay...

Thomas Gillan, standing with the white sheet which held the seed around him, took off his cap and gazed to the south and saw a dream city in the sky ... while the Marcus Igoe who had come to Harbourstown was already no more, and "the Trojan" Burke lay dead upon a green hillside a few miles from Garradrimna. To the last, the prophet had kept his fire. There was defiance still about the lines of suffering that framed his mouth, for he had remained powerful and himself to the end of his life.

He had gone into Garradrimna, once a month, to shout the things he was always shouting here upon the hillside. To keep them quiet, as he said. He had even shouted things about Marcus Igoe in Garradrimna, and now here was Marcus himself a most suitable candidate for the position he had just vacated. Garradrimna had done to Marcus the thing that it must have done at some other time to "the Trojan" Burke. He was qualified for that position now after all his various "lives." He could remember when, as a gallant and a fox-hunting man, his fear of the Trojan Burke had always been a very real thing. He had often gone for miles out of his way to avoid meeting that angry man who so affected him. When he had lived the life in Garradrimna that he might have lived but for his mother, the same thing had happened. The Trojan had said some nasty things about his beard...

At the very pinnacle of himself as "the Marquis" it was the hidden derision of the Trojan that had, above all else, given him pause, bringing him at length a curious disbelief in himself and the whole thing. When he had seen himself married to Rosalind Briody it was a thought of the things that the Trojan would say of such an alliance that must surely have taught him the lesson he had learned from the dream. It was all very well for that smart fellow, the Novelist, to write a story about him as a comedian, but it was a different thing and largely unconvincing when the Trojan was not in it, for he should be in it, even though he might not be therein depicted. He would be laughing at him in the story and not with any sort of enjoyment all the time.

And now to think that the soul of "the Trojan" had, as it were, passed into him... Already, he was engaged with the other men, who had run to him at his calling, in doing the offices by the dead body of something that he was not sure might not be himself... And he wanted to go into Garradrimna, so soon after he had just left it for good, to shout ... to tell them all what he thought of them. How would they take him now...? They would hear of him as wandering over green hillsides in the earthly habiliments of the Trojan... It seemed for the moment that he had been caught by life at last and he was filled with dread... Was this to be the end of him now, of him who had floated so successfully through various "lives"? It was a curious trick that life had played on him, Garradrimna bringing him round full circle to what he always had been, for he remembered now that on his visits to the cobbler's den, the two, the Trojan and himself, had agreed magnificently on many things, feeling themselves, in presence of his bitterness, men after one another's hearts. He would have to be very careful!

But, the Trojan becoming gradually forgotten, moods of gladness again fell down upon Marcus in Harbourstown. The people were nice to him. If he liked he could be a gentleman now, just as in the old days, but he did not want that any more.

The morning road as he came out of his house to look at the world was always lit for him by a glorious vision, the daughter of Martin Ivory, the very Martin Ivory who had been his son-in-law in the life of "the Marquis," the man who got married that time to the little girl, the daughter he had never had. So this lovely girl was in a sense his granddaughter... She was not a bit like that lassie, Rosalind, in Garradrimna anyway; she was a poor little innocent girl, without a bit of harm or "cutting" in her at all. Her father was poor despite the fact that he had once upon a time, in that queer "life," appeared a good match, but she was lovely and bits of poems would seem to come to him from nowhere as he looked upon her.

It had come into his head, for she would seem always to be going for a can of water as he came out, to call her "Rebecca at the well." It was another thought from a poem by John Cassidy, out of one of the weekly newspapers. And then he would mutter: "For when my days may fall forlorn, I'll see Rebecca at the well, and Ruth among the waving corn." His mind was breaking into sweet sympathy, and tenderness was coming to him. Was that "the Trojan" or any survival of him in the person of Marcus Igoe? Well then maybe the Trojan would have grown tender, had he lived long enough; one never knew. He began to have thoughts of going away again, of going away from Harbourstown ... of going away altogether... But then arose, more acutely, the problem of his money. He lived very simply now, and one might think of his fortune as a great sum quietly but rapidly accumulating from moment to moment... After all his mad ideas as to its expenditure he had not really spent any of it ... and less than ever now in Harbourstown, where he was rapidly earning the reputation of a miser.

Miser indeed! He was no miser. Only just that he could not help it. Having money was just wisdom if you like, what they still called sense in Garradrimna. Not having it was just foolishness, and it was the height of foolishness to engage in forms of unnecessary expenditure... Wild notions of doing things, extraordinary things with one's money ebbed from one as the years went on. They had ebbed from him; they had passed him by. But there remained memories of all his "lives," his sunny days, and he had not made of any of them a golden opportunity. Were these the "lives" he should have lived to the fullest, any of them at all, or was living just foolishness and no more?

Was the thing that made the living of any life possible merely a kind of foolishness, and that people who did not approach life that way got nothing out of it? Were the faces of happy men and women really the faces of fools...? He could behold even still, in retrospect, almost with a certain amount of pleasure, the occasions when he must have looked like one of the biggest lunatics in Ireland.

But then it was his failure in the doing of the thing that might have got the better of Garradrimna, of life, that had killed him… If it had not been for the money he might be having one of his own lives still. There was a man, "the Trojan," for instance, who had remained himself to the last, just as he might have remained himself had he continued to live on in the house of the squinting window… "The Trojan" had died, that is, his body and his personality had disappeared, but it might be that his soul still lived in the body of Marcus Igoe who was now no more.

Often it would strike him sadly, and he would think once more of going into Garradrimna to meet some one of his own lost selves. The Marcus Igoe of the dances in his young days and, later, the plums and pears; the Marcus Igoe of the time of the breach of promise action in the Four Courts in Dublin; the Marcus Igoe of the beard, and the summer morning romance upon the street of Garradrimna; the defeated Marcus Igoe of the cobbler's den; the Marcus Igoe who had been "a Marquis"; the Marcus Igoe who had pondered in "the Picture House," making life bend, as he thought, obediently to his will; the Marcus Igoe who had lived through the sorrows surrounding the death of Margo; the Marcus Igoe who had thought out a scheme for the perpetuation of his own memory; the Marcus Igoe who had failed to project himself into the part that had been written for him in the story of "the Comedian"; the Marcus Igoe who had defeated Simon Seery; the Marcus Igoe who had had the resignation to come out here.

No, he could not meet one of those, for there was something in Garradrimna that left him unable to bear even the thought of meeting them. Was it the ghost of "the Trojan" at his elbow whispering this to him that definitely prevented all this glad resumption of acquaintance? That, maybe, and the fable of the money, the destructive legend of his miserliness. No, he could not go back to Garradrimna just yet, for if he did the Trojan would be walking with him. He would be within in the very inside of him. He would be himself, and so there would be no triumph over Garradrimna but only the mad anger of a baffled prophet in his heart.

However, he would yet do one other fine thing. He would live another "life" through power of all that he still remained himself, through power of his money. No doubt they still thought of him in Garradrimna, as in retirement and defeat, like Napoleon on St. Helena's barren shore, in Harbourstown with the other old and defeated men, sometimes walking the green hillside of Mulroo, a pale and poor imitation of "the Trojan Burke." But he would show them, yes, he would show them! It would need thinking out, this new and elaborate re-creation of himself, but he was the very man who could think it out properly, now that he was put to it!

CHAPTER XLVI

SOMETIMES he thought of Bill the Savage, wondering what might have happened if that man of strange qualities had been given his way with Garradrimna... The immense thoughts about life which had, somehow, always lain behind that pallid face with its sunken eyes, like deep pools of loneliness... And now the story came over the fields to him one day that Bill the Savage was no more. He had done the uncommon thing, the thing that few, if any, of them had ever had the courage, or the cowardice, as they themselves would put it, to do in Garradrimna. They had discovered him hanged most elaborately amongst the trees of the woods, that he had hated and feared, on a windy morning. It was another night of the Big Wind with which Garradrimna had been visited, and it did not call for much imagination to realise the great bravery it must have demanded of him to have done this deed to himself at such a time.

It was from the Marlay Arms that he went to his doom, and looking at him there for the last time, he might have been seen for what he really was. The timid tragic figure with the eyes, now dark and sombre as pools, and again illuminated with the light of genius, as some spark of inspiration enkindled them, some satirical perception, some moment as when he might have got so well into the mood of life here, that he could force another man to do the very thing he was thinking, like the way he had manipulated Marcus Igoe as they said till the poor fellow had to fly beyond his

228

reach by emigrating to Harbourstown! He knew that it was he alone who had created the later "lives" of Marcus Igoe. He was an embodiment in Garradrimna of the very idea that the Novelist had in Dublin, only he was the man through whom the idea passed into reality.

His thoughts were all upon Marcus Igoe this evening. There was no excitement in Garradrimna these times at all! Marcus had gone to replace the Trojan, and so two men of parts who had amused him, although he never really laughed, were both, in a sense, dead... A certain incurable hurt to him had been occasioned by the painting of him as a savage. He had brought all his life to the accomplishment of a beautiful thing and then they had destroyed it. They had murdered his soul. He had a feeling all the same that the shattered bits of it remained and might yet have a purpose, so there was a mad notion filling all his thoughts now. With all the other wild things he had indulged in, he had thought, aye more than thought, had believed implicitly, that, at the moment of death, the soul flies to sojourn in some other habitation of clay. It was one of his secret amusements in Garradrimna to observe how the souls of the dead sometimes flew into the souls of the living and changed them—for better or for worse.

And so it was that, always, he had been seen to run out of Garradrimna whenever there was a funeral about to pass. He was afraid, as he explained to himself the reasons for his fear while hiding somewhere until the funeral was over, that he might see the *thing* happening before his very eyes... But, later, he had always been keen to watch for signs of it, and, whether he had seen them or not, he had kept the secret to himself, but, often, when they had observed him smiling his sad smile to himself they thought, maybe, that, possibly, his horror of the dead was what he had been smiling about. He was smiling now, standing there in the bar of the Marlay Arms, the proprietor, Simon Seery, maybe still pondering the big defeat of himself that Marcus Igoe had effected... He seemed to have grown balder, and, when he grappled with a thought now, his head was always bent lower down upon the counter.

Bill, whom he had permitted to forget the murderous attack he had organised against him, by allowing him again into his bar, was now thinking there in silence that, maybe, he himself had more to do with that than even Simon guessed. And there was Simon, peering forlornly at the sadly small dribble of evening customers, Bartle Boyhan and Dickeen Crosbie and Bill the Savage. He and his like had made these men; they were their artistic creations. But what a cursed lot they were to his mind now, not a bob between them, and there was the valuable lamplight absolutely wasting before his eyes with them talking, talking... Did anyone ever realise what the poor publican had to put up with through enduring the talk he had to listen to while earning his living? They wouldn't be so critical, them damn temperance fellows, if they did... He rose from his bent position with a groan... But still Bartle held sway behind his dilatory pint,

"Nothing in a name is it? Why, d'ye know what I'm going to tell you, it's all in a name.

"Look at advertisements for example! There you see my whole idea proved up to the hilt, and exactly what I mean. Look at the confidence that educated men and business men and hard-headed, knacky, commercial men place in the solid truth of everything being in a name. Sure what's the millions spent in advertising for only to prove that what I'm telling you is right, only, of course, they don't spend it in our interest only in their own. Sure the principle of it is that you have only to say a thing often enough for people to believe in it. Take any ould red-hat of a farmer now that has a daughter he's finding it middling hard to marry off his hands and what does he do?

"Well, I'm going to tell you what he does. He gets, bribes I should say, parties to run round the country telling everyone how his daughter Janeen or Margeen or Biddeen, or whatever her name may happen to be, is one of the best workers in Ireland. Up at six o'clock every morning she does be, the poor little thing, and feeds a power of pigs... And then the advertisement works out just exactly as the man intended, a fine lump of a farmer with a grand place comes along and takes the lassie 'thout a penny fortune itself, and she maybe an idle, useless strap, that never done a hand's turn in her life, only sitting in the red ashes reading Charles Garvicey novelettes..."

"Right, Bartle right!" from Dickeen, but no sound at all from Simon Seery, unless you could call a sort of heavy, stifled groan a sound.

"Look at Richard Brinsley Sheridan and his *School for Scandal*. There was a man who knew what he was about. He called his characters, chaps like Joseph Surface and Benjamin Backbite by their proper names, and no disguise whatever—"

"And Charles Dickens! Was there ever such a name for a low-down hypocrite as 'Pecksniff,' but sure there's millions of him in Ireland."

"And as I was saying when you interrupted me," continued Bartle, "sure that's the only kind of literary writing that has any sense in it. Sure we realised it long ago in Ireland. Why, look at us here in Garradrimna for instance! We scarcely ever call a man by the name he was christened. It is always some satirical appellation that reveals his innermost and most peculiar characteristics. Then, d'ye see, the suggestion of the nickname working around him always makes him go and do the things that prove the nickname to have been his true name all the time, and it only the whim of some blackguard mebbe in the first instance.

"Of course the whole mistake occurs through leaving such an arbitrary power in the hands of playwrights and novelists and blackguards, instead of putting it on a properly organised system under Government control, the Government realising the paramount importance of the whole thing and setting up boards of Psychological inquiry in every district, so that everyone would be card-indexed with his proper name. Now wouldn't that be suitable work for highly paid Civil servants instead of having it left to blackguards as in the past to perform unsystematically and indiscriminately. That'd be the way to do it, to give every fellow his correct place, according to his inclinations, in the social scheme. Look at the enormous convenience it would be to everyone, they knowing in consequence where exactly they were standing with everyone else, and the sense of protection it would be to the Government as well, they in turn knowing exactly where they stood with the whole population in general, in the case of Rebellions or declarations of a Republic."

"Begad, aye. Bartle, aye!"

This kind of talk was good enough from Bartle Boyhan, and apparently well up to his usual standard, but it lacked the sounding board of personality, urging to action, such as might be in evidence were Marcus Igoe still here. Then Bill did a queer thing. He thought of Marcus Igoe, deeply and reverently, and looked at the spot where that classical character, as he liked to think of him, had stood, on that lovely evening when he had spoken noble words on his behalf to Rosalind. Then he said suddenly:

"I'm going out to Harbourstown to Marcus Igoe."

"Y'ar like hell," said Simon Seery, with immense disbelief.

"Past the trees, this night and the storm roaring?"

"Along the wild and all the way to Harbourstown?"

"Be the Lard," said Dickeen, "there must be something devilish working to-night."

Bill was deeply silent as he looked once more to the spot where too, all lovely had once stood Rosalind, and there was a smile upon his face as he spoke the last words that were ever heard from him:

"Thou hast hung the mantles for our apparrelling upon golden pegs!"

And then he was gone in the wind and the rain.

Next morning they found him, with the knots all neatly tied, a most artistic hanging, swinging in the wind, unafraid now amongst the trees that had always frightened him... And it was this news, elaborated with lurid detail, that gave Marous Igoe the biggest disturbance of mind that he had experienced since he came to Harbourstown.

They never knew him. They began to say this immediately the body of Bill the Savage was out down and life found to be extinct, and an inquest ordered over the body in Simon Seery's stable. The Coroner made a great deal out of the expression which the dead man had used before three witnesses. He laid special stress on the word "hung." The remaining words of Bill's final speech were taken by the twelve men as merely the gibbering of a maniac in the last stages before his self-inflicted doom, and a well-worded verdict of suicide while temporarily insane returned.

But the thought that, somehow, they had never known him remained to disturb. It arose immediately by way of epitaph, by way, more likely, of a comforting prelude to forgetfulness, by way remotely, as it might be, of pity and charity. After their fashion they would have wished to develop a mood of condolence, although there was no one with whom to condole but themselves, no relative or even distant kinsman, since, so far as anyone knew, Bill had been alone in the world. And yet it became rapidly more and more evident that, although no one could possibly miss him, in some strange way he would be remembered. Indeed, within the narrow confines of this thought, there appeared a danger that his memory would grow, and so be the means of robbing themselves of some of their own immortality when they were dead and gone. They had never known him; that was true, and now there was nothing for them but to be the instruments of the shocking rumour of his death... They were a little in doubt as to whether he should get a funeral.

When the rumour reached Marcus Igoe out in Harbourstown, he knew that there was only one thing he should do ... one thing he must do... He had known well that something astonishing was about to appear in his life for since last night he had been wondering what had happened to him, what electrification of his bones, as he put it, what strange desire to be doing noble and beautiful things...? When he arose there was a feeling upon him that he had known on the morning when he had met death in the fields ... only this was like meeting life. There was an urge upon him to be moving, to be going, and he went hatless far down the road and met "Rebecca at the well."... Her father had heard the story of the suicide and she spoke of the shocking thing... Good God! Poor Bill the Savage dead! ... Dead all his life in Garradrimna and maybe only living now for the first time ... the poor unfortunate devil... There would not be many wanting to take part in his funeral of the man who had died for love of Rosalind Briody ... as Marcus knew now. But he would do it... He would see that Bill should have a wake and funeral and monument and all if need be!

CHAPTER XLVII

IN a little while he was ready for the road, going back to Garradrimna from which he had retired, dressed for the occasion and with plenty of money in his pocket... He found them still in doubt about the funeral, but the sudden enthusiasm consequent upon his appearance had immediate effect. He found himself surrounded, to an extent admiringly in the bar of the Marlay Arms, by witnesses, jurymen, policemen, and all. Even Simon Seery had shaken hands with him ... silently, as befitted the presence of death. He had the whole thing immediately in hand. It was going to be no half-hearted attempt either. By three o'clock in the afternoon the undertaker from Castleconnor had done his part of the work, and, by four o'clock, Marcus had succeeded in causing a public holiday to be proclaimed, as it were, in Garradrimna for the morrow, the day of the funeral.

It was said, perhaps uncharitably, that the crowds that gathered into Garradrimna came rather to see the return of Marcus than the departure of Bill, and it was a great sight, surely, to see Marcus himself, looking failed a bit, perhaps, but grand entirely in his funereal clothes that Margo had insisted upon his buying, and which he had never worn excepting at her own funeral. To see him walking as chief and only principal mourner! Marcus Igoe had returned to Garradrimna, and no doubt the atmosphere of the place would catch him again... He knew, God forgive him for thinking the like in such a solemn moment, that they were thinking this of him... And some of his old sense of combat rose, not without its admixture of sadness now, for here surely was a moment for a man to be having thoughts of final dissolution... And his notion of rising into combat again led him somehow that way.

The thought did not leave him after the interment of Bill; for how could it, seeing that it was nearly like a fair day in Garradrimna, like ould times, as many a man said to another, and simply all because Bill the Savage had hanged himself and he, Marcus Igoe, had declared his intention of attending the funeral, and, what was more, had attended it... Already the mood of combat stirred higher when he looked at them ... yet Garradrimna was much the same, the place was so strong a mearing fence around his life that how could it change? But the thought was upon him still that it had been given to him, of all men, to change it. He was still like a young man with brave ideas of changing the world. But an immutable and far quality had entered into his life.

He had a notion that the many "lives" he had lived here were, in a sense, but a promise of the many future lives he would yet live in various stages which would eventually place Marcus Igoe amongst the stars. There was, in a sense, a link through the office he had been performing to-day, a connection, so to speak, between the Marcus Igoe of this world and him of the next, for, assuredly, there could not be such a break, when you thought of it, between what a man might do round the corner or over the brink or up the stairs, and what he had been doing just before he took the turning or made the jump or did the climb... If only he could formulate a life for himself now that would, in some way, give him a new life or determine the quality of a life beyond and give him immortality. They must be excited because of him while he was still here, and be coming here because of him when he was gone. He had thought out plans of immortality here below, and although they had been infused by genius on the part of the Novelist and on the part of the Sculptor, they were, nevertheless, of the dust, and would pass almost as soon as himself...

It was a great evening in Garradrimna, and he had produced the necessary atmosphere, in each public-house, for nearly everyone to say: "The Lord 'a mercy on him!"— on Bill the Savage who had taken his own life... But at leaving when he had, through dint of his endeavours, to employ Wade's car to drive him out of Garradrimna, he heard everyone say that he looked very done up, but it might merely be preoccupation, if they knew, with trying to think out a complete solution, yet he would laugh to himself now and again, as if some glimmer of a solution had begun to hold his mind ... but, straightway, he appeared puzzled again, as if it were too much for him, so they said, as the car drove away, that he had much the same effect on a body as Bill the Savage, and made a body think quare things about a body's self to look at him.

He slept late next morning but when he awoke his first thought was of the report of Bill's funeral that he had arranged for the local papers, the list of people of all creeds and classes, in whose estimation moryah, the deceased had always occupied a high place! Then he got up, took his breakfast and went out upon the road, but now not as the pale imitation of "the Trojan," not even as Marcus Igoe, but as someone else, some other entity. It was well described by "Rebecca at the well" "as if he was something not right I can tell you."

"Garradrimna and the three swallows," said her father laconically, "I know that kind of stuff, and that's all that's wrong with him."

"But he's different, somehow, you wouldn't know him."

"Wouldn't you indeed?"

"I tell you he's different."

"Well, I'll see him then."

So Rebecca's father went down the road to investigate the change in Marcus Igoe.

"I'm thinking of making my will, d'ye know," said Marcus, directly that Martin asked him how he had enjoyed the funeral.

"That's bad — is it altogether as bad as that?" said Martin.

"Aye, I've seen things at last. I've seen through things... "

And then silence. Not the well-known Marcus Igoe at all, the man of parts and words.

"I see..."

"I saw it all somehow yesterday walking after the hearse. I saw something, I say I saw something..."

Then silence again.

"Begad ... so you're going to make your will?"

"I am!"

"Begad ...!"

"I saw her always as a shining thing, and I wanted ever her lovely little feet to light upon soft places... I thought and thought... And often when her picture used to be hanging before my eyes ... that is what I used to be thinking about even when I was standing lonely at the counter, looking at Marcus Igoe, letting on to see him, maybe, and I thinking of her, seeing her all the time. And to keep her always, her handsome image in my mind. How was I going to do it? Now, how was I going to do it? To take her and keep her for myself. Ah no, only to be always looking at her ... looking at her, seeing her as I first saw all lovely women, all lovely things... Did they want me to do everything that blemished beauty? They did! They did! I might have been all right if I had painted carts, and drays and wheelbarrows with yellow ochre and Prussian blue, if I had done up the fronts of public-houses and huxters' shops, if I had gone to my devotions and attended funerals, if I hadn't been afraid of voices that were always speaking to me out of the darkness. The wind and the rain and the sighing trees... Oh God, the terrible *things* that grinned at me that night I made my departure to Harbourstown with the moon shining, the racing, windy moon. Beyond the turrets of Clunnen Castle more trees and darkness and beyond that again, in the heart of Harbourstown ... the gorgeous character of Marcus Igoe."

"God, it must have been an awful day yesterday, at that poor unfortunate ruffian's funeral," said Martin, unable to keep from interrupting in his total inability to understand.

"—For I knew that I would solve the secret of Marcus Igoe if ever I came to Harbourstown... See down into that noble character whom they had never been able to understand, who had lived his life like in a dream, appearing as if he had done things that he had never done at all... No one seeing the things he had done ... the thing he was... and then the disguise of the money ... the fairy story of his money... Mebbe it is that I'd have put my eye on him there and he considering what he was going to do with it. Where her bright can caught the sun and made a dancing speck of light as from a looking glass and she going the road ... thinking of her and my eyes piercing him ... getting at the thought that he was supposed to be going to leave all his money to her.

"But from the time he came into contact with me I was always seeing through him and he knew it ... controlling his actions, making him do wild or grand things as the case might be ... trying to bring him back to himself... to the sweetness of looking at golden girls in muslin frocks on summer roads... And I'd have stopped him, surely, from doing what was on his mind to do... His lovely friend ... to think of spoiling her... When I remember all the people in Garradrimna that shocking things should be done to with the money. To do a most extraordinary thing was what I wanted. To get him to leave all his money to his enemies instead of to his dear little friend, to the people of Garradrimna, instead of to 'Rebecca at the well.'..."

It had dawned at length through the thick mind of Martin Ivory, as something which even now he was not quite sure could be true, that Marcus had taken this way of telling him, of putting an end to his expectations through his daughter Rebecca, to whom anyone would think Marcus had taken a real fancy. The devil wasn't mad at all, but absolutely sane in his madness. His period in Harbourstown had been a failure so far as the Ivorys were concerned. The kindness of his little daughter had been misdirected... Now, wouldn't anyone think...? What was he going to do with himself at all...? The thick man could not stand it longer, so he left the madman or whatever you'd call him, to his madness or whatever it was, there on the middle of the morning road.

CHAPTER XLVIII

WHATEVER survived of the consciousness of Marcus Igoe was dim, mysterious and incalculable, but there was some part of him remaining that had not become altogether Bill the Savage. And it was this part that contemplated the other part of him for days and days... It grew, at length, to seem that it was really the soul of Bill that was looking out of the flesh and qualities of Marcus Igoe at the world, at Garradrimna which was all the world he had ever known, and was maybe enough for any man to have known, when one had gone into it from all sides, as he had done... The quiet eyes that had looked upon it, long-suffering, had in the sense that had lain behind them come to sublimity, but it might be a struggle still with all that remained of Marcus Igoe to do the thing as it should be done according to his real nature.

But maybe the soul of Bill the Savage had been part of his real nature all the time, standing only just a little aloof from him as he himself was standing a little aloof from all that remained of Marcus Igoe now. Bill had been his contemporary, as old as himself, an onlooker of all his adventures from the very beginning. He remembered him standing in the street leaning against some corner looking at the figure of Marcus in the distant past at Hunt meets in Garradrimna ... looking at him with that wan, quiet smile, pitying him perhaps if the truth were known ... following his career of philandering ... seeing him at length married to Margo and collapsed from importance and appearance into poverty, yet never noticing it, treating him just the same, with the same quiet sense of pity … seeing him rise again and being not surprised or envious, only going about with his own vision wrapping him round to the end.

Yes, Bill the Savage had been most truly his closest companion down the years, even to the extent of becoming a part of himself … more than a part of himself when he thought of the way he felt now… When he thought of himself he felt a kind of pity for the Marcus Igoe who was now nearly no more, who would soon be no more. Yes, he was having thought of his contemporaries, for it was in their minds that his memory was fixed, but when all of them were gone where would he be then? What more would he be than a wisp of wind blowing over Harbourstown? So he was having thought of those who best knew all that he had been, those custodians, for the time being, of the memory that was himself. He was thinking, well to the forefront of all that remained of Marcus Igoe, of his most distinguished contemporary, Charles Delamere, the solicitor, that cogent man who said so little, but who was of such potency in the countryside… Another interview with him was beginning to be overdue… It would be, in a sense, the most important interview he had yet had with him.

It was the purpose of it, how exactly he should determine the quality of it, that had troubled him for so long, far longer than anyone around him in Harbourstown realised although they thought they did. For if he arose early and went along the road, as was his wont, laughing and pondering to himself, he would see people taking notice of him, and knew that they were excited by some suspicion, some half realisation that at last he was surely thinking it out—his will. If the smoke of any of the houses in Harbourstown had not yet begun to curl upward of a morning before his eyes … he felt that surely some of them must be lying in bed thinking it out too—his will. That he had thought it out to some extent was apparent in his outburst to the father of 'Rebecca at the well,' on the morning when he had met Martin Ivory and felt the change beginning to run through his personality...

From the moment when he had begun to consider the final disposition of his wealth amongst his enemies rather than amongst his friends, thought of his great particular friend, the girl who was the daughter of his daughter in a far-back vision, had occupied him anxiously, she being immediately the one he was most anxious to save from the disaster of money... But then they were all his enemies if you liked to look at it that way, and his fortune, big though it was, would be but as a drop in the ocean scattered over all of them ... making no appreciable difference to any of them, or in any of them... Then how could one make a selection for purposes of torture in terms of some of the passages with which he had already proposed to embellish his will:

"I have realised, just now, before I sign these lines which direct the way I am to leave it behind, that wealth is but a sorry reward for man's labour and discomfort here below... And as I should not be expected to leave this world without effecting some final vengeance on my enemies ... so strangely different are my views of wealth from the long accepted view of the world in general that the manner of my bequests should really appear as a merciful staying of my hand. Yet that is not my feeling at all, since I now definitely think of all wealth as the greatest curse with which a man may be afflicted. It is even thus that I wish to afflict them. So, therefore, it is to those who have been my greatest enemies in this life that I bequeath the whole of my fortune, in the fervent and firm hope that it may be to them, through the length of their days, the curse and torment it has been to me.

"Particularly to ———" And here, lost for a suitable name to insert, he paused and thought how unworthy of him really were the foregoing words. How untrue to all he had been, to all he hoped to remain in the next series of his lives... It had not been such a curse and torment after all: he had had good fun out of it... The sudden realisation brought him doubts, and the thought that even if he inserted the name of Simon Seery, for instance, the shrewd and powerful man, would, doubtless, find means of defeating him, the bald head between both hands bent low to the counter in immense concentration upon the problem of turning the money, after all, to his comfort and enjoyment, particularly when that pair of devils, who might have produced the necessary disturbance of any plan of his, Bill the Savage and Marcus Igoe, would, by that time, be both no more... You couldn't risk it with a man like Simon Seery... In fact, you could not risk it with any of them, his enemies, the people of Garradrimna.

It was better, rather finer to be thinking of the comic side of things... He thought of the story of himself, "The Comedian," that he had read in Andy Delahunt's, and it was some such solution he began to have hopes of evolving... Like the gods looking down from their high windy seats, he would like to be looking down—if a fellow could have it that way—on some comical sort of performance going on in Garradrimna always, the kind of thing he had been the means of producing himself from time to time... That would be some sort of achievement for a man to have added to his life, carrying it on to the next, and leaving some reflection in it of his survival here below. But how could it be done? That was the question. He gave his days to anxious cogitation.

It would have to be another meeting with Charles Delamere, a last and more triumphant appearance in a scene in which he had always triumphed... Yes, this would have to be his greatest and most perfect interview. He felt something of the artist rising in him, the thought and dream of one monumental achievement, a perfect moment superimposed upon all his many "lives." Ah yes, this was the dream of doing the ultimate fine thing such as had filled the mind of Bill the Savage. It was in a sense to be a perfect collaboration between them, such as might never come again out of Garradrimna, could never come, for the purposes of it were deathless beyond description. They would know then whether Garradrimna had defeated him and driven him into retirement... He would look down at them for evermore with wise eyes, with big eyes of pity, and the thing that had troubled him as Marcus Igoe could trouble him no more.

CHAPTER XLIX

AT last the great day came. His plans for the future were fully matured and prepared on the side of the comic, and an appointment had been arrange with Charles Delamere... He wondered what his solicitor would think of it. But of a certainty, so carefully had he planned it, there could be no demur on Charles Delamere's part, for it was, in a way, an arrangement which must appear most satisfying to him, too. A will, and, thereafter, a period of fees and that sort of thing would be the end of Charles Delamere's connection with him, as well as the end of the money. But surely Charles Delamere must have had better hopes of him than that, and maybe he was not going to be disappointed, for it might be something more than a will that he was going to make.

He had made the most exhaustive preparations sending for the solicitor's beautiful car, so that he might do it in real style, going to the greatest pains with his personal appearance, even to the extent of putting on his funereal clothes ... feeling fine as he sped in the road ... passing splendidly up the street of Castleconnor ... gliding softly to the solicitor's door ... feeling reminiscent of the day he had come here for the fortune ... remembering the eyes of Bill the Savage as they had observed him at his setting forth and at his coming home to Garradrimna upon that occasion.

"Why, I thought you were lost out there in Harbourstown," said Mr. Delamere, dropping suitably into the vernacular of the

246

countryside, for this was Thursday, the market day, when an ordinary easy County Meath manner was the best one for his particular brand of client.

"No, I was only making up my mind about it properly," said Marcus.

The solicitor scented trouble. Making up his mind about what? he thought. Some other damnable plan?

"I'm going to give you less trouble this time than ever before. It's not often a man like me resolves to make his final settlement the easiest thing ever you heard."

"Not often perhaps, but did I hear you say *final* settlement? Tut, tut, Mr. Igoe ... you might easily put off this day a long while yet," said the solicitor comfortingly, although a little nervously returning to the grand manner, in deference to the distinction of his client in an important and anxious moment...

"All the same there's no time like the present. I was thinking about it this long time, and as a certain famous man of Garradrimna once said, 'thinking is bad wit.'"

"A will then?"

"Well not exactly what you'd call a Will, a Bequest, perhaps more correctly an Endowment."

"Excellent, I knew you'd come to a better frame of mind about the whole thing eventually."

"Better than what?"

"Than wasting your money on monuments or empty houses."

"That remains to be seen... But it's purely for the fun of seeing it working out that I'm going to arrange it the way I am."

"To take effect before—"

"No, *after* my regretted demise, some years hence."

"I hope so."

"You do?"

"I mean I hope very many years hence."

"If at all!"

"If, as you say, at all!"

"Mebbe not at all."

Charles Delamere looked blank and dismayed before the jubilant smile of Marcus, who could not help feeling some sense of his legal adviser's inferiority for the moment, a maddening realisation for the other—on a market day.

"And what, might I ask, do you propose to endow?"

"Myself."

"I see..." They were getting near it now, whatever it was, so Mr. Delamere thought it safer merely to say, "I see," pausing for a moment before again saying, "I see," even more blankly, for he didn't, so far, see anything or any sense in his client at all.

"I must go on in Garradrimna."

"Although you may be in another, shall I say, sphere."

"Exactly—looking down at myself going on in Garradrimna. They would say they missed me for a few days, of course. But I'm not going to be missed, I'm not going to let myself be missed at all."

"But how do you propose to survive the—I personally, for one, hope you will—the stage of mortal dissolution."

"My money, what else?"

"Well, I've heard of money doing many things, Mr. Igoe, but I have yet to learn that it has ever done that."

"No one ever went the right way about it. They always approached it from the serious angle entirely."

"But I think it is of its nature not unrelated to seriousness, Mr. Igoe, and I hope you will agree."

"No, I read a story one time in Dublin, by a great character, a Novelist, no less, about myself ... well, no matter about the story. I got the idea from it that's all, and I have thought of it several ways..."

Here Mr. Delamere leaned back, tapping his smiling lips with the pen, for he knew that Marcus had, quite definitely, settled down to talk now ... although there was some curious difference in his manner, sufficient even to disturb the equanimity of a family solicitor... Extraordinary ways some of them had in the country... This Marcus Igoe had given him the devil's own amount of trouble.

"But I want to see if it's really possible for a man to have a look at himself, and the result of himself, after he has shuffled off this mortal coil, that is to die and not to die."

"That is the question," said the solicitor smiling somewhat feebly. "It has been done in novels and plays."

"Never, not what I'm going to do. It's the most absolutely original thing that any man ever thought of doing. I'm going to die; I'll be actually dead before the thing happens, and gone over to have a look at myself going on. Not so much myself, as the conception of myself, for what are we all, Mr. Delamere, but our own conceptions of ourselves? I never saw that properly till Bill the Savage hung himself."

There was something in the words of Marcus and his manner now which frankly puzzled Mr. Delamere ... something that was subtle—or mad—beyond realisation, and which made him thoroughly uneasy.

"Have I not, tried various 'lives' in my own one little bit of a life? What I want is the image I created here to keep on living and keep going on, with Garradrimna and all about it that made me what I am still going on too. I have loved my native village more than words can tell, or how else could I have hated it so much for what it would not be? A godly place, something so lovely that it would give one nearly a feeling of music round one's soul to look at it. But it is my hope that I may be able to make a place like that of it some day ... and it will be with this firm and earnest belief in Garradrimna that I propose my plan..."

Charles Delamere thought he could detect a flicker of the well-known smile of Marcus Igoe, as he drew the paper to him and poised his pen to make notes of his client's instructions.

"I have brought it down to the choice of two alternatives. The first is representative of many notions of the kind which I have had, and it is simply this that, with the income accruing from the capital sum invested, which is now pretty tidy, a cobbler, such as I unfortunately became at a certain period of my life, is to be subsidised, *in secula seculorum,* in Garradrimna, that he is to behave as much as possible like myself, for instance, to work as hard as I had to work, and never to think that he can go around at any time like a gentleman, even though he is subsidised, and whenever he feels like that, and thinks he has had enough of playing that part of me, he is to be fired out of it and the position is to go to the next deserving applicant..."

"You have rejected this notion?" timidly questioned Charles Delamere, somewhat painfully in the presence of the pretty complete return to earlier-character Marcus Igoe, which was embodied in the suggestion.

"I have, simply because I have thought of a better one."

"Oh, I see."

"And this is where you'll come in, too, my sweet fellow. This is where the Endowment is going to begin. There must be three Trustees to see that the money is spent exactly as I desire, and after yourself I was a bit puzzled for a while about the selection of the other two."

"Solid men," ventured Mr. Delamere.

"No, not too solid," replied Marcus. "Not men of the earth earthy, not, for example, as might be usual in such a case, men with a stake in the country like Simon Seery or John Higgins. But I have left nothing to chance, and I have the men in my mind, your co-trustees, two men who must have thought I had forgotten them this long time, although I hadn't, for I was merely thinking out some proper way of honouring them and distinguishing them— Bartle Boyhan and Dickeen Crosbie, two men who have lived all their lives without ever doing a hand's turn in Garradrimna."

"My God," said Charles Delamere, groaning inwardly and saying, with an uncontrollable relapse into the Thursday provincial manner, "them two?"

"Them two, exactly, observers and critics of my youthful prime, men with a knowledge of me and therefore most suitable men ... men who have steadily observed, down the years, the course of the various aspects of me, that is my one only self presently."

Mr. Delamere did not know what to make of this, so he just waited patiently for more...

"They'll be the very best advisers you can possibly have in the course of any action you may find it necessary to pursue if you are to retain the administration of my fortune."

Mr. Delamere winced a little but waited, playing with the pen.

"They'll be the men to spot the right material for the character I have in view, the men to make him continue to be the right material when they get hold of him in Garradrimna..."

This was still all very vague, but Marcus presently continued:

"My money is to be invested in such a way as will bring in as much of a yearly income as will correspond exactly with what I had to spend when I began life as a young man of means and leisure. It is to be devoted towards financing the enjoyment and the upkeep of the most promising specimen of a second Marcus

Igoe that can be selected by the three Trustees aforesaid. This young man, whoever he may be, is to effect a deed poll, if that's what you call the legal formula (Mr. Delamere nodded his head) and advertise that he will be in future known by the style and title of Marcus Igoe.

"Should his original inclinations run astray he will retire from the Marcus Igoe-ship, and you'll see that he does it damn quick, too, and the next most promising specimen will have then to be selected by the three Trustees hereinbefore mentioned, and so on… Should a perfect replica of myself be at length discovered, that is to say, myself exactly, in all my moods and tenses again, the capital sum is to be handed over in its entirety to him and the Endowment as such lapses. For I, that is, my fully resurrected self, will be well able to do what I think best with it, if there should be any of it left at all at my second going."

This was certainly more than Charles Delamere bargained for to-day, even from Marcus Igoe… There were little beads of perspiration on his forehead which the effort of concentration, the effort to realise or understand, had produced.

But Marcus was not finished even yet:

"And, if one or other of the Trustees should drop out, through dint of the effort to administer me, so to speak, the surviving two are to select another trustworthy man with a clear knowledge and appreciation of the institution known as Marcus Igoe, so that he may bring his enthusiasm for me to bear upon whatever further selections of myself which may be necessary. The sooner all this happens for the sake of Garradrimna the better, for I hear that it hasn't been quite itself this long time, missing me … but still not altogether devoid of my presence since it has had no conception of what I am going to do eventually with myself or my money, and that, in itself has been, I am sure, a great excitement for it all the time… But it will recover its real personality with the beginning of me again, and it will never be quite certain, will it, what the shadow of me on this earth is going to do next, and I'll have the best of sport looking on at it all, until such time as I'll absolutely have to return, mebbe, and put an end to the farce, in a more exhaustive and suitable manner, if even that should be necessary.

"Now, Mr. Delamere, I've given you a rough, but fairly complete, outline of what I want you to do for me. Will you have that drafted in the proper legal manner by next Thursday and ready for sealing and signing, delivering and witnessing?"

"Certainly, Mr. Igoe," said Mr. Delamere with a kind of desolate alacrity, making unintelligible scrawls, which he took to be notes, upon his pad.

He stumbled rather than rose from his chair to show Marcus out of the office.

"Certainly ... everything ready next Thursday... Fixed up perfectly ... quite," he stammered, showing Marcus into his own car.

CHAPTER L

THERE was a happy smile upon the face of Marcus as he turned out of Castleconnor. He would go the long way home this time, as they did with funerals, do a big round... over half the County Meath nearly, if he could keep the driver to it... It was a lovely autumn evening. The car moved swiftly beyond green fields and swept the sudden purple of the bog of Ballycullen. There was a touch of gold upon the autumn hedgerows. His mind was like that this evening, green and purple and gold, full of a rich sense of immortal quality, like that of some king who had done well in battle going home... But was he not more than any king, and his complete career more magnificent than any reign, for had he not vanquished life itself? Green fields again and a glimpse of low, distant hills, and cattle lowing... words out of books coming back to him, noble thoughts and lines of poetry... That young fellow, John Cassidy, the schoolmaster's son, had done this better than any of them... this sense or whatever you'd call it of the fields of Meath. This heart-melting country-side! What about that poem he had called "Cattle in Meath"? The lines came easily to his memory in the opulence of his mood:

"I wonder why the cattle call
To reach the heavens far above
While round them flow the fields and all The
lovely quiet that they love.

And yet at eve the cattle call;
So lonely does their lowing sound
Where, dim, the evening shadows fall
To fill the world that's wheeling round.
Or do they think of all their kind
Who trod these fields of grass of yore
Or does their calling bring to mind
The echo of the great herd's roar
That sweeps the world in wilder climes,
And now they grieve that they grew tame
And, grieving, do they low by times,
And wonder whence their kindness came
 That they should give their milk at eve,
And spring so fine for man to fall.
For this, maybe, the cattle grieve,
For this at eve the cattle call."

Nice things in it, he thought, but lonely ... lonely like the fields of Meath, and why was he remembering such a thing this evening?

He must have been a long time driving ... dreaming... through the evening when he realised at length that he was drawing near home.

A few lights were breaking out upon the sides of the gently hilly country around Harbourstown. In the half light that was falling down, he saw a few pine trees stealing lonesomely away across the hills... Peering out he could see some of the men of Harbourstown coming home from their day's labour ... they knew nothing of the tumult in his mind, poor, quiet fellows that they were. Near the road, in the demesne land of Captain Ludlow who had married Olive Fetherstonhaugh he saw an old herdsman moving with an air of providence through the cattle... Captain Ludlow's cattle had reminded him of something, of someone else, of another day... This road, too, he had travelled going to and coming from the great breach of promise action in Dublin... Lost loves! But he was not really thinking of such things now. His whole consciousness had flowed, as it were, into the mood of dream... Curious wisps of imagination flitted across his mind ... like the poem he had remembered outside Castleconnor, lonesome things, thoughts that suggested endings ... words out of a book by some poet that the schoolmaster's son had lent him. That was a queer jumble of a thought, too, with wild notions in it, not at all like the whole of his own mind this evening.

"With the last breath all is done: joy, love, sorrow, macaroni, the theatre, lime-trees, raspberry drops, the power of human relations, gossip, the barking of dogs, champagne."

The moon was beginning to rise big and misty beyond Garradrimna and, far off, already, the answering barking of the dogs... High over Garradrimna, there was one star. His head bent to his chest and muttering to himself, so that the driver might not hear, he called it "Margo of the Skies."... There was that to be said of him anyhow—he had remained faithful to the memory of Margo. No, that poet fellow was wrong all the same... lonesome devils, the whole of them... There were ways, there were plans, and he had surely thought of a good one. It had left even Charles Delamere speechless with admiration... Now, just past two fields of corn, was his quiet house. The light in the upper storey made it like a little lighthouse above the golden sea of ripening grain...

Quiet... and still quieter in the house... A great stillness, and just himself laughing in the very middle of it... laughing, Marcus Igoe laughing... yet, in the long curious silence after each laugh, rising and looking in the overmantel at himself... Seeing the sad, quiet smile of suffering above the mouth, the smile of Bill the Savage...

Charles Delamere would have all prepared by Thursday, but there were a few other instructions that he might have to think of still... All the worry that was Marcus Igoe, the thing which was that part of himself still, must be cleared and settled... He wanted to be free and quiet... Bill the Savage was free and quiet now... There could be lovely days then as his spirit hovered over these fields at rest, when, most truly, he had made them Harbourstown. The old men would bless his memory for such addition to their place, and say a prayer for the repose of his soul ... or wish him good health and a long life, but no ... he was going to a place where there were no years.

Every instruction must be handed to Charles Delamere. If he died any time shortly there might be mistakes made, but he would make every provision against them, down to his own very obituary notice for the papers. You never could tell how they might spoil even the words of that...

He took a sheet of paper and wrote, without having to pause to think of a word, the following:

> IGOE.—(A blank for the date, whenever it might be.) At his residence, Harbourstown, Co. Meath, Marcus Igoe, only son of the late Denis and Delia Igoe, in the (a blank again) year of his age. R.I.P. Deeply regretted (he laughed quietly as he wrote these words). Funeral at 2.30, Summer time (It would be nice to die in summer when Meath was greenest!), to-morrow from the Church of St. Lonan to the Family Burial Ground, Garradrimna. American papers please copy.

A curious prelude, surely, to a comic beginning... But melancholy would not take him even at the last... nor even in his lonely mood at this late hour of the evening... Yet, on the point of going to bed, when he pondered the notice more calmly, and with something less of laughter moving him, it appeared just a little too much like an ending and he was not ending... He had arranged that most cleverly... So this notice appeared of a sudden to be out of place... He laughed again... and paused, candle in hand, at the foot of the stairs... Another surprise for Charles Delamere and something that would suggest his real beginning... He put down the candle and, coming back into the room, began to write another announcement. This, instead, was what he would hand to Charles Delamere... It would give him a bit of a shock, keep him in suspense a little longer. It would have to be put in a sealed envelope, to be opened only at his death... The Death of Marcus Igoe... He would be dead and so unable... oh yes, he would be able to see Charles Delamere's face, as well as the face of all Garradrimna, when it appeared in the papers... Of course, you had to pay for a thing like this, just as if it were an obituary notice, and so it would be inserted without doubt, in company what the fashionable people and the professional people, like doctors and surgeons and dentists, got in about themselves from time to time. ... Maybe it would put a little touch of the fear of God into the usually so undisturbed countenance of Charles Delamere when his solicitor came eventually to see it... He read it over and over again, smiling pleasantly at this final effort of his foresight:

"Mr. Marcus Igoe, preparatory to taking up his residence in Garradrimna again, has left Harbourstown for an indefinite period."

Yes, that was the touch about it he liked best—for an *indefinite* period.

THE END.

Dublin, New Year's Eve, 1928.

AFTERWORD
by Michael McDonnell

If one thought, letting cold reality into one's mind, instead of dreaming, one was likely to remember that, by hurriedly adopting a means of release from the life he had lived, he would be, in a way, confessing the failure of his life. He had not accomplished his twisting of Garradrimna into complete accordance with its own squint... And he was seeing now that it might not be so easy for a man to relinquish the dream of an ideal that has given him much anxiety, and into which he has put much earnest endeavour, even in the very presence of a certain way of relief from every trouble of the mind... Maybe that poor devil, the Savage, going about with the evening wind shivering through him was still warmed by his dream, which he might never hope to achieve, but which he had not surrendered, however mad it might be.

The Various Lives of Marcus Igoe (1929)
Brinsley MacNamara

Re-reading *The Various Lives of Marcus Igoe* today, one appreciates how acutely self-conscious Brinsley MacNamara was in this ambitious reassessment of his life and literary career.

In 1928, new editions of his *The Valley of the Squinting Windows* and *The Mirror in the Dusk*, each well received and reviewed, spurred MacNamara's resumption of earlier inclinations that expanded the range of Irish fiction to accommodate the labyrinth of one's ego. This renewed curiosity led primarily to exploration of one man's perception of reality and its incompatibility with his inner, delusional world. With characteristic defiance and iconoclasm Mac-Namara carefully examined and re-examined his peculiar literary milieu; he properly acknowledged his astonished intuitions and abandoned derivative narrative conventions to herald the cautious postmodern emergence of an existential Irish meta-fiction.

Resolutely, MacNamara took a discriminating look at the man he had become since the idealistic, ambitious days of his early novels. In so doing, he placed himself at great emotional and intellectual risk. To his credit, he honestly admitted the gap between the earnest dreamer, the disillusioned romantic of *The Irishman* (written in 1916 but not published until 1920) and the successful playwright and citizen of Dublin he had become. A significant portion of *The Various Lives of Marcus Igoe* concerns itself with MacNamara's personal reproach and chastisement at having allowed himself to descend into the life he had so expressly rejected in *The Irishman*. In that earliest of his novels (using another pseudonym, 'Oliver Blyth'), MacNamara's youthful desecration of pretentious, post-Synge Dublin, with its loud twaddle of idle, would-be authors, was sadly prophetic of a redounding pub literati. *The Irishman* was an early, unheeded warning to future generations that they disdain self-admiring, insular complacency.

Pursuing the methodology which he had utilized in his last published novel, *The Mirror in the Dusk* (1921), MacNamara assimilated several previously written short stories into *The*

Various Lives of Marcus Igoe to elaborate its major themes. A difficult novel to read and to follow (Bertie Smylie, then editor of *The Irish Times*, referred to it as the novel Brinsley wrote back to front), *The Various Lives of Marcus Igoe* meanders casually by design among the worlds of Garradrimna, Dublin, and Illusion. Conveniently pigeonholed as a fantasy, this novel nonetheless admits those rural tensions which had always preoccupied MacNamara — accidentally, he remains at odds with Garradrimna's inhabitants, with their legacy of petty vices and spiteful villainies. Seriously convinced of the ultimate sadness of human destiny, MacNamara occasionally smiles here to keep from weeping, but a shuffling sigh becomes the audible insinuation in the novel. *The Various Lives of Marcus Igoe*, for all it was dismissed as merely a comic-fantasy, is really far more drolly melancholy for that charge alone than Brinsley MacNamara's other novels.

By 1928, MacNamara had developed a speculative philosophy very much in sympathy with his reading of the Spanish philosopher and writer, Miguel de Unamuno y Jugo, called 'Unamuno.' Unamuno's *The Tragic Sense of Life*, first translated into English in 1921, contains several ideas with which MacNamara was personally in great sympathy. 1921 was a pivotal year for both Ireland and Brinsley MacNamara. He had been perilously near death from rheumatic fever that same year and spent a lengthy period of time in convalescence and contemplative recovery. Also, On December 6th a desperate Michael Collins agreed to 'The Treaty,' saying 'I just signed my death warrant' — in London. And James Joyce was 'elaboratively' reading and re-writing galleys of *Ulysses* — in Paris. *The Tragic Sense of Life*, an essential text for MacNamara, reveals that Unamuno was an existentialist long before that mode of thought became popular in

European thought. Leo Hamalian and Edmond L. Volpe, commenting upon *The Tragic Sense of Life*, write:

> Though he assailed rationalists before it was common to do so, he also saw that "the demands of reason are fully as imperious as those of life. The most potent urge of life," he says, "is not only to continue living, but to transcend the mortality of the flesh." This urge is the origin of religion and the spur of all individual endeavor. The artist... creates out of his anxiety to perpetuate his name and fame, "to grasp at least the shadow of immortality."...
>
> Hence, the only really burning problem for man is death and the possibility of life after death. The will to live, vital and affirmative, hungers after such immortality, but reason, unable to rise higher than scepticism, discounts it. Whether he knows it or not, man must live with the agony of this conflict. This agony is a necessary condition of existence. Yet, it is out of this transcendental pessimism that Unamuno creates "a temporal and terrestrial optimism." In his will to live, which survives the onslaught of reason, he finds the basis of belief — or rather of the effort to believe, which he regards as the same thing.

I propose that the artistic personality which MacNamara explores in *The Various Lives of Marcus Igoe* is his own. Because he was working out intimate philosophical problems of a confusing and ultimately unsolvable nature in this novel, the plot deliberately mirrors that confusion and frustration. A major concern of the author is that of mutability and how best to survive death — how best to be immortalized. As Marcus Igoe, Brinsley Mac-

Namara confronts man's dilemma of defining himself between the celestial and the secular, the ephemeral and the eternal; he explores the necessity for man to forsake his neat, parochial assurances in order to pursue his true nature: "Where was the real Marcus Igoe now? Aye, where was he indeed? He would often set out, as it were, to find his own lost self, wherever it was gone to in Garradrimna."

The initial difficulty in addressing the novel lies in determining the reader's point of view. Precisely where are we when Marcus appears to be creating recollections of former experiences? Are we inside his mind? Where is Marcus when we are apparently off visiting one of his many dream projections of exorbitantly non-existent, unrealized lives? Where is the 'dramatic now' of this novel? Where is Marcus Igoe's reality — in his mind exclusively? Simply, how, when, and where does the reader ever confidently enter this fiction? Whom do we trust?

In *The Various Lives of Marcus Igoe*, MacNamara's *mise-en-scène* looks neurotically distorted; a silent, patient cast uneasily await scripts; they appear to inhabit a seemingly familiar, rural Irish village, though coldly refracted or stylized here. The whole arrangement might presuppose an audience of strangers watching and dreaming this novel independently, enjoined at last to identify as one with the narrator. *The Various Lives of Marcus Igoe* transcends its Irishness by appearing to be 'in' but not necessarily 'of' or 'about' Ireland. The novel's disillusion and intellectual doubts are thus allowed to imbue us all with their insolent, immortal misgivings. The influences of this chilling, extra perspective are cinematic to me. In the 1920s, German cinematic expressionism seemed to demonstrate a Freudian conjecture about altering states of mind, taken to the point where directors maneuvered and rearranged external reality to reflect a clinical, inner reality. I am thinking of Robert Wiene's *The Cabinet of Dr.*

Caligari (1919) or F.W. Murnau's *The Last Laugh* (1924), for example. In these early films, we experience actuality and imagination simultaneously, an unseen presence constantly being implied by a shifting camera. An insinuated, manipulative intelligence became cinema's central mystery, a visible portent of some powereful, unknowable world.

Moving from some real to some illusory realm, with only the vaguest rehearsal and without reliable exposition or perceptible alteration in style or tone, makes this a most demanding fiction. Such liberties evoke the ambiguous recollections associated with dreams. Consequently, *The Various Lives of Marcus Igoe* must be read with full, if bemused, attention. After all, we submissively descend into an implausible, evanescent, gentrified sub-culture. Linear suggestions of truth seem inconsequential; our spatial ramblings are effortless; spontaneous and spectral; indeterminate and soundless. Unaccountably, we seem always attired in appropriate *fin de siècle* fashion. I suggest that reality and illusion here, form and content, weave as nebulously as MacNamara intended. Lacking a Vergil, much forbearance is required.

Marcus Igoe's determination to survive his death seemingly reflects MacNamara's apprehensions as he faced his fortieth year. In the light of what he had to know was the perishability of his dramatic work, Dublin boulevardier MacNamara seems frightened by realization of that work's vanishing literary relevance. His anguish may have brooded upon questions of life and death; the vestigial horrors of a Catholic conscience vacillating among 'then,' 'now,' and 'forever'; or endured a more primal anxiety with our whirling transience. I believe a fearful pursuit of artistic commemoration impelled MacNamara's reversion to the more intuitive and reclusive, if less public, genre of fiction.

My interpretation of *The Various Lives of Marcus Igoe* proposes that this novel is an aesthetic, intellectual dialectic, a picaresque novel of the imagination. It endures as a meditation and evaluation by Brinsley MacNamara of his literary reputation, his peculiar genius and their joint prospects for immortality. The existential quandaries that beset Marcus Igoe, his ephemeral solutions for them and his lifelong grievance with the dim, disfigured Garradrimnians, are reflections of similar preoccupations in MacNamara's life.

When Marcus fatefully ruminates, 'There was no doubt about it; one way or another, Garradrimna had made bits of him. No matter what he might have done, it would, most likely have made bits of him,' MacNamara is musing on the original of Garradrimna and his relationship to that notorious village: Delvin, Co. Westmeath, MacNamara's native place. When Marcus ponders his own inconsequence, 'He had done a poor mean thing with his life, and the thought of it continually burned into his mind as punishment,' it is not difficult to extend that sentiment to MacNamara and his own estimate of himself in the late 20s; or, projecting much further as I feel MacNamara would have us do, it is not difficult to understand the plight of Marcus Igoe and Brinsley MacNamara as the plight of every man.

In none of Marcus's extensions of himself do things really work out any better for him than they have in his actual life, the imagination of an unsuccessful person pitiably tending to produce unsuccessful alter egos. Marcus pursues lost time not as it was, nor even as it seems to have been but, more despairingly, as it never could have been. Though, how unusual is it for a person to fabricate a romantic past, successful or unsuccessful, to ease the memory of youthful insignificance or the paralysis of dull reality?

We engage this novel as if by accident. We appear to be late, shamelessly uninvited, certainly strangers, though not unwelcome. We are as incidental intruders, surprising another's canvas, our uncomfortable silence mute witness to his repetitive, bounded scepticism. There is such an unworldly, surrealistic quality to the novel's ambience that several readings are required to determine the tangible, dramatic circumstances of the plot. One must have patience with MacNamara's unhurried, non-linear dissemination of hard evidence. However, gradually and deservedly we are richly rewarded.

In John Banville's *Birchwood*, how many pages does it take the narrator to explain this cryptic line from the first page: 'When I opened the shutters in the summerhouse by the lake a trembling disc of sunlight settled on the charred circle on the floor where Granny Godkin exploded'? One must be willing to participate as indulgently in MacNamara's novel as in Banville's, comprehending symmetrical conformations rather than demanding traditional, " 'Listen now, let ye listen, this is what happened and I coming over here from—' " exposition. Our perseverance ultimately provides a focus for unraveling, if not for solutions then for dignified commiseration. One does not casually participate in this fiction — one assembles it with glad misgivings.

The reference to his shop intimately surrounding all that Marcus's life had been and to the pleasures experienced in his mind, furthers my belief that the only reality in the entire novel is that Marcus Igoe is an aging, philosophizing cobbler probably married to a childless Margo. When Marcus describes the monument of himself he plans to have erected in Garradrimna, he describes it in these telling terms:

> ... the figure of Marcus Igoe, as he used to be
> and always was, with the last between his knees
> and the sole of the boot uppermost with a half

finished track of nails around it;... my head bent
like my mind inside upon my business that was
never anybody else's business, and a fierce, determined expression upon my face...

The confusion in this predicament with identity and seem-
ing dramatic circumstances is the confusion peculiar to dreams
and their countless interpretations, the confusion which inevitably occurs when there are such gossamer scrims separating fact
from fancy. Could the entire novel be an interior monologue?
Whose? Is MacNamara evaluating the relationship between in-
ternal and external reality, only discoverable in time and memory? Is he observing that time mocks man's knowledge and his
yearning for assurances? MacNamara comprehends that memory
may assimilate but probably discriminates. What are his artistic
alternatives? Perhaps this novel defied adherence to traditional,
sequential expectations or conventional logic. Most likely this
novel comprises only the unique, inner logic of its dominant,
authorial personality. Is MacNamara parodying this subjugation
of man's pitiful strivings, or compassionately empathizing? Or
both? I cannot offer any irrefutable analysis — that may have
been MacNamara's best judgment: there are no absolutes — so,
what now? Or he may merely have been portraying man's temporal desires as the chief cause of his suffering. I simply note
speculation's perilous inferences and suggest that such mystifi-
cation intensifies MacNamara's intricate, ambivalent meditation.
The tangible result is a remarkably introspective, soulful, and
challenging novel.

As Marcus peers out in rational cynicism through his squinting contortion of existence, reviewing his irrevocable past, so
MacNamara was gazing into himself, uncertainly puzzling that
uncharted world. He would discover that the profound and insolv-
able perplexity of this abyss has no artistic correlative — like

infinity, it is inimitable, except as derision. Inevitably, Marcus's and MacNamara's obsessive misgivings nervously correspond, for they are truly both one and universal. MacNamara emphasizes his awareness of the confluence between creator and created, between that part of Marcus Igoe which is conventional invention and that part of Marcus Igoe which is Brinsley MacNamara. The two men are extensions one of the other, eternal companions, extending to us puzzled, but companionable hands.

Marcus feels himself completely segregated from his village and its spectral, cartoon inhabitants. He has further impaired his relationship with them during the hiatus between the 'death' of Margo and the present, for '...his soul had been groping towards some kind of recovery of itself, towards some fine or startling thing that he yet might attempt to make himself Marcus Igoe once more.' Is the physical novel (itself merely an artisan's vain impersonation of life), the 'fine or startling thing' Mac-Namara himself was fiercely groping towards through Marcus? I am convinced MacNamara thought so — I am equally convinced that he was successful.

MacNamara here painfully acknowledges the feigned, ineffectual simulation that is all literature, the profound, urgent impertinence that is every artistic endeavor. Bill the Savage posthumously intones through Marcus/Brinsley subliminally: 'Aye, I've seen through things at last. I've seen through things...' But rather than meekly succumbing to an ineffable resignation, MacNamara knowingly bequeaths us this hieroglyphic affirmation of man's imperishable doubt.

By plot connivance, Marcus becomes involved with literary, affected Dublin and MacNamara produces an intriguing piece of reflective writing, resembling the prophetic satire he achieved in *The Irishman*. Candidly, he recognizes and acknowledges the fact that he himself has become an integral part of that which he once so savagely ridiculed for its shallowness and lack of enduring accomplishment.

In one of the highlights of the novel, set in Andy Delahunt's, a pub where 'at every word a reputation dies,' Marcus, a man in search of his identity, meets the man ultimately responsible for his one-dimensional existence, 'the Novelist,' or Mac-Namara himself. MacNamara pillories 'himself,' petulantly developing a convenient literary thesis:

'No damn good... they don't want novelists in Ireland. What can you do, when every old woman and every harnessma-ker and every cobbler is a better novelist than we are? There's a better novel in every one of these than we could ever do. What's wrong with them in the villages is dint of literary energy. Each one tries to get his novel over on the other, and they're continually trying to talk down one another with their unwritten novels. That's how they play hell, and the real reason why we novelists ourselves scarcely ever write anything at all.'

I suggest this is an original, innovative demonstration by MacNamara of artistic self-consciousness in Irish fiction. Here is an artist deconstructing himself, a writer's textual acknowledge-ment of his awareness that he is writing 'writing.' MacNamara endures the anguish of the void open before his pen, deliberately engaging the audience in their willing manipulation. Signifi-cantly, he utilizes his own earlier fictions for corollaries, literature made from literature, or what perceptive contemporary critics such as Rudiger Imhof refer to as 'inter-textuality.'

The Novelist informs Marcus, not without relevance, that he has already written about Marcus and describes a further instance of life imitating art:

'Yes, I had you imagined as a suitable County
Meath character. That has often happened. I project a creation out of nothing, and then the actual

character himself comes up from Garradrimna to meet me.'

The true decadence, Oscar Wilde noted, is the trespass of life into art. Marcus learns that the story in which he has been written of is called 'The Comedian,' first published in the August, 1921 *Banba*. Marcus must react to yet another alternative for the life to which he is barely clinging. The blending of real and illusory, image and imagined, deepens to a perplexing, comic fusion when The Novelist leaves Marcus the story about himself to read: '... the figure of the ex-cobbler from Garradrimna in the Midlands, now hovering perilously upon the verge of... actually falling into it from moment to moment... as he sat there reading the story of himself.' Is life the mirror here or the reality? Did French women, as Proust deliciously suggested, suddenly begin to imitate Renoir's conception of them? MacNamara seems always to have ambivalently wavered upon this Wildean epigram:

'By the artificial separation of soul and body men have invented a Realism that is vulgar, an Idealism that is void.'

I propose that in *The Various Lives of Marcus Igoe* Brinsley MacNamara is conspicuously derivative only of himself, while predictive, in his isolated venture into fiction's limitlessness, of others to come in self-reflexive Irish fiction: problematically, Joyce, *in absentia*; Beckett, *in dubio*; and Brinsley's great friend and adherent, Flann O'Brien. (MacNamara's novel fulfills O'Brien's theory of fiction delineated in *At Swim-Two-Birds* while pre-dating that masterpiece by nearly a decade. Actually, how dissimilar is MacNamara's introductory quotation from Montaigne, 'We are never present with but always beyond ourselves,' from Flann O'Brien's Euripidean epigraph in *At Swim-Two-Birds*, 'All things are separated from themselves'? The favorite diversion of MacNamara's Marcus, as well as the narra-

272

tor of O'Brien's later, anti-fictional work, is 'retiring into the privacy of [his] mind,' whence he indifferently tempts us to join him.) It is as well a Beckett-like world, freely admitting the contrivances of fiction, that telling stories is telling lies. In that world, artificiality is the given from which one proceeds, not a criticism which repulses.

I include Aidan Higgins in *Langrishe, Go Down*, and the Benedict Kiely of *Proxopera* or, especially, of *Nothing Happens in Carmincross*. I particularly consider it no exaggeration to suggest that MacNamara was a commendable precursor to John Banville's estimable meta-fictional canon. Marcus Igoe has a great deal more in common with Copernicus, Kepler, or the narrator of *The Newton Letter*, with what Professor Imhof has incisively termed 'redemptive despair,' than ever previously elaborated: 'Whither [indeed] is fled the visionary dream?'

What Marcus fails to comprehend in his quest for identity and immortality is what MacNamara stressfully realizes when he produces this novel — that the immortality of the one would doubtless depend immediately upon the immortality of the other. If MacNamara was ever to attain the enduring recognition he sought to deserve, there could be no question but that by chance Marcus Igoe, not unlike Tristam Shandy or Leopold Bloom, would attain his own lasting, distinctive celebrity. Unfortunately, Marcus equally reflects the common failing of his own purblind Midland people, that collective unconsciousness, to appreciate what MacNamara was attempting to accomplish: 'I have loved my native village more than words can tell, or how else could I have hated it so much for what it would not be?'

After Marcus reads 'The Comedian,' the Novelist returns somewhat unsteadily from the Palace. Marcus makes a suggestion concerning himself which the Novelist feels would appeal to the young sculptor friend with him: 'How would it strike you,' says Marcus, 'if someone was to put up a monument somewhere in Ireland to a man that was supposed to write a book that was never written?' The broad implication of this remark, of course, is that there would then be infinitely more monuments of this type in Ireland than there are Celtic crosses. Arrangements are made between the Novelist, the Sculptor, and Marcus for a future visit to Garradrimna, bringing preliminary sketches of the monument which will perpetuate Marcus.

Marcus returns to Garradrimna, the Garradrimna which has remained his overwrought obsession, with a new purpose in life, a new determination: the erection of a monument to himself which would stand as an affront to Garradrimna always. (The correlation between Marcus's visit to the Phoenix Park monument and this novel as immortality-insuring is noteworthy.) The only remaining problem is to determine which aspect of Marcus should be most prominent in the memorial, which of his numerous facets uppermost.

The visit of the two Dublin notables affords MacNamara another opportunity of laughing at himself as he amiably describes his own casual route on numerous jaunts from Dublin to Delvin with a party of friends:

> 'We're a bit late,' said the Novelist, 'but the lad here wanted to have a drink in County Meath, and I was glad of the opportunity to revive old acquaintances... characters of mine... We stopped at Blanchardstown, Mulhuddert, Clonea, Dunboyne, Summerhill, Rathmolyon, Trim, Aarboy, and here we are! We had a great day... Not alone had we to go through towns and villages, but we had to go through whole novels. I thought some of my characters would bate us, — the dirty ones, but they were all very nice.'

An appreciation for the significance of an inquiry made by Marcus of the Novelist is critical to my exegesis: 'I wonder what'll they do for yous at all when yous have done for me?' MacNamara's earnest regard for this work, the obsessive longing of all creators, is echoed in the Novelist's reply: 'You'll have made us immortal.' The plural 'us' reaffirms the inseparability of creator and created in *The Various Lives of Marcus Igoe* — their destinies were fused. How different, really, is Kepler's cold jubilation in John Banville's novel *Kepler*: '... and he thought, with rapturous inconsequence: I shall live forever.'

The Sculptor has come prepared. His sketch is described and recalls us to MacNamara's obsession with inexpressible, unimaginable time out of time, to his yearning for perpetuity which inspired this novel and should be its consequence. Mac-Namara is reprising the common trepidation of Marcus and himself with transcending mortality — how best to soften Unamuno's 'eternal persistence of consciousness.' We pensively appreciate that what MacNamara attempts to embody in this novel is self-consciously the soul of any ordinary, Being-trapped, illusion-requiring person:

> This exquisite little drawing showed a bird in flames, and if one looked long enough one saw a curious resemblance to Marcus, rising from the ashes of a book. There were grinning, leering faces below the book... Faces of people in Garradrimna. 'How the hell did you get them all in so well?'
>
> 'Well, if a man is a genius,' said the Novelist, with a most hopeless gesture by way of explanation...
>
> 'It is, but the bird isn't a bird exactly.'
>
> 'Of course not, that's your soul.'

275

'Me poor ould sowl... is that so? Is that it?'

The multi-levelled conversation between Marcus (the creation) and the Novelist (his creator) continues to a marvelously absurd conclusion. Marcus alludes to a sketch that exists only in the Sculptor's mind and the Novelist, who is also the Sculptor's creator, replies:

'It goes beyond anything he has yet conceived. It would be too terrible for Garradrimna. Too bloody awful for words. It would demolish the place... '

'Would it? Sure that's what I want!'

It was an unlucky stroke for the Novelist to have spoken of the imaginary conception... They had to do now with a man on his native heath, with a character whom the Novelist had really endowed with too much life.

'Didn't you say something about a statue to a book that was never written? Wouldn't it be a great notion now, never to put up a statue, that was never designed, to a book that was never written by a man that never lived... ?'

One might delay a lifetime or two in Davy Byrnes's discussing such inviolable equivocation.

This final question by Marcus does encourage further deliberation on the philosophical implications of MacNamara's novel. There are similarities, not perfectly ordered but suitably ontological, between this work by MacNamara and the subsequent works of those who came to be known as 'absurdists.' If, as I have suggested, MacNamara is characterizing Marcus's condition as that of a purely passive cobbler, persisting in reverie, altogether trapped behind the window of his shop, mired in a sterile marriage and life, then we should understand Marcus's fearful speculation: if one day is just like any other, then he need never have suffered existence but for one day — or, better still, no day at all. Is Pozzo's furious shout at Vladimir in *Waiting for Godot* appropriate here?

> 'Have you not done tormenting me with your accursed time! It's abominable! When! When! One day, is that not enough for you, one day he went dumb, one day I went blind, one day we'll go deaf, one day we were born, one day we shall die, the same day, the same second, is that not enough for you?'

Marcus is alienated man in search of his identity, cut off from his religious, intellectual, and transcendental roots — he is lost, abandoned, his actions consequently senseless, impotent, and absurd. There is as much point to not erecting a statue as there is to erecting a statue. It is highly significant to me that, uniquely, *The Various Lives of Marcus Igoe* contains absolutely no visible incarnation nor hint of a clerical presence, no sign of meddlesome clergy, MacNamara's traditional antagonists. There is no mention of any Church — the damage appears all to have been done irreparably. Marriages abound without ritual; Marcus is married but we witness no ceremony; Margo dies but there is no service. There is local memory of a prophecy from Jeremiah once quoted by a holy man in utter denunciation of Garradrimna: 'Moreover I will take from them the voice of mirth, and the voice of gladness, the voice of the bridegroom, and the voice of the bride, the sound of the millstones, and the light of the candle.' In this village wilderness, seemingly forsaken by God, Man is obliged to create himself. Are we post-apocalypse here? Does Marcus Igoe embody the spiritual solitude in which man conducts his futile search for personal salvation?

I am not insisting that MacNamara belongs in the philosophical company of Beckett, Sartre, or Camus, who would define and give definite literary expression to the Absurd. However, it is certainly conceivable that the doubts, the questionings, the sense of estrangement and exile felt both by Marcus Igoe and later by Pozzo, are reflections of MacNamara's ominous sense of metaphysical isolation by 1928. The ideologies, the unshakable assumptions and infallible faith, already discredited by the anguish of logic's treachery, were visibly dishonored by the feudal slaughter of rational behavior and innocence that was Ireland's Civil War (1922-23). Perhaps the unquestioned, imperturbable assurances shattered utterly by the inconceivable atomic climax to World War II were cracking for Brinsley MacNamara as early as 1920-22 — the years from which I date Marcus Igoe's intellectual evolution. As Yeats wrote in his *Autobiographies*, 'It is so many years before one can believe enough in what one feels even to know what the feeling is.'

The inescapable preoccupation with time's sovereignty has a great deal to do with Marcus's obsession with identity. Marcus, MacNamara, and all mankind endure a condition bruited by Samuel Beckett in his 1931 study of Proust:

There is no escape from the hours and the days. Neither from tomorrow nor from yesterday because yesterday has deformed us, or been deformed by us... Yesterday is not a milestone that has been passed, but a day-stone on the beaten track of the years, and irremediably part of us, within us, heavy and dangerous. We are not merely more weary because of yesterday, we are other, no longer what we were before the calamity of yesterday.

Marcus's difficulty in recognizing himself completely in any of his own imaginings or in the Novelist's sketches partially stems from this irreversible condition of Being. Change is our only constant. As surely as the vain flower, which blushes at the artist's glance, alters from his whimsical contemplation to his swift reproduction, so Marcus changes page by page, line by line, till we never know him — any more than he can truly know himself. Art is merely approximation, speculation, conjecture, till we never get it right — '... a never-ending process of failure,' as Rudiger Imhof writes in his seminal work, *John Banville: A Critical Introduction*: 'the artist in the end must come to terms with his predicament in redemptive despair.'

MacNamara was vainly attempting to fix ceaseless transience within the immutable context of art. Consider Martin Esslin's comments on Beckett's *Proust*:

> The flow of time confronts us with the basic problem of being — the problem of the nature of the self, which, being subject to constant change in time, is in constant flux and therefore ever outside our grasp. Being subject to this process of time flowing through us and changing us in doing so, we are, at no single moment in our lives, identical with ourselves.

If not exclusively postulating a philosophical thesis, *The Various Lives of Marcus Igoe* nevertheless whispers questions and poses circumstances that illustrate an absurd condition. In his own way, MacNamara anticipates Sartre, Camus and Beckett, parallels Kafka and Hesse and remembers the spiritual limbos inhabited by Dostoevsky's angst- and doubt-ridden intellectuals. Italo Calvino and Brinsley MacNamara would have recognized one another immediately — and gladly. Milan Kundera would wire his acknowledgment — as would Vladimir Nabokov. The worthy comparisons seem endless, academic grist for scholars unborn. I trust the uncomplicated joys derived from frequent readings of Calvino's *If on a Winter's Night a Traveler* will not be compromised by referring to just one sympathetic passage in that wondrous novel's Chapter 8, 'From the Diary of Silas Flannery':

How well I would write if I were not here! If between the white page and the writing of words and stories that take shape and disappear without anyone's ever writing them there were not interposed that uncomfortable partition which is my person! Style, taste, individual philosophy, subjectivity, cultural background, real experience, psychology, talent, tricks of the trade: all the elements that make what I write recognizable as mine seem to me a cage that restricts my possibilities. If I were only a hand, a severed hand that grasps a pen and writes... Who would move this hand?

Yes, they would recognize Brinsley MacNamara, as well as one another, across any abyss of time — surely, it would have been wonderful, too, if Leopold Bloom suddenly had spun around outside of Mulligan's, fired a quick glance over his shoulder and politely asked, 'Are you not coming in for a jar, Mr. Joyce?'

Based on these observations, I submit that Brinsley MacNamara approaches much nearer Camus's 'If the only significant history of human thought were to be written, it would have to be the history of its successive regrets and its impotence,' than he does Liam O'Flaherty's 'As Michael was going out the door he picked a piece of loose whitewash from the wall and put it in his pocket.'

The final six brief chapters contain the most complex and provocative writing that Brinsley MacNamara ever produced. I do not presume to fully understand what he intended, nor that he accomplished what he intended, but it is well to bear in mind the importance of the opaquely circuitous framework, not unlike the workings of Marcus's mind.

Selling what he has, Marcus retires from Garradrimna and moves to Harbourstown. He is not long in this retreat when an extraordinary event befalls him. Walking abroad on a spring day, Marcus notices the gaunt figure of 'the Trojan' Burke. 'The Trojan' Burke had retired years ago from Garradrimna only returning periodically to nobly denounce the town. Sensing that 'the Trojan' is in some way himself, Marcus goes forward to meet him, but Burke staggers and falls dead. We are told of Marcus: 'He was now like one walking into the shadow of himself, or else a ghost going forth to inhabit clay.' In a sense, Marcus encounters death, for his old self as well as his old life has died. Marcus is now prepared to receive the torch from 'the Trojan' Burke who dies fulfilled, knowing his ideals will survive in the person of Marcus Igoe. Marcus's enigmatic private life now appears to have been a preparation for just this ceremonial transubstantiation, real or imagined.

The conversion in Marcus returns MacNamara to his concern with the demands of artistic integrity, the necessity of being true to one's self:

> ... the Marcus Igoe who had come to Harbourstown was already no more, and 'the Trojan' Burke lay dead upon a green hillside a few miles from Garradrimna. To the last, the prophet had kept his fire. There was defiance still about the lines of suffering that framed his mouth, for he had remained powerful and himself to the end of his life.

Feeling that the soul of 'the Trojan' Burke has passed into him, Marcus, far from resuming his flight from intimidating reality, begins for the first time in his life to face responsibility, 'And he wanted to go into Garradrimna, so soon after he had just left it for good, to shout... to tell them all what he thought of them.' But Marcus grows scared and confused by these unique emotions:

> It seemed for the moment that he had been caught by life at last and he was filled with dread... Was this to be the end of him now, of him who had floated so successfully through various 'lives'? It was a curious trick that life had played on him, Garradrimna bringing him round full circle to what he always had been...

Momentarily ignoring 'the Trojan,' though retaining the alteration to his character, Marcus soon settles into a mood of sweet sympathy and tenderness in Harbourstown, admiring the young daughter of Martin Ivory, the man to whom Marcus's imaginary daughter was eventually wed in his reverie as 'the Marquis.' Living modestly, Marcus predictably soon earns a reputation for frugality as the multiplying villainies of men pursue him to his hideaway and he is driven to brooding reminiscence and misanthropic pessimism:

> But there remained memories of all his 'lives,' his sunny days, and he had not made of any of them a golden opportunity. Were these the 'lives' he should have lived to the fullest, any of them at all, or was living just foolishness and no more? Was the thing that made the living of any life possible merely a kind of foolishness, and that people who did not approach life that way got nothing out of it? Were the faces of happy men and women really the faces of fools...?

Not quite at the stage of presuming upon the absurdity and vacuity of existence, MacNamara seems nevertheless to be seriously questioning the nature of being, the devaluation of ideals, purity, and purpose, the inadequacy of any rational approach to incomprehensible existence. Remembering 'the Trojan,' Mac-Namara has Marcus insist upon his new being and reflect, really for each of them, upon what might have been:

> But then it was his failure in the doing of the thing that might have got the better of Gar-radrimna, of life, that had killed him... There was a man, 'the Trojan,' for instance, who had re-mained himself to the last, just as he might have remained himself had he continued to live on in the house of the squinting window... 'the Trojan' had died, that is, his body and personality had disappeared, but it might be that his soul still lived in the body of Marcus Igoe who was now no more.

Now the great blow in Marcus' life occurs — Bill the Savage hangs himself most elaborately. Marcus had been think-ing, not unlike MacNamara must have, of what might have happened if that man of strange qualities had been given his way with Garradrimna — that man, with the immense thoughts about life hidden behind sunken, lonely eyes. Looking at Bill in the Marley Arms, from which he had gone out to his doom, Bill might have been seen for what he was, an aspect of the personality of Brinsley MacNamara,

> The timid tragic figure with the eyes, now dark and sombre as pools, and again illuminated with the light of genius, as some spark of inspiration enkindled them, some satirical perception, some moment as when he might have got so well into the mood of life here... He was an embodiment in Garradrimna of the very idea that the Novelist had in Dublin, only he was the man through whom the idea had passed into reality.

A most significant paragraph, these remarks guide us towards what I comprehend as MacNamara's sincere, complex misgivings.

The entire novel may be read, I suspect, as a convergence of the reader's personality with the personalities of Marcus, Bill the Savage, 'the Trojan,' the Novelist, and Brinsley MacNamara, who lives in each of them. Bill, as an idea passed into reality, represents pure ideal, that to which both Marcus and MacNamara aspire. The novel, in its 'lives,' provides alternatives, possibilities wherein men remove themselves from the ideal by placing perishable, material acquisition before immortal and spiritual speculation. Bill the Savage has faith that 'at the moment of death, the soul flies to sojourn in some other habitation of clay,' and this is what happens when Bill hangs himself — his soul seeks out and unites itself with Marcus Igoe, who knew that something strange had occurred to him even before hearing of Bill's death:

> He had known well that something astonishing was about to appear in his life for since last night he had been wondering what had happened to him, what electrification of his bones, as he put it, what strange desire to be doing noble and beautiful things... ?

Marcus arranges for Bill's funeral and returns to town, where his former combative mood is aroused by the thick intransigence of Garradrimna and its inhabitants, though he seems confused:

> ... the thought was upon him still that it had been given to him, of all men, to change it. He was still like a young man with brave ideas of changing the world. But an immutable and far quality had entered his life.

Marcus's attitude towards immortality has turned as well, for he now appears to reject notions of earthly immortality as being of the dust. Marcus ponders long and deeply upon his plight until he realizes what he desires. In an eerie scene, the soul of Bill the Savage speaks telepathically through Marcus as medium:

> 'For I knew that I would solve the secret of Marcus Igoe if ever I came to Harbourstown... See down into that noble character whom they had never been able to understand, who had lived his life like in a dream, appearing as if he had done things that he had never done at all... No one seeing the things he had done... the thing he was...

In uniting Marcus, Bill, 'The Trojan,' the Novelist and himself, their creator, MacNamara achieved the collaboration of which Marcus had dreamed:

> Ah yes, this was the dream of doing the ultimate fine thing such as had filled the mind of Bill the Savage. It was in a sense to be a perfect collaboration between them, such as might never come again out of Garradrimna, could never come, for the purposes of it were deathless beyond description. They would know then whether Garradrimna had defeated him and driven him into retirement.

Marcus senses an immortal quality about himself for, he exults, had he not vanquished life itself? Or, by chance, Marcus has achieved Unamuno's transcendental pessimism, his own 'temporal and terrestrial optimism.'

In discovering an indifferent universe, stripped of illusion and promising light, perhaps MacNamara recognized his existential isolation in a dislocated and insubstantial world. Marcus Igoe has been driven so deeply into illusion by the somnambulant nightmare of Garradrimna that he strives to ignore the ultimate reality — death — through a fancy he derives from reading a story about himself written by the man who is writing this story about everybody. Such stratification illustrates how Brinsley MacNamara bravely challenged and expanded the provincially comfortable, linear and topical conventions in Irish narrative exposition. This he accomplished while pursuing the untraveled margins of his fictional horizons towards literary immortality.

Concluding this adventurous line of reason while recalling MacNamara's major concerns in this novel, might he not be vigorously asserting the supremacy, reliability and permanence, the greater tangibility of characters in literature over the inconstancy, mutability and unreliability of characters in reality? Like bringing the blurred and disjointed images in binoculars slowly together, MacNamara gradually fuses the character of Marcus as he seems and as he aspires with the benign character of Bill the Savage, who has always been a part of Marcus's nature, and with the prophet's spirit of 'the Trojan' Burke. Thus, MacNamara completes his composite profile of the personality of Marcus/Brinsley/Everyman, real and potential.

The Various Lives of Marcus Igoe provokes many more misgivings and questions than it does solutions. One finishes the novel unsettled, retaining the uneasy suspicion of something unutterably shared, some mutual sense of personal loss or incompleteness. But that is often the way one awakens from a disquieting dream. Whatever MacNamara's personal motives for his book, he has willed us a provocative, softly comical, visually expressionistic, and verbally stylized 'critical' fiction.

In the multiplicity of its concerns, in its undeniably existential musings, and in its ultimate universality, *The Various Lives of Marcus Igoe* emerges as Brinsley MacNamara's most profound work, a brilliantly challenging, iconoclastic post-modern masterpiece. Today, we presume on the now familiar techniques which resonate from MacNamara's novel; they endure through the seven decades of literary sophistication since his lonely, dissociating inquiries. MacNamara's uniqueness was both exaggerated and exacerbated by the dilemma of having no one with whom to exchange philosophies of fiction, no sounding-boards, no proximate barometers against which to measure his singular investigation. *The Various Lives of Marcus Igoe* engages us as a most personally dramatic and profound expression of genius in tragic isolation.

Nowhere in MacNamara's *oeuvres* does one come so near confronting the essential, creative man, facade removed, fears bared — the artist convinced of the necessary insufficiency in any human or artistic endeavor. Brinsley MacNamara is Marcus Igoe and perhaps in our fears, in our terror that we must cease to be, in our own craving after immortality, we are all Marcus Igoe.

Michael McDonnell
Fairfield, CT
1995